The Italian Connection

By
Jill St. Anne

Airleaf
Publishing

airleaf.com

Author's Note

The Italian Connection is a novel that I wrote based on my first book *The Riviera Conspiracy*. After its release, a Hollywood screenwriter, Vicki Howie, wrote a screenplay treatment based on this book. Her plot points were brilliant, and I used many of them in writing *The Italian Connection,* which therefore dramatically changed the story. For those of you who have read *The Riviera Conspiracy*, you will notice many similarities between the two books, although I have rewritten every word. Christina, the heroine, is just as fun and feisty as the first time around, but I've added a few significant changes to her character. I hope you enjoy this reincarnation as much as I enjoyed writing it.

Also, I would like to thank all my die-hard fans for their encouragement and support; especially my parents: Judy Fairchild and David Zajicek, who have read and re-read my books to the point where they know each sentence by heart, and Lucrezia O'Brien Zajicek, who loves Italy as much as I do!

Chapter One

Christina Culhane maintained a heart-pounding pace until she broke her stride to glance at her plastic Swatch. If she pushed herself, she'd finish the six-mile loop to the Golden Gate Bridge and back in less than forty minutes.

Another runner pulled alongside her, his t-shirt dark with sweat and his red face dripping. "Nice," he huffed. "Streamlined. Real smooth."

Christina smiled but was in no mood to talk: she ran to get fresh air, not fresh men. This was her time, and she didn't want to share. She sped up and left him in the dust. She had an eight a.m. presentation today and she needed this half-hour to prepare mentally, not to chitchat with some random runner.

The physical discipline of getting up at five-thirty every morning to run had become an addiction. She'd have been lost without the squawking seagulls and the deep groan of foghorns out in the Bay. Even when the fog grew thick and cold, she wouldn't miss a day. A cold splash of salty water sprayed her face as a large wave crashed onto the path. She jumped aside to avoid it and continued running.

After a ten-minute, cool-down walk back to her condo, Christina stepped into a steaming shower. She had just finished rinsing the shampoo out of her hair, when the telephone rang. Cutting her shower short, she wrapped herself in a towel and dashed to the phone.

"Sounds like you just ran a marathon," said her childhood friend—and now client—Peter Carmaletti.

Christina caught her breath. "What's up, Peter? You're never awake this early."

"I have a lot on my mind. Can we meet for breakfast?"

She wiped her face with the towel. "My presentation with your company is this morning. If the president agrees to sign with us, this will be my biggest deal yet."

"Christy, I forgot. Sorry—"

"Hey, don't worry about it. I could meet you after the market closes. How about one-fifteen?"

"Just tell me where."

"Beldon Alley. Tiramisu."

Christina put the phone down slowly. Peter didn't sound like himself, and getting a phone call from him before nine was more than unusual.

She hurried back to the bathroom. She calibrated her mornings to the second, and even a two-minute phone call could put her behind schedule. Instead of contacts, she opted for the quicker alternative and grabbed her titanium glasses. Luckily, Rosa had picked up her suits from the cleaners. She slipped into her charcoal-grey, pinstriped Armani, and then opened a pack of nude stockings and pulled one up her leg.

"Shit," she said, as her nail tore through the nylon. She grabbed another pack from her drawer and popped them into her black Birkin. Now where were her shoes? Droplets of perspiration formed above her lip as she hunted, and the frantic thirty-second search felt more like thirty minutes. At last, she located her black leather pumps under her bed, slipped them on and raced downstairs to the garage. Good—the fog was starting to burn away. She could lower the top on her Saab. For the next twenty minutes, all the way from the Marina to her office in the Financial District, strawberry-blonde tendrils snapped at her cheeks, but by the time she arrived, her hair was dry and full of body.

Just before seven forty-five, Christina pushed through the heavy mahogany doors and strode across thick Persian carpets into the foyer of her office, the West Coast branch of Kingstone and Company, a powerful New York investment bank. A client had once joked that the last time he'd seen so many Oriental carpets, there'd been a 'Going out of Business' sign painted on the front window. Christina could live with the pretentious-is-best decor, but she always felt a bit guilty walking into the reception area. The rain-forest destruction required to panel the walls was enough to cause a full-scale Greenpeace rally.

"Good morning." She smiled at Nancy.

"It won't be good for long," Nancy said, adjusting her headset. Middle-aged and conservatively dressed, she had been a receptionist with the firm forever, her domain a massive Louis XV desk. Above her, large bronze letters spelled out the firm's name. "Jacobs has been calling non-stop for you. I transferred him through to Bart."

Christina's muscles tightened. Andrew Jacobs was her supervisor in New York. All he cared about was his year-end bonus. He needed it to maintain his 5th Avenue apartment and the beach house in the Hamptons. He had two children in private school and a Park Avenue princess for a wife; rumor had it that her salon bills exceeded five grand a month. His bonus was contingent on the amount of new business his group booked each quarter, and while Christina was the lead banker in San Francisco, her numbers had dropped from last year.

Jacob's keeping-up-with-the-Trumps lifestyle was beyond anything Christina could comprehend, or aspire to. She had grown up in a middle-class Philadelphia suburb. Her mom was a schoolteacher and her dad ran the family's trucking business, and although the Culhane Trucking Company was one of the biggest on the East Coast now, it hadn't started out that way. Her grandfather had founded the company with one Ford pick-up. Christina had worked summers at the company all the way through college, even driving a long haul herself if one of the drivers called in sick. While not exactly a glamorous internship at a glossy fashion magazine in Manhattan, her father paid her well, and she'd learned the value of hard work—something that had helped her land a scholarship at Wharton, where she'd earned her MBA.

The more business Christina brought in for Kingstone, the more she got paid; but she was still young and single, and as far as she was concerned, she earned plenty for her family of me, myself and I. Not yet thirty, she owned a comfortable condo in the Marina District, a cool car and a fabulous wardrobe. And though she could afford five-star vacations, making time to take them was another matter.

"Hey Bart." Christina acknowledged her assistant, who sat at the end of the long marble corridor, otherwise known as the Hall of Fame.

Polished brass plaques, commemorating the billions of dollars raised by Kingstone for their clients, hung like Madonna's platinum records on the walls. For Christina and Bart, this was their home-away-from home, and the epicenter of the corporate finance division.

"Hey—where's my latté?" He looked up and ran a hand through his hair, worn short with blonde highlights. Although in his mid-thirties, he looked younger.

"We're both out of luck this morning." Christina crossed the threshold into her office. "But I still owe you. Call the nail bar and tell Nga to give you the works, on me."

Bart grinned. "Don't *you* know how to keep a boy happy."

"No problem." Christina looked at her chipped French manicure. "And while you're at it, get one for me."

*

The executives from Symex already sat around the massive cherry wood table when Christina walked into the conference room at precisely 7:59. She took a deep breath and looked past them at the stunning view of the Golden Gate Bridge. She took a few deep breaths to calm her nerves, and then she presented a thorough and convincing analysis: how much money she'd raised for previous clients, and how high their stock had risen after their shares went public. Within a half-hour, she had the group eating out of her hand. Symex had agreed to let Kingstone finance the deal.

*

When the stock market closed at one p.m., Christina walked the few short blocks to Beldon Alley, still in the Financial District. Ten restaurants shared the alley, all with outdoor tables and umbrellas, and all packed with people. But for the adjacent skyscrapers, she could have been on a cobbled street somewhere in the south of France. She had chosen Tiramisu because she loved Mediterranean food—and of course, for the eponymous dessert, something she could never resist.

She arrived a bit late and spotted Peter sitting at one of the outdoor tables, squinting in the mid-afternoon sun. Christina loved Peter to death, but even she had to admit he looked out of place among all the well-groomed and smartly dressed business people. An engineer in San Jose, the heart of Silicon Valley, his work attire consisted of jeans, t-shirts and more t-shirts. She hadn't seen him in a while; he wore his brown hair as messy as always, but his face was paler, his cheekbones more pronounced, and the half-moons under his eyes looked purple and pillowy. Christina's stomach lurched. She hoped to God he wasn't sick.

"Peter." She sat down. "Is everything okay?"

"Everything's fine," he said. "I've been working hard. Not sleeping much." He picked up his glass of water with a shaky hand. "That's one of the reasons I asked to see you. I need your advice. How quickly can I liquidate my Symex stock?"

"About as soon as the top guys from Enron are back trading energy futures."

Peter raised one eyebrow. "That long?"

"Seriously? The papers for the new company have already been filed with the SEC. You're restricted under rule 144a. You can't sell until well after the new division goes public."

"Okay, so how long?"

Christina sipped her water. "About a year."

Peter shook his head and leaned back in his chair. He looked up to the sky, heaved a great sigh, and shook his head again.

"You must have some unrestricted stock," Christina said. "Didn't you get some shares when you joined the company five years ago?"

"I did, but I sold them when Mary and I bought our house."

Christina leaned over the table. "Peter, if you're having financial problems, I'll lend you some money. No questions asked. How much do you need?"

"I wouldn't feel right about that. And I don't know when I could pay you back."

"I'm not worried about the money. I'm worried about you." She looked directly into his eyes. "What's going on?"

He looked away. "I just need a vacation."

"We could all use a vacation." Christina looked around the bustling tables. "In fact I'm long overdue. I'd love to go back to Italy. I can't get enough of the food. And I've heard the men aren't too bad either." She winked at Peter, who was half-Italian.

"Anywhere but Italy," Peter said.

The waiter approached, interrupting their conversation. Christina ordered a Salade Niçoise and Peter a focaccia sandwich with a side of fries.

"Let's forget about my stuff for a minute," he said. "I have a present for you."

"A present?" Christina smiled. "What for?"

"Your birthday."

"My birthday isn't for three months."

He reached into his pocket and pulled out a dark-blue velvet bag. "Let's call it an early birthday present. Just in case I decide to take that vacation we talked about."

Christina, as excited as a little girl emptying her Christmas stocking, opened the bag. Inside was a gorgeous watch with a blue crocodile band and a diamanté face as large as a silver dollar.

"For the woman who's always concerned about time," Peter said. "I even included a spare battery, because I knew you'd never take the time to go to the jeweler's and have it changed."

She laughed. Leave it to an engineer to think of a spare battery. "Wow, Peter. Very bling bling." She strapped it on her wrist. "Sure beats my plastic Swatch. But I should be buying you a gift. If it weren't for you, I wouldn't have landed the Symex deal."

"That may not be as great as you think."

"What do you mean?" Christina asked.

"I can't go into it now." Peter looked around for the waiter. "I'll get the check."

"But we just ordered our food!"

*

Christina nibbled fries off Peter's abandoned plate and tried to make sense of his mystifying behavior. First the comment about Symex, and then he had apologized and begged off, leaving the table without touching his lunch. *What's going on with him?*

Maybe he was about to get fired. But that wasn't likely. He'd just been promoted to senior engineer a few months ago. She munched another fry. Was he so unhappy with his job that he wanted to move on already? Again, not probable—he wasn't fully vested. All employees in the Valley pretty much acted the same. Unless they were being tortured on the job, and being sleep-deprived didn't count, they stuck it out until the bitter end—or at least until they could sell their stock options. Only *then* did they box the contents of their office and give notice.

She had nearly polished off Peter's fries by the time the waiter returned with her card—she had insisted on paying—but so much for having a healthy salad for lunch.

*

Christine dropped off her handbag and collected a stack of papers from her office. She needed to get them to the firm's high-tech analyst, Suzan Anders, and not coincidentally, her best friend. They had been pals since their early twenties and had worked their way up through the ranks of various investment firms, sharing their personal trials and tribulations along the way.

Suzan was on the phone when Christina entered her office, most likely talking to a CEO or CFO of one of the companies she followed. And, as was her habit, she absently twisted long spirals of hair around a pencil as she listened. She had her African-American mother to thank for her skin, smooth and the color of light cocoa. The heart-shaped face and amber eyes came from her father.

And though Christine didn't know how she managed, her lips were always a perfect shade of red, regardless of whether she wore lipstick or not. Actually, neither of them wore much make-up: they didn't have a spare minute to worry about it.

Suzan held up her index finger and motioned for Christina to sit amidst the stacks of prospectuses and research reports piled on the chair opposite her desk.

Christina sat and crossed her bare legs. She had forgotten to put on her stockings once she got to work—not a very professional image, but she hoped no one else had noticed her *faux pas*. While Suzan talked, Christina flipped through the prospectuses. Each of the small companies was a potential candidate for another IPO or a private placement. While she glanced at them, she simultaneously watched the Bloomberg monitor that sat on the side of Suzan's desk.

A familiar Nasdaq symbol flashed on the blue screen. "Yes!" Christina shook her clenched fists. "Comtech is up another two points today."

Suzan smiled at her from behind her cluttered desk and gave her a thumbs-up. They had taken that company public last June, and since then the stock had tripled.

After a few more minutes, Suzan slammed down the phone. "Finally! What's up?"

"Well, besides Comtech, I just landed the Symex financing."

"Isn't Symex a defense contractor? As in bombs and missiles?"

Christina smiled back at her. "Very good, you know your stuff. But this company's entirely different; it's a new division that manufactures microprocessors."

"Okay; but still, won't we need special clearance to work with them?"

"No, not at all. The new company will have nothing to do with the Department of Defense."

"That's a relief—I hate that vetting process." Suzan pulled her hair into a bun on the top of her head and secured it with a pencil. A row of silver rings pierced the cartilage above turquoise-studded earlobes. She leaned forward onto her elbows and whispered, "So—what's this new chip they're making?"

"Sorry," Christina shook her head. "I signed a confidentiality agreement." Changing the subject she said: "By the way, I met Peter Carmaletti for lunch." She held out her wrist. "Look at the watch he gave me."

"It's gorgeous. But a bit extravagant, isn't it?"

"It's an early birthday present. After all, I'll be thirty soon."

"Don't remind me. My big three-oh is also just around the corner. But next time you see him, tell him I said hello."

"Moving on to another client," Christina said, "I asked Bart to call Brandy Jensen to see if she could join us for dinner."

"*Dinner?*" Suzan winced. "Thanks, but no thanks. I've been here since the crack of dawn and I'm exhausted."

"Hey, I'm tired too." Christina took off her glasses and massaged the area under her brow. "I'd rather go home and watch a movie, but the three of us have been trying to get together for months. C'mon, Suzan, what about her firm's multi-million dollar retirement fund? She's in a position to turn it over to us."

Just as Christina was ready to go for the close, Bart poked his head into the office. "Eight o'clock. That's the best I could do."

"Well?" Christina looked over to Suzan.

Suzan leaned over her desk and set her chin on her hand. "What restaurant?"

"Bix."

Suzan removed the pencil from her hair and let it cascade past her shoulders. "I'll do it for your sake." She dialed the number for Brandy's real-estate firm on the speakerphone.

"Brandy Jensen." Her voice was low and raspy.

"Hi Brandy," Christina said into the speaker. "We have everything set up. Bix at eight."

"Nice work. I haven't been there in ages. How did we get in on such short notice?"

"I left that to Christina," Suzan said, "our resident A-list socialite."

Christina shook her head. Hardly. She had a certain amount of clout at many of the best restaurants because she entertained clients so often, but she was no socialite, nor did she want a reputation as one.

"I'll meet you there," Brandy said. "And make sure you've got a double martini waiting for me."

"Now I've gotta run," Christina said to Suzan. "Let's meet in my office after work."

*

It was getting dark when Suzan let herself into Christina's corner office, but she didn't turn on the lights. The last glowing embers of the day were fading on the horizon behind Alcatraz Island, leaving the Bay dressed in ruffled black velvet. She kicked off her shoes with a sigh of relief, and padded over to investigate the contents of Christina's bar fridge: several bottles of Perrier, a Diet Coke, and a bottle of champagne. Veuve Clicquot, too. Suzan popped the cork, poured herself a glass, and then sank into the leather club chair by the window. It took some experimentation with Christina's remote control, but in a minute or two, she got the Samba Kings playing softly over the wall speakers.

With her feet propped on the windowsill, she closed her weary eyes. She could get used to this: an impressive office, sales calls by day and dinners with clients by night. On the other hand, the glitz and glamour were deceptive; Christina was out almost every night wining and dining clients. Was it any wonder she never dated?

Suzan's own job wasn't without its perils—her career was on the line every time she offered a professional recommendation; one inaccurate sell could cut a small company's market capital in half, an overzealous buy could catapult a shaky stock to a dangerous, overvalued high. But even so, given a real choice, she'd take her analyst job and cluttered office over Christina's high-profile sales position any day of the week. She held her champagne glass to the Bay and the lights from the sailboat masts winked back at her.

Christina arrived to interrupt her momentary bliss. She kicked off her Ferragamo pumps as she entered. "Great Salsa music."

"It's Samba music. I can't believe you don't know the difference."

Christina poured herself a glass of champagne, opened the bottom drawer of her desk and pulled out a pair of Christian Louboutin stilettos with their trademark red leather soles. She rarely had time to change after work, but putting on a pair of elegant shoes helped her make a mental shift.

Suzan finished her drink and heaved her leather bag over her shoulder. "Let's get outta here."

Christina sipped her champagne. "What's with the backpack?"

"You makin' fun of my backpack, girl? I've had this since college." She ran her fingers along the tan leather. "It's taken years to get this hide soft as butter. And look who's talking, you practically live out of that overnight bag of yours."

"Overnight bag? Hermès has a six-month waiting list for one of these."

"Puh-lease." Suzan adjusted her backpack and walked out the door.

*

Bix, located in an obscure alley of the Financial District, was one of Christina's favorite spots to grab a drink and listen to jazz. The two-story restaurant gave her a sense of stepping into a 1930's supper club. Men and women dressed in smart business attire lined the polished mahogany bar, where they sipped drinks and exchanged empty pleasantries.

Sergio, the slim, dark-haired maitre d', greeted Christina with an air kiss. "Nice to see you again, Christina. We've saved your favorite table."

"Thanks, Sergio. Have you met Suzan?"

He picked up her hand and kissed the back of it. "No. But the pleasu*rrrr*e is all mine."

Suzan gave him a coy smile and rolled her eyes with as much bravado as he rolled his R's.

Sergio showed them to a corner table overlooking the restaurant and bar area. "Enjoy your evening, ladies." Before he left, he leaned down and whispered into Christina's ear. "Tell that naughty boy Bart to call me tomorrow."

Christina laughed. "Will do, Sergio." Though a lot of good it would do—Bart had more men after him than a Victoria's Secret model in a Manhattan night club.

Now a boyishly handsome waiter approached the table. He was dressed head to toe in black, with just enough facial hair to make him look hip, but not homeless. Christina ordered a double martini for Brandy, a Cosmopolitan for herself and a beer for Suzan.

As the waiter turned away, Brandy burst into the restaurant. A tough New Yorker, she had moved to San Francisco ten years ago. For many of those years, she had worked for several local real-estate agencies, and then she started her own firm, specializing in the sale of multi-million dollar homes. As usual, she wore oversized sunglasses propped on frosted blonde hair, expensive costume jewelry and a serious amount of makeup.

She yelled across the room. "I hope my martini's waiting. Traffic was a bitch and my day the worst."

She fell into the nearest chair and lit up a cigarette. Polished red fingernails rivaled the glowing tip for color. "It's great to finally see you two." She took a long drag.

Christina fanned away the smoke. "Brandy, smoking's been outlawed in California for years now."

Brandy ignored her and took another drag. "So—how's my portfolio doing?"

"Try reading your statements," Suzan suggested mildly.

"You know I never open those things."

"Statement or no statement," Christina added, "it's still up over twenty percent."

"Fabulous. Much better than that money-market account."

Suzan changed the subject. "What happened today that was such a downer?"

The drinks arrived, and Brandy drained half her martini. "Let's just say that my clients from Wisconsin found out the hard way that their home-buying dollar is worth next to nothing here in California." She took another sip. "And to top it off, good ole Maxwell informed me that he wanted to start seeing other women."

"Brandy, that's awful."

"Which? The family from Wisconsin or Maxwell?"

"I guess both," Christina said, "but I'm sorry to hear about Max."

Brandy took another drag from her cigarette and blew the smoke toward the ceiling. "I could use some new blood." She glanced toward the group of men leaning against the bar. "Maybe I'll take a vacation or something."

"Peter and I were talking about that just this morning," Christina said. "If I don't take a break soon I might end up dead in my condo with rats crawling all over me." She had dreamt

14

once that paramedics found her eaten alive by rodents in a pile of dirty clothes on her bedroom floor.

"Now that's a lovely thought." Suzan poured the remainder of her beer into a glass. "A friend of mine just got back from Europe. She said she came back feeling ten years younger."

Brandy cupped her neck and tightened the loose skin along her jaw line. "I like the *ten years younger* part. What's your favorite country? I've never been anywhere but Mexico."

"Definitely Italy," Christina answered. "The food is fabulous, and the men to die for. I backpacked around Europe after college, and loved it."

Brandy stubbed out her cigarette. "Men to die for? Tell me more."

"First of all, everyone smokes. No one would think of giving you a hard time for lighting up in a restaurant."

"Believe it or not," Suzan said, "Italy just passed a law banning smoking in public places."

Brandy gave her the eye. "Like that's going to stop me? How 'bout we all go together?"

Suzan and Christina looked at each other. They both liked Brandy but she was at least ten years older than they were, and the words *high maintenance* didn't begin to describe her. Christina couldn't imagine the three of them traveling together.

"Well?" Brandy said. "What do you think?"

"Uh—yeah, Brandy." Suzan stole a glance over at Christina and mumbled into her beer. "Couldn't think of anything better."

Christina didn't say a word, but she gave Suzan a look that could shatter a mirror.

With dinner, they ordered a bottle of champagne. As the waiter poured the bubbly, Brandy jumped up from her chair and nearly knocked the bottle out of his hand.

"I see a friend of mine." She waved her arms above her head and shouted across five tables of diners. "Rob! Rob Carmichael!"

A man turned around, looking startled to hear his name. But when he recognized Brandy, he broke into a smile and walked toward the women.

"My God, Brandy." Christina gawked at the approaching man. "He's a dead ringer for Cary Grant."

"He's also an incredibly rich movie producer," Brandy whispered. "The last I heard, he was spending more time at his beach house in Malibu than in the fabulous penthouse I sold him here in San Francisco."

Rob arrived at their table. "Brandy, how great to see you." He touched his cheek to hers.

"You too, stranger." She patted the empty chair next to her. "Christina, Suzan. Meet Rob." She poured champagne into an empty water glass for him. "Spill it, Rob. How long have you been in San Francisco and why haven't you called me?"

Rob shook his head and smiled at the other two women. "I flew up yesterday. Our latest movie just went into production."

"That's so exciting!" Christina thought how dull banking must seem to the people she met for the first time.

"It sounds more glamorous than it is," Rob said. "We're still a bit disorganized now, but in a few weeks, when I have more time, I'll give you three a tour of the movie set. Maybe you'll even meet Brad Pitt or Sandra Bullock."

"Brad Pitt," Christina said. "You're on."

Rob stood and shook hands with Suzan and Christina. "I better get back to my table. Nice to meet you ladies." He blew Brandy a kiss. "Call me when you're in LA."

When he was out of earshot, Suzan said to Brandy, "Forget Max. Why the hell aren't you dating Rob?"

"Well, as luck would have it," Brandy said, "I'm pretty certain he prefers the company of men."

The three of them let out a slow sigh, held their glasses high, and toasted all the gorgeous unavailable men.

*

When Christina arrived back at her condo, she threw her suit onto a chair and put on a t-shirt. She was dead tired, and barely had the energy to wash her face.

Her mobile rang just as she was ready to crawl into bed. She saw it was Suzan.

"Miss me already?" Christina asked.

"Turn on the news. Channel Seven. I think something terrible has happened to Peter."

Christina ran to the television and pressed the power button. She couldn't find the remote, so she had to change the channels manually, which seemed to take forever. Finally, tuned to the right channel, she saw a reporter standing in front the Symex office building. Yellow police tape flickered in the background.
The man spoke into a microphone. "It appears that a young computer engineer, identified as Peter Carmaletti, jumped to his death earlier this evening."

Chapter Two

Christina dropped the phone. When she had processed the horrific reality, she picked up the receiver. "This can't be right. I just saw him this afternoon."

"I know. I couldn't believe it either. Do you want me to come over?"

"God, yes."

"Sit tight, I'll see you in a few minutes."

Christina immediately thought of Peter's wife, Mary. She snapped shut her mobile, which was nearly dead, and reached for her home phone. Her fingers flew over the keypad, but although she knew the number by heart and had dialed it at least a thousand times, it was suddenly as unfamiliar as the number of the convenience store down the street. She plugged in her mobile and pressed the speed dial assigned to Peter's home. There was no answer, so she spoke briefly. "Mary, I'm so sorry. Please call me."

Her head spun, her arms and legs felt like lead, and she began to shiver uncontrollably. She collapsed into her down-filled sofa and wrapped herself in a cashmere blanket.

When the front-doorbell rang, it took a few seconds for the sound to register. Still wrapped in her blanket, Christina shuffled to the entry hall and buzzed Suzan in.

Suzan gave her a big hug and then ushered her back into the reception room. "You're in shock," she said. "Stay there. I'll make us some tea."

Christina's teeth chattered as she waited; time suspended in thick, heavy air. She couldn't tell if Suzan returned within minutes or an hour. Either way, she held two cups of green tea.

Christina accepted one and wrapped her hands around the mug. "I've known Peter since tenth grade. I would've known if he was suicidal. He was strange at lunch, quite worried in fact, but he wasn't despondent, and he certainly wasn't suicidal."

"Maybe he just fell."

"But why would he be out on the roof? Seriously Suzan, *why*? He didn't smoke. It's not as if he needed to sneak out for a cigarette."

"Do you think he was in some kind of trouble?" Suzan asked. "Maybe something at Symex? Or maybe with Mary?"

"Not with Mary. No way. He loved his wife. And he was just promoted two months ago."

"Did he gamble?"

"Not a chance. He lived a simple life. Mary told me that he turned down a bachelor party to Vegas because he'd rather spend the weekend with her, fixing up their new house."

Suzan sipped her tea. "I don't know, Christina. There must be some explanation."

"He did seem concerned about money." Finally a bit warmer, Christina let the blanket drop from her shoulders. "He asked me how quickly he could liquidate his Symex stock."

"Do you think he was facing bankruptcy?"

"I offered to lend him money, no questions asked, but he didn't take me up on it." She held her wrist in the air. "And look at this watch. This isn't a gift someone buys a friend if they're having money troubles."

Suzan nodded. "Good point."

Christina sat trance-like, her eyes focused on nothing, her brain churning. So many questions tumbled through her mind. Poor Mary. Peter meant the world to her, and she meant the universe to him. He took care of the bills, the taxes, investments, *everything*. They had met in college, and after their second date, there was no looking back. All Mary talked about was having children with Peter. She had even picked out wallpaper for the baby's room. Yellow, blue and pink. Boy or girl, she'd be prepared.

"I don't know how Mary will cope."

Suzan reached over and hugged her. "She'll get through this, and so will you. You lost a dear friend. No words will ever help. Especially now, but hopefully time will."

When Christina stopped shaking, Suzan released her. "Would you like to go see Mary now?"

"I called, but she's not home. Maybe in the morning."

"I'll drive you," Suzan said. "Do you want me to crash on your couch tonight?"

Christina nodded. "Thanks, I'd appreciate it."

*

In the morning she and Suzan walked the two short blocks to Chestnut Street in the Marina, a lively thoroughfare filled with trendy boutiques, coffee shops and restaurants. Even after all the fresh air, she had the worst hangover of her life. A sip of champagne in her office, a glass with dinner and one Cosmopolitan wouldn't cause her head to pound this much. Grief, she supposed, must be a more potent assailant than alcohol.

An SUV loaded down with surfboards drove past them; it reminded Christina of the days when she had time to go windsurfing in the late afternoon at Chrissy Field. The wind was always wicked around four, but lately she hadn't been able to leave work early enough to enjoy it.

They sat at an outside table at Starbucks, where she drank a double espresso and watched all the active people around her. By the time she finished her coffee, Christina felt better, and good enough to drive to Mary's house alone.

*

The Carmaletti house was modest, a light brown bungalow on a tree-lined street in Noe Valley.

Mary answered the door in her robe, looking much older than her twenty-eight years. Her eyes were puffy and red, and her short blonde hair looked tousled and uncombed.

Christina immediately gave her a hug. "I'm so sorry."

Mary's petite frame trembled in her arms. "What am I going to do without him, Christy?"

As much as she wanted to, Christina couldn't answer that question; she could only hold her.

"I knew Peter was stressed," Mary said, "but I didn't think he was suicidal."

Christina pulled away and held Mary by the shoulders. "I refuse to believe he jumped off that building."

"That's what I tried to tell the police, but they said the evidence suggests that he deliberately jumped."

"There weren't any witnesses?"

Mary shook her head. "Apparently a wino told the police he saw a man running from the back of the building. They took his statement, but I have a feeling they're not taking him seriously."

"He's still a witness, drunk or not." Christina looked at Mary and remembered how she had felt last night when Suzan came to the door. Mary needed to be comforted, but Christina was at a complete loss for the words. What does one say to someone who has just lost her young healthy husband? In the end, she offered to make tea, as Suzan had done for her. "Let's sit down in the kitchen, Mary. I'll start some hot water."

"I haven't been able to eat or drink anything since last night."

"That's why you need to now. You can't let yourself get sick."

Mary sat at the pine table and buried her face in her hands.

Christina, not that familiar with Mary's kitchen, took a few minutes to locate tea bags and mugs. She filled the stained kettle with water and tried to turn on the old metal stove. No flame appeared, but she smelled gas fumes. Instinctively, she turned off the knob.

Mary saw her struggling. "Sorry Christina, that range is ancient. You need to start it with a match." Her shoulders shook. "Our next project was to remodel this kitchen. I love to cook, and Peter promised to buy brand-new appliances."

Christina walked back to Mary and put her arms around her shoulders. She wished she were capable of articulating comforting words suitable for such an emotional and life-altering time. She didn't want to say, *but you can still remodel the kitchen*, because that would only remind Mary that she would never cook for Peter again. Rather than say anything, Christina gave Mary a reassuring squeeze on her shoulders. She returned to the stove, found a box of matches, and ignited the blue flame. Within minutes steam rose from the spout. Remembering milk and a packet of Splenda, she handed the mug to Mary and sat down. "I know you don't want to think about this, but do you need me to help you arrange Peter's service?"

Mary shook her head. "Thanks, but my parents are flying out tonight. They'll help with all that."

Christina took a sip of her tea. She had no taste for it at all; her stomach felt queasy, but she hoped Mary would see her drinking and do the same. "Does that mean they'll stay with you tonight?"

Mary drank a bit and nodded.

"Good, you'll need someone here. In the meantime, I'll drive down to Real Foods on Castro and buy some food." The Real Foods market was the one place she knew she'd find a huge selection of healthy, ready-made meals.

She put up her hand to stop Mary from protesting. "You may not be hungry, but I'm sure your parents will be. And besides, you'll need to eat at some point. Also, show me where your linens are. I'll make up the guest room and do some laundry. In the meantime, why don't you get back in bed?"

The relief on Mary's face spoke for her. Together, they walked to the bedroom, and Christina helped Mary into bed. She put the covers around her neck and brought in an extra blanket from the hall closet. Photographs of the couple were scattered around the room. At first, seeing them comforted her, as each one showed them smiling or laughing together. Then the flip side of this reminder slammed home the truth: Peter was gone forever. All they had left of him were colored snapshots, and thankfully, wonderful memories.

"Try to get some sleep, Mary. I'll be back in an hour."

Mary's eyelids closed even before she left the room. Tamping down her own feelings of sadness, she threw a load of laundry in the washing machine and headed out to the grocery store.

When she returned about an hour later, Mary slept soundly. Christina unpacked the groceries, finished the laundry and made up the guest bedroom. She found some barely used linen spray in the drawer of one of the end tables, sprayed the sheets with the fresh citrus scent and fluffed the pillows. She checked on Mary one more time, and seeing that she still slept, she left a note asking Mary to call when she awoke.

As she drove up the hills of Pacific Heights, she phoned Bart. She wouldn't make it to the office today. He'd have to do his best to field her calls.

*

Mary woke Christina the next morning with an early call, not unlike the one she had received from Peter just two days ago.

Christina could tell from her voice that she felt a little better. Apparently, she had slept from the moment Christina left her house until her parents arrived later that evening. She had eaten a bite or two of the vegetarian lasagna Christina had left, and then had gone straight back to bed.

"I'm glad to hear that you're eating again," Christina said.

"It's good to have my parents here. They're a big help."

"Is there anything I can do?" Christina asked.

"There is," Mary said. "We touched on this yesterday, but I can't believe for a second that Peter committed suicide. I want to clear his name." She paused, and Christina heard her struggle for control. "I *need* to clear his name, and I'd like you to help me."

"Of course. I agree with you one hundred percent. I'm not sure exactly how I can help, but I'll try."

When she hung up, she glanced at her watch. She had time for a quick run if she hurried. And once she hit the path, her mind raced faster than her legs. She knew Peter hadn't jumped from that building. Now all she had to do was help Mary prove it.

Chapter Three

Mary wore a Giants' sweatshirt and baggy sweat pants when she opened the door. Her eyes remained red, but her hair was wet. That was a good sign, Christina thought. At least she had the energy to shower. The two women sat on a worn sofa in a room filled with a collection of hand-me-down tables, chairs and lamps. Magazines and newspapers were piled everywhere.

"I think we both believe that there's been some foul play here," Christina said, "so let's start with the most obvious question. Do you know if he had any enemies?"

Mary shook her head.

"What about any changes in his daily routine? Did you notice anything different?"

"Not really." Mary's eyes filled with tears. She wiped them with a tissue. "He worked late every night this past month, but that's not unusual for the Valley. I remember when he first started at Symex he worked nearly eighteen hours a day for an entire week."

"I don't want to pry into your personal life too much, but I need to know who he's recently been in contact with."

"Since he's been so busy at work, we haven't had much of a social life. The only person I've heard him talking to was George Stinson. He's an engineer at Symex, like Peter. They've known each other for years."

"I'll give him a call today. Anyone else you can think of?"

Mary shook her head. "Sorry."

"Do you have your most recent phone bill?"

"Sure," Mary said. "It's back in Peter's office."

"I'd like to take a look at it."

Mary eased up from the sofa and led Christina back to Peter's home office. Papers so completely covered his desk Christina couldn't tell if the tabletop was wood or metal. He also had papers strewn all over the floor, and the waste paper basket overflowed with leftover take-out wrappers.

"Sorry," Mary said, as she tried to clear a space on the desk. "I learned a long time ago to not come in here and tidy up. He said he was like an archaeologist and knew exactly what was buried under each layer of paper."

"Don't worry about the mess. I just hope we can find the phone bill."

After a few minutes digging, Mary located the telephone statements under a pile of unopened mail. She handed Christina two bills, one mobile and one home.

"What about files?" Christina asked. "Did he keep any work files at home?"

Mary opened the bottom drawer of his desk and pointed to a pile of papers, some in folders, but mostly not. "I guess you could say they're files. I tried to help him organize when we first moved in, but he obviously hasn't kept it up very well."

"Well, let's have a look." Christina thumbed through his file folders.

"Are you looking for anything in particular?" Mary asked.

"Not sure," Christina said. "Let's start with *S* for Symex?"

Mary got down on her knees and reached over to the P's. She held up her finger. "I think I know what you're looking for." She pulled out a thick file folder marked: PITA.

Christina looked confused.

"It was Peter's nickname for his latest project."

"Pita?"

"Pain In The Ass," Mary said. "He always had such a good sense of humor." Her voice broke. Christina hugged her, holding back her own tears.

"May I take this?" Christina asked, holding the folder.

"Take whatever you want."

"This and the phone bills will be enough to get me started."

*

On her way home from Mary's, Christina called Bart. He didn't answer, so she left a message saying she'd be in late. He knew where to find her if any emergencies popped up.

Back at her condo, Christina dialed the phone numbers on Peter's bill. She recognized both her work and home phone. As she went down the list, she dialed the numbers and wrote names next to them: pizza, Chinese, bank.

A voice recording answered the next number she punched in: "You've reached George. Leave a message and I'll call you back."

Probably George Stinson, Peter's colleague at Symex. The number she just dialed looked like a mobile number, so instead of leaving a message, she hung up and called the Symex Corporation directly, a number she knew by heart.

She left a message for George and moved on with her list. She noticed an international number listed at least twenty times as an incoming call to his mobile phone. Strangely, she didn't notice any outgoing calls to the same number—either from his mobile or home phone. She remembered from her European travels that the '39' prefix was assigned to Italy. Without thinking about the time change, she dialed the number.

A dignified female voice answered the phone. "Hotel della Luna et Stelli."

"*Per favore*," Christina said in rudimentary Italian. "*Parlate Inglese?*"

"*Si, un pocco.*"

"Where is your hotel located?"

"Forte dei Marmi, Madame, on the sandy beaches of Tuscany. The weather is beautiful and the sun shines each day."

Hmmm, this didn't sound all that bad. Maybe she could combine a little investigating with that much needed vacation she and Suzan discussed at Bix the other night.

With no further consideration, Christina made a reservation.

"For how much people?" the woman asked in awkward English.

"Uh—two," Christina replied.

*

"You did what!" Suzan shouted into the phone.

"I know I tend to be a bit impulsive, but I think there's a link between that hotel and Peter's death." Christina paused and took a breath. "And Suzan, I'd like you to come with me."

"Are you crazy? I can't pick up and leave on such short notice."

"I know it sounds insane, but I want to get to the bottom of this, for Peter and for Mary."

"Let's back up a minute. First, you don't know that Peter's death was anything other than a fall or, I'm sorry to say, maybe a suicide. Second, even if it was something more clandestine, you're a banker, not a private eye, and third, those calls from the hotel may have simply been vacation research."

"That's where you're wrong,' Christina was curt. "I know it wasn't vacation research. When Peter and I were at lunch, he said he'd go anywhere *but* Italy. It sounded a bit odd when he said it, but I definitely remember hearing it."

"Christina, your imagination is getting the best of you. Why don't you just let the police deal with this?"

"Because they've already written his death off as a suicide. Oh, and did I forget to mention, I'll buy your ticket if you come with me."

"First class?"

"Business."

"First or nothing." Christina heard Suzan's chair creak and then a faint thud. She could just picture Suzan gloating, leaning back in her chair and propping her feet on her desk.

Christina chewed the end of her eyeglass frame. She had accumulated enough United miles to upgrade the two of them, but their trip would wipe out her entire Mileage Plus account. On the other hand, this airline, like so many others, was flying under the protection of the US Bankruptcy laws. And with the price of oil climbing every day, the airline could easily crash and burn by the end of the year. Probably not the best choice of words to describe an airline going out of business, but that's how it was these days. "Okay, fine," she said. "We leave Monday. That gives you four full days to pack."

*

"You did what?" It was Christina's turn to scream into the phone.

"I was bullied into it," Suzan said. "When Brandy heard that wc were going to Italy, she wouldn't let me forget our conversation at Bix."

"I knew that would come back to haunt us," Christina said, "but this isn't really a vacation. We're flying by the seat of our pants. You know how she is. If everything isn't perfect, she tumbles into a tizzy. As far as I know, the hotel where I made a reservation could be a total dump."

"Christina, save your breath. She already bought her ticket."

"Did she know that I booked a ticket to Nice instead of Pisa?"

Christina had asked her travel agent to find her the best upgradeable fare for a non-stop flight from San Francisco. It turned out that ticket took them to Nice. The agent suggested they take the train from Nice down to Forte dei Marmi, which she assured Christina would be a relaxing and scenic journey along the Italian Riviera.

"You can count on it," Suzan said. "Remember, you two use the same travel agent. In fact, I think you told me Brandy recommended Skye Travel to you."

"Damn. You're right. At least I didn't have to buy her ticket too."

Christina's next call was to George Stinson. He had still not returned her call, and she wasn't one to sit around and wait.

Luckily, he answered on the first ring.

"Hello, George, my name is Christina Culhane. I work for Kingstone & Company. I was a very good friend of Peter's and I understand you were too. I'm very sorry about what happened. Mary told me that you two have worked together for years."

She heard some tapping at a keyboard but no speaking.

"George, are you there?"

"Oh, yes—Christina. Sorry about that. I meant to call you earlier." He cleared his throat. "It's strange not having him here. He always sat in the next cube over."

"I don't know about you, George, but I'm fairly certain Peter didn't commit suicide. What do you think?"

She heard more keyboard tapping but again no words. *Was this guy completely out to lunch?* She understood how some people were distracted at work, but it wasn't as if they were talking about the weather.

He cleared his throat again. "Uh—yes, real strange. But you never know how some people handle stress, and there's been a lot of it around here lately. This last project nearly pushed me over the edge."

"Can you tell me a little about what you were working on?" Christina asked.

"Fraid not, you know how it is around here. Everything's top secret."

"I understand." Peter had a high-level Department of Defense clearance rating. The FBI had interviewed her when they vetted Peter for his rating. They interrogated a number of his old high school friends, as well as neighbors and relatives.

"What about outside the workplace?" Christina asked. "Did he get involved in anything—how shall I put it—clandestine?"

George let out a low whistle. "Who, Peter? No way. All he did was work. There wasn't anything going on *outside the workplace* in that guy's life."

"I'm not so sure about that. Anyway, George, I should also tell you that I'll be taking a week off work. I'm assuming that with Peter gone, you'll be our point-person at Symex."

"Yeah, you're right about that. But to tell you the truth, I'm already stretched to the max. I'm not confident I can fill Peter's shoes on this one."

"I'm sure you'll do fine."

"So, you taking a vacation or something?"

"Yes, I'm going to Italy. Forte Dei Marmi. Have you ever been there?"

"Can't say that I have. Ah, listen Christina, I need to go. I'll see you Sunday at the funeral." He hung up without saying good-bye.

*

True to form, the weather in the Marina was cold and foggy the morning of Peter's funeral. She picked up Suzan at nine-thirty and headed over to the Mission Delores Basilica, an old Spanish-style building situated on a hilly, palm tree-lined street next to the Mission Delores, a white adobe church, which happens to be the oldest structure in San Francisco. The Mission survived the 1906 earthquake because of its four-foot thick adobe walls and wooden beams. After the earthquake, buildings made of brick crumbled in minutes. Mary had chosen this church because it wasn't far from their house, and in a neighborhood Peter had really begun to call home.

As Christina drove over the hill to Noe Valley the sun burned its way through the fog. By the time she and Suzan reached the Basilica it was downright hot. Inside, the church was nearly full with people. The moist, earthy smell of incense permeated the warm unventilated room and streams of sunlight shone through the stained-glass windows, casting dusty diagonal beams throughout the church. A few people were lighting white candles in front of the altar; but most talked in small groups by themselves. Christina recognized some of Peter's friends, but not more than a handful.

She walked over to Mary and gave her a kiss on the cheek. A little color had come back to her face, but she had aged ten years in the past three days. From not eating, she appeared gaunt, and the lines around her mouth, eyes and forehead were more visible. Her mom, who looked like Mary, but with a full head of grey hair and more expression lines, came over and greeted her. They had met eight years ago at Peter and Mary's wedding.

A man she didn't recognize approached Mary to offer some words of condolence. Christina guessed he was a colleague of Peter's from the way he had dressed in a light blue windbreaker with wrinkled khakis. It was difficult not to judge. Valley geeks may not have the first clue about fashion, but still, this *was* a funeral, not happy hour with the guys.

"Thank you George," Christina heard Mary say to him.

George Stinson from Symex? She stepped over to him. "Hello, George." She held out her hand. "Christina Culhane. We spoke Friday."

"Nice to meet you. Not under the best of circumstances, but still good to put a face with the voice." His eyes darted around the room. "So, you're headed off to Italy?"

"That's right. But first we're making a stop in Nice, on the French Riviera."

"When you coming back to work?" George asked.

"Not for at least ten days."

"Well, think of me slaving away, while you're frolicking on the beach."

"It's not a pure vacation; I think there's a connection between Peter's death and something going on in Italy."

He frowned at her. "What makes you say that?"

"I'd rather not discuss it now," Christina said. "But I'll fill you in when I get back."

"Fair enough." George looked over his shoulder toward the front of the church. "We better sit down." He turned away and joined a group of men seated in one of the pews.

After a few more minutes talking with Mary and her mother, they all sat down and listened to his friends eulogize Peter. Christina couldn't hold back the tears. She purposely hadn't worn any mascara, knowing that it could streak down her face in seconds. After a short sermon by a priest, Peter's two best friends—one from his softball team and the other his college roommate—gave a short presentation. The kind words were comforting but they didn't help numb the pain. After the last man spoke, Christina's tissue was so wet it shredded to bits. During the remainder of the presentation, she resorted to using the ends of her hair to wipe away her tears.

The service didn't last more than an hour, but Christina dragged herself from the pew, every muscle aching. And still there was the barbeque at Mary's house, on the deck—the one Peter had just finished building in the spring. He would've liked it, a casual get-together with great friends.

She and Suzan stayed until mid afternoon. By then, the fog had rolled back in and Christina could barely keep her eyes open. They would leave for Europe in the morning and she hadn't even begun to think about packing. Maybe after a nap she'd have enough energy to throw some clothes into a suitcase. In the meantime, she closed her eyes while Suzan drove them home and hoped that for just a few short minutes she would be relieved of this terrible nightmare.

Chapter Four

The cab arrived at Christina's house in the Marina first; several steep hills later, they pulled up in front of Suzan's place in Russian Hill. Brandy lived in Pacific Heights, just a few minutes away. Both Suzan's and Christina's jaws dropped when they saw Brandy standing on her front step with three pieces of brass-bound Louis Vuitton luggage.

"How in the hell will she carry all that?" Christina said.

On the plane, the flight attendants in first class went overboard pampering their passengers. Between continuous rounds of drinks, they served a gourmet meal. Christina couldn't get used to cutting into a filet mignon with a plastic knife but she supposed it was a small price to pay for security. Brandy, who washed down a Valium with a glass of champagne, slumbered in the anesthetized state of a stressed-out housewife.

Suzan sipped a mimosa while she watched a film on the portable DVD player. Christina decided to stick with water—she always had a horrible time with jet lag—and instead of watching a film, she read the PITA file, which had a red Confidential stamp on it. After just a few minutes, she could tell that even though the Symex spin-off was strictly non-military, Peter's notes in the file clearly indicated his involvement in some sort of anti-ballistic missile research and development. One hundred percent of the company's contracts were with the U.S. Air Force, Navy and the Army, who had commissioned them to provide technology for various military applications. She also read, from an internal office memo in the file, that potential uses of this technology included guidance systems for ground-to-air missiles and interceptors, air-to-air missiles, and threat warning devices.

Christina thought of the possible ramifications and shuddered. If a terrorist organization got control of this technology they could cripple the United States Armed Forces instantly, and thousands of American and allied soldiers would be killed in the process.

She took a deep breath and put down the file. Peter had written many of the pages in some sort of computer code, which was quickly putting her to sleep. She made a mental note to ask George for his help in deciphering the jumble of numbers and letters. In the meantime, she needed to stretch her legs and use the bathroom before she settled down to sleep.

She walked down the aisle to the back of the plane. Most people were asleep, but one man, a heavyset bald guy, sat on the aisle in the business class section. When she walked by him, he stared at her long enough to make her uncomfortable, but she kept walking. After she used the lavatory and crossed through the small galley kitchen at the back of the plane, the bald guy stood in front of her, blocking the aisle.

"Excuse me," she said. She tried to pass him. Instead of making room for her, he stepped directly in front of her. When she stepped to the other side, he mirrored her movements. "Excuse me, sir," she said forcefully. "I'd like to go to my seat."

He didn't move or say a word, only stared at her with steely black eyes. She pushed past him, brushing her shoulder to his chest, and hurried back to her seat. What a creep.

As the plane started its descent, Christina woke up groggy. She had only caught a few hours sleep. Brandy complained about still being dizzy from the Valium, but Suzan, on the other hand, seemed to be in the best spirits, as if she'd slept a full night in her own bed.

Given that they each had first class tickets, they expected their baggage to come off the carousel first, with the orange, airline-issued *priority* tag. Brandy's three pieces and Suzan's backpack all shot down the ramp within minutes of them arriving at the baggage terminal. But after ten minutes of watching the same bags circle the carousel, Christina's still had not appeared.

Brandy, already on her third cigarette since deplaning, said, "Now what are we gonna do? Do you think your bag is lost?"

Christina pushed her glasses onto the top of her head and rubbed her eyes. The smell from the crowded airport and the cigarette smoke was giving her a headache. "Let's give it a few more minutes."

Finally, Christina's bag slid down the ramp. Her peacock-blue pashmina stuck out from the corner of the bag.

"Why's my pashmina caught?" she asked. "And why would my suitcase have been opened after we went through security?"

"You know how it is these days," Suzan said. "Security personal think they have carte blanche."

Christina grabbed her bag and they navigated their way through customs.

*

"At least that's finally over." They walked outside the terminal to a road lined with palm trees. The sunshine and fresh air was a welcome relief after ten hours on a stuffy airplane. Several Mercedes taxis sat parked in a line; they piled into the first one.

"L'Hotel Negresco, si'l vous plait," Christina told the driver. Instead of immediately catching a train down to Forte Dei Marmi they'd spend a day in France recuperating from jet-lag.

About fifteen minutes later, they arrived at the heart of the French Riviera. Their hotel, which occupied the corner of the block, was an elegant white *Belle Epoque* building with a peach roof trimmed in green tarnished copper.

The cab driver turned to Christina. *"Cent Euros, s'il vous plait."*

From the back seat, Brandy poked Christina in the shoulder. "What did he say?"

"One hundred and twenty-five American dollars, please. That's what."

Christina reluctantly handed him the fare. "This must be the special rate he charges American women," she muttered. No tip for this guy.

She approached the desk clerk and gave him her name. The man pursed his lips together and slid his fingers along a skinny black mustache, greased to curl up on the ends. "Mademoiselle, I'm sorry, but I don't see your reservation."

"Excuse me?" Brandy glared at Christina. "Are you telling me we don't have a reservation?"

Christina gave Suzan an "I told you so" look.

"Calm down." Christina dug in her handbag for the confirmation number.

The clerk pursed his lips again and scanned the page. He handed it back to Christina. "I'm sorry Mademoiselle; this reservation was for last night. Americans often make this mistake. They forget that they lose a day traveling."

"Anne Skye would never make that mistake."

"She didn't." Christina looked at Brandy. "I did. I only used her to make the airline reservations. I prefer doing my own hotel research. Sorry about this, guys. I've had a lot on my mind." Shit. Here it was high season on the Riviera and they didn't have a room. "There must be something," Christina pleaded with the clerk.

He let out a deep sigh. "Let me check." Fastidiously, he tapped the keyboard. "Ah—here we are." He held up a well-manicured finger. "We have one room left. I'm afraid it's quite small for three people, but there is a sofa by the window." He looked up from his monitor and smiled. "And, I might add, it has a spectacular view of the sea."

"We'll take it." Christina turned to Brandy. "I'll sleep on the couch."

The room was bright and sunny, and the view reminded Christina of the David Hockney paintings she had seen at a recent Museum of Modern Art exhibit.

"Let's hit the beach," Christina said. "It's a gorgeous sunny day, and I'm not going to waste it in here."

Brandy pulled herself up from the bed. "After seeing all those women prance around in their hip swim suits, I think I could use an authentic French bikini."

They tried on several swimsuits: one-pieces, thongs and strings, all of which left little to the imagination.

Brandy held up a bottom that consisted of a piece of dental floss on the backside and a small triangle of material on the front. "Even if I lost those last ten pounds, I wouldn't be caught dead in this." She hung it back up and pointed to the rack of one-pieces. "I think that low-cut black tank is more my style."

Suzan, the most voluptuous of the group, settled on a cream-colored, macramé two-piece. She held it next to her body and looked in the mirror. "On second thought," she patted her hips and shook her head, "I'm not taking off my shorts unless I'm flat on my back."

"You've got great curves, plus a tiny waist," Christina said. "That's more than I can say."

Christina, who had a thin runner's body, but not much of a chest, bought an orange and pink string bikini with a matching floral sarong that she wrapped around her waist.

Armed with towels, tanning lotion and magazines, the women dodged speeding cars and mopeds to run across the busy Promenade des Anglais.

At the beach, Brandy scooped up a pile of tiny pebbles. "What's the deal with these boulders?"

"Oh, I forgot to tell you," Christina said, "you won't find many sand beaches here. But the hotel beach club has lounge chairs we can use."

They staked out a space and slathered their skin with banana and coconut-scented oil and watched the scantily clad people parade across the beach.

"I've never seen so many tanned, hard bodies in one place," Christina said.

"And the women are topless," said Brandy.

"When in Rome…" Suzan whipped off her macramé top and tossed it in the air.

"Nice tattoo," Brandy said, noticing a small black marijuana leaf inked above Suzan's right breast.

"Please, don't remind me." Suzan covered the design with her hand. "It's an indelible souvenir of my wild and crazy days at Berkeley."

Brandy pulled out the *Marie Claire* she'd bought at the airport and began flipping through the fashion ads. Christina started reading her PITA file.

"Christina. What are you doing?" Suzan snatched the papers from Christina's hand. "I know that this is supposed to be a working vacation, but can't all this technical garbage wait until later?"

Christina caught Suzan's wrist and took the papers back. "When I went to Peter's house last week, Mary gave these to me. It's pretty clear that Symex has been getting some serious money from DARPA and the B.M.D.O."

"I don't mean to sound disinterested, but I need to concentrate on people watching and my tan."

"No, you need to listen to this. It's important."

"Okay." Suzan groaned. "I know what DARPA is, but what the hell is the B.M.D.O?"

Brandy shot up from her white wooden lounge chair. "Hey, I don't know what DARPA is."

"The Defense Advanced Research Projects Agency."

"A lot of good that does me." She fell back onto her chair and resumed reading her magazine.

"It's a small division of the Army's R & D department," Christina explained. "And the B.M.D.O. is the Ballistic Missile Defense Organization. The Cold War may be over, but the war against terror sure isn't. From what I can tell, I think it's one of those top secret Black Projects the government commissions from time to time."

Brandy threw her magazine onto the ground. "I can't believe you guys. This is the last thing we should be focusing on. Look around us: Water. Beach. Men. That's why I'm here."

"Me too." Suzan pushed up her sunglasses and looked at Christina. "But I admit; it *is* kind of scary."

"You bet it is. This technology could be used against us in the worst way." Christina applied another thick layer of lotion to her legs. Without this protection, the sun would turn her pale skin into a mosaic of rust-colored freckles, but at least her naturally cinnamon-colored hair turned blonde.

Brandy rolled onto her stomach. "If you two will excuse me, I'm going to get back to my article: *The 10 Best Ways to Please Your Man in Bed.* From what I've read so far, I could give them a few suggestions."

Several drinks, and four hours later, Christina noticed Brandy pressing the red skin on her arms, leaving white oval prints.

"I'm frying out here," Brandy said. "Let's go back to the hotel and get something to eat."

Back in their room, they looked at each other with sunburned faces and tired eyes.

"We've all been awake for nearly forty-eight hours," Christina said, "and I'm not really in the mood to party all night. How 'bout we grab something quick on the street and call it an early night?"

They ran down the stairs instead of waiting for the antique elevator, and found a local *boulangerie* and *fromagerie* that were still open. They bought a baguette, some mineral water and a wedge of Brie.

"So much for experiencing the gastronomical wonders of France," Christina said.

Famished, they devoured every last morsel of cheese and the entire baguette the minute they hit the sidewalk. Feeding time at the San Francisco Zoo would seem sedate in comparison.

"Hey," Suzan said, "let's stop and listen to this guy. This is my kind of music." She pointed to a black man, with long dreadlocks and a bright white smile. He tapped a steel drum and played reggae music in front of an outdoor cafe. Back in their fast-paced world in San Francisco he would've been invisible.

After a few minutes, a young schoolboy ventured outside with his harmonica. The spontaneous energy became contagious and a small crowd formed. Soon after that, Suzan and Christina began dancing and tossing coins into the drum case.

Then Christina saw Brandy across the street talking to the bald guy she'd seen on the airplane. She stopped dancing and sprinted over to them. By the time she reached Brandy, he was gone.

She caught her breath. "Who was that guy you were talking to?"

"Didn't get his name." Brandy fluffed her hair with her fingertips. "He was pretty sexy, don't you think?"

"Sexy? Are you crazy? That guy totally harassed me on the plane."

A group of boys on mopeds whizzed past them, honking their horns. Brandy responded by giving them the finger. "He was on our plane last night?"

"Yes," Christina said, "and he was extremely rude. By the way, what were you two talking about?"

"Not much," Brandy said, "but he did ask me how long I was going to be in Nice. I think he was going to ask me to dinner— until he saw *you* running across the street."

"Well good thing I did. He really gave me the creeps. And besides, you're here to meet European men, not professional wrestlers."

Brandy tapped a red nail against her cheek. "Come to think of it, he did look a bit like Jesse Ventura."

Christina shook her head and smiled. "I can assure you, he wasn't the ex-governor of Minnesota."

They walked back across the street to join Suzan. Brandy held her forefinger and thumb an inch apart. "Didn't you think he was just a little bit sexy?"

"Like a bouncer at a strip club."

"Where'd you guys go?" Suzan asked.

"I met a real hottie," Brandy said, "but Christina scared him away."

"Let's go back to the hotel," Christina said. She looked back over her shoulder, but saw nothing out of the ordinary.

Suzan's long hair swirled around her shoulders as she continued dancing in front of her. "In a few minutes."

*

Christina's back ached from sleeping on the small love seat— hardly a sofa by American standards. And why was it so blasted hot? She looked at her watch. Twelve-thirty! She jumped up so quickly that she almost blacked out. She ran over to the double bed where Suzan and Brandy slept and shook it. "Wake up! We'll miss our train."

Suzan pulled the sheet over her head.

Christina yanked it back down. "No more sleeping. The last direct train to Italy is in an hour."

Chapter Five

When their train rolled into Massa Carrara, the train stop nearest to Forte dei Marmi, Christina understood why the town's name translated to 'marble fortress.' She saw wall-like slabs of cut marble and granite stacked along the tracks for miles. Behind them, white-capped mountains rose in the distance. Could that possibly be snow?

The train came to a screeching halt. "Okay troops, this is it," Christina said. "I checked the map, and we have at least five kilometers into town. We need a cab."

"You can say that again," Brandy said. "There's no way I can drag these bags more than a few feet."

A blast of hot air assaulted them as they stepped outside. Christina walked over to a tourist information kiosk. Closed. But luckily, a posting of several local cab companies hung on the outside wall. She called all of them, but after nearly a half-hour, she threw her hands in the air. "We'd have better luck finding a cable car. Let's forget the cab idea and hit the road."

With her free hand, Christina grabbed Brandy's hanging bag and slung it over her shoulder. "Suzan," she said. "Maybe you could take one of Brandy's bags."

Suzan picked up Brandy's cosmetic case, which resembled a carpenter's toolbox, if not for the beige LV's stamped all over the brown leather. "What are you carrying in here, girl? Solid gold bars?"

Armed with her handbag and a trunk large enough to hide a dead body, Brandy trudged onward.

Twenty minutes later, after trekking in ninety-degree heat, the women experienced firsthand the derivation of the word luggage: *to lug.* They collapsed on the side of the road to rest. Ripples of hot air hovered above the pavement, and Christina's shoulders felt as if they had been pulled from their sockets. Her t-shirt was drenched in perspiration where the luggage straps hung from her shoulders, and she could feel the skin on her face burning.

"I can't go any farther." Brandy sat down on her bag and pulled off her shiny new Prada's. Her feet were as pink as her shoes, and watery white blisters had formed on her heels. "I wish I could ditch my luggage." She rubbed her swollen feet. "This steamer trunk I'm dragging around weighs a ton." Small droplets of foundation dripped down her face. She dabbed her chin and forehead with a tissue. "I'm not used to all this exercise. Biking, hiking—what's next: climbing the Mount Vesuvius? I feel like a contestant on *Survivor*."

"Listen, girlfriend." Suzan swung her hip out to the side and pointed her finger at Brandy. "None of us wants to take another step, and I'm in a ton of pain. Why don't we just hitch hike? I'm willing to try anything at this point."

They stood on the side of the road and stuck their thumbs out. A train whistled in the background.

"Matchbox cars," Brandy fumed, as she watched the miniature cars whiz by. "There's no way they could pack in the three of us and our luggage."

Luckily, a farmer transporting a load of fresh melons in his pickup truck noticed them. When he pulled over, his tire hit a large rock, which sent a metal hubcap reeling. It skirted across the cement and spun like a top before it settled with a clatter and a final loud clink. The farmer hopped out, collected the hubcap, and motioned for the women to get in.

"Christina," Suzan said, eyeing the short-haired terrier on the seat of the cab. "You speak some Italian. Why don't you squeeze up front? We'll climb in back with our luggage."

Having grown up in Philadelphia, it would've been nearly impossible not to learn at least a little Italian. Christina had often joked that there were more Italians in South Philly than in Milan.

45

She crawled in the front seat and patted the dog's head. "Hi, Scruffy."

Over the noise of the engine, which clearly lacked a muffler, Christina tried to communicate that they would like the driver to drop them in the center of town. *"Centro, per favore, centro."*

The farmer stopped abruptly in the middle of a busy intersection. Irate drivers popped their heads out of their car windows—yelling, shaking fists and honking horns.

Suzan quickly threw their luggage onto the side of the road.

"Brandy, jump!" she yelled.

Christina shouted *"grazie"* to the driver and leapt out the door.

The farmer sped away, waving in his rearview mirror. They sat down amidst their pile of luggage and watched a parade of Italians pass by on foot and bicycle.

Christina noticed Suzan's puzzled expression. "What's bothering you?"

"I thought this was supposed to be a beach town."

"It is, the water's just a few blocks away." She could smell the salty scent of the sea and feel its cool breeze.

"Why is everyone so dressed up?"

Women peddled by on their bicycles, their hair perfectly slicked-back, wearing black skin-tight dresses and shiny gold jewelry. Suzan was right. Who would dress like that to ride a bike? The men appeared no less casual. They strutted by in white linen shirts, freshly pressed khakis and shiny brown loafers. Their hair was also perfectly coiffed and their eyes hidden by the latest style of designer sunglasses. She even noticed a couple of them wearing silk scarves, neatly folded into the collar of their unbuttoned shirts.

Most noticeable of all, everyone who peddled, strolled or strutted also talked on a mobile phone. One man, who wore the Riviera shabby-chic uniform of leather Tods, faded jeans, and a rumpled, navy linen jacket talked on one mobile while he sent text messages on another.

"The brain cancer in this town must be off the charts," Christina said.

Suzan nodded. "This sure ain't Santa Cruz."

That was the understatement of the millennium; no wet suits, hippies, surfboards or beat-up VW buses. They looked at themselves in their shorts and t-shirts and laughed. Forte dei Marmi was one chic beach resort.

"I'd love to sit here and watch this fashion parade all day," Christina said, "but we need to find our hotel."

They lifted themselves off the sidewalk and looked behind them. A light pink, Mediterranean-style hotel across the street caught their eye. Flower boxes dripping with scarlet geraniums hung under windows framed by faded green shutters. The hotel sign displayed an ornate, celestial array of stars, a moon and the sun. *Hotel della Luna et Stelli*. Hotel of the Moon and Stars.

"Hey, the farmer didn't do too badly." Christina pointed. "That's our hotel."

"Please tell me we have a reservation." Brandy lifted herself up from her trunk.

They dragged their bags across the sidewalk and into the hotel. An Italian woman, with the name "Donatella" sewn onto her uniform, saw them struggling and rushed out of the hotel to help.

"Prego, prego, i bagagli, prego!" Thin and slight, she held her hands out to take one of Christina's bags.

"Thank you," Christina said, "but I'm okay. My bag is almost bigger than you are."

"Not to worry, a boy help me."

She ran back to the hotel and returned with a strong-looking young man. He loaded the luggage onto a cart and wheeled it into the lobby. Donatella scurried back to the front desk to check them in.

The hotel lobby, expansive and airy, contained a large atrium filled with fully-grown potted palms and ferns. A tumbling waterfall, cascading adjacent to the plants, contributed to the earthy aroma of a tropical rainforest. The floors, covered with rose and gray marble, looked as smooth as bone china. Christina stopped and marveled at the twenty-foot ceilings adorned with ancient frescoes, and the walls, lined with gilded mirrors and white marble statues.

At the reception desk, Christina remembered that in her impulsive call, she had reserved rooms for only two.

"Signora, I'm sorry, but we're a party of three now," Christina explained. "Is it possible to get another room?"

"Not to worry," Donatella said. "I ask." She smiled, picked up the phone and rattled off something in Italian.

A young sultry-looking man emerged from a doorway and walked over to the front desk. He wore his wavy black hair chin-length, and had large almond-shaped brown eyes. Christina poked Suzan in the side and discreetly pointed at him.

The darkly handsome man walked behind the desk and took the women's passports from Donatella. He opened each one and stared at them, individually, for several seconds. He gave the passports back to Donatella and said something in Italian to her; then he left the reception area.

Donatella smiled at the women and handed them each a key. "Room thirty-one for Ms. Culhane, thirty-two for Ms. Anders, and thirty-three for Ms. Jensen. Your baggage will be delivered shortly."

"Any room sounds good to me," Brandy said. "I'm ready to collapse."

"Who do you think that guy is?" Suzan asked Christina as they rode the elevator to the third floor.

"I don't know. The manager—or maybe the concierge."

They found their suite of rooms on the top floor in the corner facing the sea. The three bedrooms shared a luxuriously furnished sitting room, and they each had their own bathroom.

"What a place!" Christina sank into a white, over-stuffed sofa that sat in front of a granite fireplace. She put her feet up on the marble coffee table and pulled a floating gardenia from a crystal bowl. It smelled like perfume of the gods. She pulled herself up from the heavenly sofa to inspect the bedroom. The sheets on the bed were smooth and fresh, and sunlight streamed in from a skylight. A large west-facing window looked out on the sea and filled the room with fresh air.

She washed her face, and was on her way downstairs when Brandy called out from her bathroom. "Hey, wait. Try getting us some reservations for tonight. I read about a restaurant called Castelli in *Town and Country*. It got a great write-up."

"I'll do my best," Christina said. "Maybe the concierge can help."

When she reached the lobby, no one was at the front desk so she ventured into a room that seemed to be the library. It smelled like old leather and cigar smoke. Rows of antique leather-bound books lined the walls, and in front of them, the man from the front desk sat at an oak library table, sipping an espresso. He smoked a cigarette and appeared engrossed in some papers. Nevertheless, Christina pulled up a club chair and sat next to him. When he saw her, he took off his wire-rimmed reading glasses.

"Hello." She smiled and extended her hand. "Christina Cul— I mean, hi, I'm Christina." She almost kicked herself for reverting back to her business persona.

"I'm Franco. Nice to meet you."

"Thanks for arranging our rooms. That was a wonderful surprise."

"It was my pleasure." A purring cat could not have competed with his sultry accent.

"Could you do us another favor?" As concierge, she figured he probably knew all the hot spots. "Have you heard of the restaurant, Castelli?"

"Ah, Il Castello." He let out a deep sigh. "Yes, of course."

She felt her cheeks flush over her mispronunciation. "My friend read about it in a magazine. I wondered if you could get us a reservation for tonight."

Franco's cigarette smoldered in a marble ashtray. Christina frowned when the smoke blew toward her face.

"I'm sorry." He took a quick drag, blew the smoke away from her face and held the cigarette under the table. "I forget, American women don't smoke—especially women from California."

"Well, they do," she said, smiling. "In fact I'm traveling with one of them; but she's actually from New York, and they're a different breed altogether."

He stubbed out the cigarette. "Better?"

Christina smiled. "Much."

He leaned back in his chair and crossed his legs. "I could arrange for you and your friends to have dinner at Il Castello but the three of you should not go there by yourselves."

"Why's that?" Christina watched his mouth. His words resonated so eloquently along her spine that the hair on her neck tingled, as if he were reciting poetry or singing.

"It is the most romantic and expensive restaurant on the coast. You need to go there with a man you are in love with—or with a man who is in love with you."

"Thanks for the warning." How was it that everything he said sounded so damn sexy? "So, where do you suggest?"

"There's a little restaurant on the beach, called La Barca, and I think it would be more pleasurable for the three of you. If you like, I'll make a booking for you."

Only after she left did it occur to her that perhaps she should've tipped him for securing the reservation.

Starving, as usual, the three women wasted no time walking over to the *trattoria*. The homey aroma of roasting garlic and rosemary welcomed them as they walked through the heavy oak doors. Large glass balls and fishing nets, made from thick coarse ropes, hung on the walls, and the maitre d' was unexpectedly accommodating. He sat them at a table by a floor-to-ceiling window that opened onto the sand.

The sea air smelled fresh and clean, and the breeze felt cool, but not cold or uncomfortable. Christina gazed out at a lone man swimming in the rippled sea, his dark form silhouetted by the glowing orange sun setting behind him. He swam rhythmically, his stroke as steady and peaceful as a metronome.

The minute they sat, their waiter brought them a bottle of Barbaresco, saying that Franco, from the Hotel della Luna had sent it over.

"How thoughtful," Christina said, as he poured her a small amount to taste. She always felt so pretentious swirling and sniffing the wine. Instead, she took a sip, and allowed the liquid to rest on her tongue for a second or two. As it didn't burn her lips like acid or choke her to death, she figured it was good enough for everyone else to drink. "Thank you. It's fine."

The waiter nodded and poured them each a glass.

"Franco is certainly making sure that we're well taken care of," Suzan said.

Christina drank more of the robust red wine. "Maybe he can help me figure out the connection between Peter and whatever else has been going on down here."

Suzan winked at Christina. "And maybe he can help you figure out your love life while he's at it."

"Suzan! A bottle of wine doesn't mean he's interested in me. He's just taking care of us, like he would any other guests."

"Yeah, right." Suzan drank her wine and picked up the menu.

*

When they got back to the hotel that evening, Donatella was still working. Suzan and Brandy went up to their room while Christina waited for Donatella to finish her call.

"May I help you?" Donatella asked.

"You're sure burning the midnight oil."

"I'm sorry?" Donatella cocked her head.

Christina smiled. "Oh nothing. Just an American colloquialism. Anyway, I was wondering—have you ever heard of a man named Peter Carmaletti?"

"An Italian man?" Donatella asked.

"No, he's American. From California."

Donatella shook her head. "I'm sorry. I not hear of this man."

"What about a company called Symex?"

Again Donatella shook her head. "No, I not hear of this name either. But maybe Signore Doria knows."

"Is Signore Doria a guest here?"

"No, but you meet him this afternoon. Franco Doria. Maybe ask him these names."

*

As Christina fell asleep, Franco worked late in his office. He smoked his last cigarette of the night, and mused about the American girl, the friendly one with the great legs. Something about her caught his attention. Was it her smile, or the way the light bounced off her hair? Sometimes it looked blonde, other times as shiny as copper. Or again, maybe it was just the great legs. Regardless, he needed to stay focused.

He stubbed out his cigarette and placed his call to the US. Every night the same call, the same time. There was nothing unusual to report tonight, but he was still obliged to call.

*

The scent of freshly baking bread wafted through the open window from the kitchen downstairs and enticed the girls into waking earlier than usual.

"I'm going for a run," Christina said, as she laced up her shoes. "On my way back I'll pick up some Italian newspapers and the European *Wall St. Journal*. Any requests?"

"The *Wall Street Journal*?" Brandy said. "No thanks. Pick me up one of those slick fashion bibles I keep seeing at all the kiosks."

Christina left the hotel and walked toward the sea. The air was hot and muggy by San Francisco standards, by any standard really. She almost turned back, but forged ahead. She knew if she skipped her run, she'd feel sluggish all day, so she tried to stay in the shade by hugging the buildings and ducking under restaurant awnings. Once she hit the beach, already packed with sunbathers and swimmers, she walked to the hard sand by the water and started running. Little boys kicked about red and white balls while little girls, some in swimsuits, some *au natural*, made sandcastles. Crowds of people waded in the waves or surfed on boogie boards. And although a bit of a sea breeze ruffled her hair, the late morning sun was blistering. After thirty minutes, the heat grew too much for her. She stopped running, took off her shoes and walked into the water. The cold water so exhilarated her that she dove into the waves fully clothed. After a few minutes playing in the waves and bobbing around like a buoy, she walked to the shore and grabbed her shoes. By the time she made it back to the hotel, her clothes and hair had nearly dried. She asked the young man at the reception desk if Signore Doria was available.

"I'm sorry, Madame, but he is occupied now. He has asked not to be disturbed. Is there anything I may help you with?"

"Does the name Peter Carmaletti mean anything to you?"

The man shook his head.

*

Later that afternoon, after a two-hour sizzle on the beach, Christina and her friends took relief back at the hotel. They ordered a pitcher of ice-cold lemonade made with real lemons, probably picked from one of the trees outside.

"Who's up for hitting some of the boutiques?" Suzan asked.

"I am," Brandy said. "I got some great tips from *La Moda.*"

"I think I'll stay back and read some more from Peter's file," Christina said. "Also, since I dragged an Italian grammar book over here, I should probably spend some time brushing up."

As promised, when Suzan and Brandy headed out for their fashion expedition, Christina gathered her Italian book and Peter's file. She explored the hotel grounds in search of a cool and quiet place to read.

She opened a door on the far side of the lobby that led to an internal courtyard. Magenta bougainvillea clung to the crumbling stone walls. A marble fountain gurgled in the corner, and mature grape vines, hanging from a pergola, shaded the area over a wooden bench. Taking a deep breath, she savored the fresh scent of jasmine. She had found her sanctuary, and she knew she would be comfortable there for hours.

She looked over the file and jotted down some notes. Still frustrated about not understanding the computer code, she made a mental note to call George later in the day, when it would be morning in California. Then, putting Peter's file aside, she moved on to Italian.

As she read her Italian lessons aloud, Christina felt the palpable presence of another human being encroaching on her space. She looked up to see Franco leaning against the arched stone doorway, staring at her. She had no idea how long he had been watching her, but her stomach fluttered when she noticed him. She smiled, and he walked over to her.

"I'm charmed to see an American wishing to learn our language," Franco said. "Would you like some help?"

"That would be very kind," she replied, uncharacteristically flustered. "Only if you have time."

When he sat on the bench next to her, she noticed the subtle fragrance of musk, rather than the cigarette smoke she'd smelled yesterday.

He took the book from her and helped her get through a few chapters. But his seductive Italian accent made it nearly impossible for her to concentrate—that and the way silky dark lashes framed his almond eyes. In fact, given the time she spent admiring his smooth brown skin, she may have been better off without his assistance.

After about forty-five minutes of speaking and reading a foreign language, Christina's brain felt like mush. She took the book back from him, closed it and fumbled through asking him what he'd done this afternoon: *"Che hai fatto sta sera?"* She wanted to know and understand him better, but that was all she could pull from her vast repertoire of Italian phrases and words.

"Very good, Christina. You learn fast."

"No-o-o." Playfully, she pounded her book. "Answer in Italian. It's the only way I'll learn."

"Very well then: *Io ho dipinto il mio studio dietro il giardino.*"

His response, flowing like an operetta, explained that he had spent the morning painting in his studio behind the courtyard.

"May I see some of your paintings?" Christina asked in English, already giving up on a meaningful conversation in a language she didn't fully understand.

"You're kind to express interest," Franco said softly, "but I rarely show my paintings to anyone. I fear that other people would not understand their meaning." He smiled slightly and pointed at her nose. "You look like a clown."

Christina covered her burnt nose. "I overdid it our first day on the beach."

"I think it's *carina.*"

"What's that mean?"

"Funny, yet cute." He shifted closer to her. Faced with his seductive lips, her own felt dry and colorless. She wanted to apply lip-gloss, but knew it would be awkward to reach for her Strawberry Lip Smacker.

"So, Christina," said Franco. "What brings you to Forte dei Marmi?"

"Actually, I'm here in your neck of the woods because—"

Franco frowned, looking perplexed. "What does this *neck of the woods* mean?" He wrapped his hands around his neck as if he were trying to strangle himself.

Christina smiled, delighted that this very sensual man could also act so goofy.

"I'm sorry," she said. "I guess I should've said that one of my dearest friends brought me to your lovely village by the sea."

Franco raised his eyebrow. "Oh? How is that?"

Christina looked down. "Actually, it's tragic. My friend died last week, and I don't think his death was accidental."

He put his warm hand on her thigh, and her skin tingled instantly. "I'm very sorry to hear that. Was he a guest at this hotel?"

"No," Christina said, "but I noticed from his phone bill that several calls to him were placed from here. I'd like to know who made them."

"Would it help you if I checked the hotel records to see who stayed here on the days of these calls?"

Christina hoped that he would keep his hand on her leg. "That would be a huge help."

"My pleasure." Franco leaned closer to her. She felt the heat of his body next to hers. "Now tell me, what do you and your friends have planned for the evening?"

"Nothing whatsoever." She pushed her hair behind her ear and let her sandal dangle loosely from her foot.

"There is a nightclub on the water I think you would enjoy. If you like, I drive you and your friends."

"That sounds like fun. What time do you get off work?"

His sensuous lips curved slightly. "Whenever I want, my Christina. I'll meet you downstairs at ten." He softly touched her face, brushed her hair away from her forehead, and whispered, "Ciao, dolcina," in her ear.

A wave of warmth passed through her at this unexpected gesture of affection. Unable to study any longer, she watched Franco walk away from the bench and disappear into the long shadows of the late afternoon sun.

Chapter Six

The Hotel della Luna had reciprocity with the exclusive beach club Twiga, owned by the Renault Formula One team manager, Flavio Briatore. Each afternoon, around four, guests gathered on the terrace to enjoy freshly cooked antipasto dishes, prepared with locally grown herbs and fish caught that morning. The world's most gorgeous men and women filled the open-air, Moroccan-style tent, and while neither Suzan nor Brandy had sighted Naomi Campbell or Heidi Klum, two of Briatore's former flames, they reported that everyone looked as if they had stumbled straight off the catwalk.

Before Christina had even entered the club, she smelled pizza bread baking in the wood-fired oven. A deejay in the corner played sexy chill-out music, its rhythmic beat undulating through a room decorated with low round tables and mountains of cinnamon and persimmon-colored pillows. She pushed her way through a billowing silk curtain to the outside dining area and approached Suzan and Brandy, already surrounded by six male-model types.

Half-filled glasses of red wine crowded their table, along with bottles of sparkling water, small pizzas and a platter of sizzling fish and vegetable kebobs.

"It looks like you two are learning to soak up the Italian way of life." Christina poured herself a glass of water. "We've been invited to go to this night club, La Capannina, tonight—with Franco and some of his friends."

One of the men interrupted her. He had short dark hair, bright blue eyes and a dark tan. "La Capannina is the most popular club on the coast—you'll never get in tonight. Annabella is performing. She's Italy's most famous pop star, and the show has been sold out for months."

"It's sounding more fun than I thought." Christina chewed a mouthful of the warm, crispy pizza. The crust was so thin she could almost see through it.

"We might as well try, what do we have to lose?" Brandy poured another glass of wine for herself and for the man next to her, a muscular fellow clad only in black swim trunks.

With her fork, Christina slid some fish pieces off the metal skewer and popped one in her mouth. "Franco told us to meet him downstairs in the lobby around ten, so we better grab something to eat here. I have a feeling we'll be out late tonight."

*

As they primped for their big night, a combination of hairdryers blowing full force, curling irons heating and the CD player blasting blew a fuse and knocked out the electricity to their suite.

"Party's over." Christina searched in the dark for the one dressy outfit she'd brought: a silk, apple green, spaghetti-strap dress. She opted for contacts instead of glasses, and rather than let her hair dry naturally, she turned the ends under with Brandy's warm curling iron.

Brandy wore a Roberto Cavalli dress sporting more animal print than one would expect to see on safari in Africa. When the fuse blew, she still had hot rollers in her hair. Red nail polish in hand, she merely moved closer to the window to finish painting.

"You look fabulous," Christina said to Suzan, who had dressed in an ankle length slip dress. "That caramel color flatters you."

"Thanks," Suzan said. "Now if only I can get my hair to cooperate." Several silver bracelets, formed like a Slinky, slid on her wrist as she straightened her hair with a hot styling iron. At last, she secured her masterpiece with hairspray.

Christina smoothed on some lip-gloss. "Let's get downstairs and wait for Franco."

In the library, a young Italian man stood up to greet them. He had a black goatee and hair so short he must have to shave it daily. "You must be the three American girls. My name is Stefano—I'm a friend of Franco." His accent, though Italian, sounded less refined than Franco's. "And you must be Christina." He looked at her with obvious approval. "Who are your lovely friends?"

Christina barely had time to introduce Suzan and Brandy before Stefano pressed himself between them. He locked his arms into theirs like an escort at a debutante ball and accompanied them down the hallway to the bar. When he poured them each a glass of the Italian champagne, Prosecco, a shiny gold Rolex flashed at his wrist.

Christina took a sip of the sparkling wine just as Franco descended the massive marble staircase into the lobby. She held her glass to her lips and stared. His hair, always wavy and shiny, looked sleek and damp, as though he had just stepped from the shower. He wore a pale-yellow linen shirt with neatly pressed cream trousers.

"Is everyone ready?"

The group walked outside behind the hotel and squeezed into an older-model Volkswagen Jetta. They followed the coast down about a mile to La Capannina. The club, built on stilts to let the water flow underneath, appeared packed with people. Outside balconies spilled over with patrons who couldn't find a place to sit indoors, and they couldn't get near the parking lot for the crowd of hundreds standing on the pavement. Franco left the car on the side of the road, and the five of them got out and pushed their way through the fans of Annabella.

Above the noise of the crowd, Suzan shouted to Christina. "There's no way in hell we'll get into this place."

And yet, as they approached the entrance, the bouncers left their posts to help the group break through. Inside, the music was deafening. A man in a white dinner jacket and black bow tie escorted them to a table at the corner of the stage.

Once again, Suzan leaned over and shouted to Christina, "I guess this is one of the perks of working in such an upscale hotel."

Unbidden, two waiters brought over a platter of shellfish arranged on crushed ice and placed three bottles of champagne into silver buckets. Franco held a chair for Christina and then sat next to her. He poured her a glass of champagne and looked into her eyes.

"Your emerald eyes are beautiful." He leaned closer to her. "They match your dress perfectly."

"Thank you."

"So," he said, "did you notice the stars shining through your skylight?" He put his hand on her thigh and spoke into her ear. "I gave that room to you because I thought you would find it romantic."

Blood rushed to her cheeks, and again that warm feeling she'd experienced in the courtyard flooded through her. She took a nervous sip of champagne. It tasted wonderful and delicate, much more refined than the champagne she had drunk back at the hotel. She often drank Dom or Cristal when Kingstone closed a huge deal, but never simply for a night out on the town. When Franco turned his head to talk with the waiters, she pulled the bottle up from the ice bucket. The glass was indeed a dark olive green, and the familiar antique gold Dom Perignon label peeked out from the ice.

A man approached their table and asked Brandy to dance. He wore jeans, cowboy boots and a cowboy hat. Without hesitation, Brandy jumped up, and within minutes, they were bumping and grinding on the dance floor.

Christina had so fixated on Franco that she didn't notice when Suzan and Stefano also hit the dance floor. She shifted in her chair to move even closer. "Franco. I have a silly question for you."

"No question is too silly for a clown." He smiled and lightly tapped her nose.

"Since you've lived here all your life, maybe you could tell me why there's snow on the mountain tops in the middle of summer?"

He looked puzzled and then smiled. "Christina, my dear, that's not snow. That's marble. White, Italian Carrara marble."

"Marble! Now I understand." She sipped her champagne. "Are the statues in the lobby made from the same marble?"

"Indeed."

Was it Franco's hypnotic stare or the champagne that made her feel so dizzy? She yearned to know more about him. Did he have brothers and sisters? What did he do when the hotel shut down in the winter?

"Franco, I was wondering…"

He put his warm hand on hers. "I must go now. Stefano will make certain that you and your friends get home safely."

He touched the tips of her nails and then moved his fingers under her palm. He lifted her hand to his lips and gently kissed the back of her hand. Before Christina could utter the words *good night*, he touched his fingers to her lips and walked away from the table. *Why did he have such a numbing effect on her?* Never in her life had she had the sensation of melting when a man touched her hand.

Suzan and Brandy returned from the dance floor to find Christina sitting motionless, staring into her champagne glass. She looked up. "Have fun dancing?"

"We had a great time. Stefano's hilarious." Suzan devoured a cracker covered with caviar. "He couldn't stop dancing."

"What about Cowboy Joe?"

"After he tried to stick his tongue down my throat for the second time, I thought I'd better ditch him." Brandy lit up a cigarette. "Where's Franco?"

"He had to go back to the hotel. I guess Stefano will take us home." Christina scanned the room, looking for him. "Where'd he go?"

Suzan waved her hand toward the bar. "He ran into some friends and he's buying them a drink."

Christina looked in the direction of the bar, where Stefano talked with a slightly overweight Italian man. And in the background, wasn't that the bald guy from the plane? He wore a knit cap, so she couldn't be sure.

She poked Brandy in the arm and pointed toward the bar. "Is that the same guy you were talking to in Nice?"

Brandy turned toward the bar. "Yeah, that's him."

"Don't you think it's a bit weird that he's here too?"

"Not at all. He had the hots for me. He probably followed me down here."

Christina didn't comment; the man in the knit cap had just handed Stefano a white envelope. Stefano shook his hand and put the envelope in his breast pocket.

Christina turned to Brandy. "Let's go. There's something going on here and I need to find out what it is."

They shot up from the table and pushed their way through the crowd to where the bald guy stood by the bar. But by the time they reached the vicinity, he had disappeared.

Christina grabbed Stefano's elbow. Some of his drink splashed onto his hand. "Who was that guy you were just talking to?"

Stefano looked around the bar. "No one. I'm here by myself."

"Stefano." She looked directly at him. "I saw him hand you an envelope."

Stefano put his hand on her shoulder. "Okay, California girl, if you must know, he's just a man who owes me some money."

"I saw him on our plane from San Francisco, and in Nice."

"Where he was flirting with *moi*," Brandy added.

"What's his name?" Christina asked Stefano.

"What is this? The Spanish Inquisition?"

"I just want to know his name."

Stefano threw back the remainder of his drink. "Really, Christina. It's only business." He looked straight at her. "And it's none of yours." He placed his empty glass on the bar. "Now, how about I buy you two a drink?"

"No thanks," she said. "I'm ready to go back to the hotel."

Brandy pointed to herself. "Excuse me? I'm not." She smiled at Stefano. "I'll have a vodka tonic."

"How 'bout trying a Negroni? It's the house specialty, named after Count Negroni. He used to be a regular here." Stefano looked at Christina. "Christina, can I interest you in one?"

"Oh, why not?" They weren't in California anymore. With dinners starting at eleven p.m., it was often two in the morning before port and petit-fours were passed around the table.

"That's my girl." Stefano held up his hand and snapped his fingers at the bartender. "Three Negroni's."

*

The sky had begun to brighten when Stefano dropped them off in front of the hotel, said his goodbyes and drove away. Christina could hardly wait to crawl into bed, but when she walked into her room, the shutters on her window flapped and the room was cold, not warm and toasty like she had hoped. She went to the window and found it wide open, but she remembered closing it earlier when the sea wind blew strongly. Also, the clothes she had placed on the chair beneath the window had been knocked to the floor.

She walked into Suzan's room to tell her about it, but Brandy had got there first. She smeared an oil spill of mascara off with a tissue, and filled in Suzan about the mystery man who'd been talking with Stefano.

Christina interrupted Brandy's tale. "I think someone may have been in my room."

"Yeah, the maid," Brandy said.

"Since when does a maid come through the window?" She motioned for Brandy and Suzan to follow her back into the bedroom, where she pointed at the open window.

She went over to the desk and opened the top drawer, but the PITA file wasn't there, so she opened the drawer below it. That was empty too. She banged it shut and then opened the bottom drawer. Again, empty. "It's gone."

"What's gone?"

Christina slumped onto the desk chair and looked up at Suzan. "The file that Mary gave me."

"What's so important about that file?" Brandy asked.

"From what I read so far, Peter was designing the highest technology missile defense system ever made. And I know it has something to do with his death."

She picked up the phone on the desk. "I need to call George Stinson. Maybe he can help."

It was nine p.m. in California, so Christina first tried his office, which went right to voice mail.

She slammed down the phone. "He must have already left."

Suzan said, "Try his cell."

"I would, but I didn't memorize his number. I had it on an old phone bill Mary gave me, but that was in the file." She looked at Brandy and put her hands on her hips. "Which walked off with the maid."

*

Christina forced herself to go for another run in the heat. But instead of making her feel better, the sun and oppressive noon heat gave her a splitting headache. Unless she got up to run early in the morning, she'd have to forget working out until she returned to San Francisco.

She took a quick shower, towel dried her hair, and threw on a loose fitting sun-dress. When she walked downstairs to get something to eat, Suzan and Brandy were not far behind.

Brandy lit a cigarette. "God, I feel like I just went to bed."

"Me too," Suzan said. "I could use a triple espresso."

They ordered a round of coffees, three large bottles of mineral water and individual-sized pizzas for lunch.

Just as Christina was about to devour her first bite of pizza margherita, Franco and Stefano walked over to the table.

"Good afternoon, ladies," Franco said. He let his gaze linger on Christina.

"More like *good morning*." Suzan pointed to her cup of coffee.

Franco set a slim leather briefcase on the table. "I trust Stefano got you home safely?"

"Right on time for their five a.m. curfew." Stefano grabbed a piece of bread from the basket and shoved it in his mouth. He clapped his hands together and said with his mouth still full, "How about we all go to the beach?"

Suzan looked over at Brandy and Christina. "Are you two up for it?"

Brandy jumped up from the table, but Christina didn't. "Not me. I want to call George and maybe practice a bit of Italian."

After the others left the table, Franco sat next to Christina. Just as the previous night, she felt a physical surge. "We had fun last night, Franco. Thanks for inviting us."

"My pleasure, dolcina."

"So how do you know Stefano?"

"We've been friends since we were little boys." He held his hand to the height of the table.

Christina was about to ask how well they knew each other when he opened his briefcase and handed her an envelope. "Here's the list of people that stayed at the hotel when your friend received those calls. I hope this will help."

She took the envelope from him. "Do you by any chance know a friend of Stefano's from America who's here in town now? He was at the night club last night."

"I'm sorry Christina, but I don't know all Stefano's friends."

"Someone broke into my room last night and stole some important documents." As soon as she told him, she wondered if she should have. She wasn't certain whom she could trust, including Franco, and if he and Stefano had been friends since they were little boys, their bond of loyalty could be as strong as that of two brothers.

But Franco recoiled. "I apologize, Christina. This has never happened before. I'll investigate it immediately." He stood. "Excuse me; I'll be right back." He walked to his office, where she heard him shout in rapid Italian. Again, she had second thoughts. She needed to keep a low profile.

A few minutes later, Franco returned to where Christina sat. "I arranged a staff meeting this afternoon, and I assure you, I will find out what happened. Also, I just spoke with the police; they'll be here this evening."

In this matter, she didn't have much confidence in the Italian police. She had a pretty good idea why the thief took the file, and he wasn't a petty thief looking for jewelry. The local *carabinieri* couldn't help her situation in California.

She touched Franco's arm. "I appreciate how decisively you've acted, but it's not necessary to involve the police. I have a feeling this is a personal matter, and I'd prefer to leave it at that."

"I don't like the idea of someone breaking into my hotel."

"I understand," Christina said, "but I'd rather keep my name out of it."

"I didn't mention your name when I called the police. When they come to investigate, if you like, I'll tell them that the matter has been resolved."

"Thank you."

Franco eyed the Italian grammar book Christina had brought down to lunch with her and picked it up. "Would you like some help?"

She rested her elbows on the table. "Aren't you busy?" She wanted to open the envelope, but Franco's hypnotizing stare trumped that. As for George, it was still only six a.m. in California. She'd let him sleep a bit.

Franco closed his briefcase. "In the summer I get up early to work, and leave the afternoons free to paint." He reached out and touched the tips of her fingers. "How often do I have the honor and pleasure of helping a beautiful young woman learn my language?"

That did it. Maybe his lines were a bit corny, and maybe he did hang with a few unsavory characters, but she found his charming ways impossible to resist. Franco rose, extended his hand and led her out to the courtyard.

As they walked down the corridor, she paused to ask Franco about an enormous portrait that hung above the mantle, framed in gilded gold. The painting depicted an aristocratic-looking woman with a long elegant neck and thick raven hair pulled tightly away from her face. Dark eyes, almost black, peered out into the room as though alive and aware of their surroundings; and her incredible jewelry was impossible to ignore. A magnificent pair of diamond and ruby earrings hung from her delicate ears, and a substantial diamond ring, surrounded by rubies, clung to one finger of her gracefully folded hands.

"Ah, yes. This is a picture of my great-grandmother, painted within months of her marriage."

Christina noticed the resemblance between her and Franco. The eyes, especially, were similar: dark, warm and penetrating. "What a powerful looking woman. She must have commanded a great deal of respect."

"She certainly did. She was truly the matriarch of our family."

Franco's gaze lingered on the portrait of his grandmother, and then they continued walking down the cool marble hallway. In the courtyard, the silence of the corridor and the sharp smell of citrus-scented floor cleaner segued into the soft sounds of the trickling fountain and the fragrance of flowering jasmine. They sat on the wooden bench under the pergola and studied for nearly an hour, until Franco closed the book. "Two chapters are enough for one day." He inched closer to her. "What are your plans for this evening?"

Christina eased the book back from him. "I don't have any plans."

"No?" He brought a finger to the corner of her lips, ran it along her cheekbone and then to the edge of her eye. His mouth hovered inches from hers. "How come such a beautiful woman never has any plans?"

She could hardly speak. "We're playing every day by ear."

"By ear?" He touched his ear. "I'm sorry I don't quite understand."

Christina laughed and thought how cute it was that he took her literally. "That's an American expression, like *neck of the woods*." In the future, she'd better stay away from using body parts to describe her actions or feelings.

"Ah, I see." He settled back into the bench and put his briefcase on his lap. "Very well then, we will have dinner at Il Castello."

She felt a small patter in her stomach when he asked her to this restaurant, supposed to be the most romantic on the coast.

"Your smile could brighten a moonless night. Does it mean yes?"

She nodded.

"I'll meet you downstairs at nine." He took off her glasses and kissed her lightly on the cheek. "Until tonight."

Christina remained in the courtyard for several seconds. What kind of spell had he cast upon her, and why was she so incredibly attracted to him? She hardly knew anything about him, only that the chemistry between the two of them sizzled.

She returned to her room and opened the envelope Franco had given her. One name, Curtis Saunders, looked familiar, but she couldn't place it. She circled it and made a mental note to ask Brandy and Suzan if they had heard of him. Or she could Google him if she could get access to a computer. Maybe Donatella could help her out; she didn't want to keep pestering Franco.

Next, she reached for the phone and called George Stinson. Luckily, he was at his desk and answered on the first ring. She heard the familiar tapping of the keyboard in the background.

"Hi George. Christina Culhane."

The tapping stopped. "Christina, I thought you were in Italy."

"I am, but I needed to talk to you about something."

"Fire away."

"I know Peter was working on something important before he died. Mary gave me one of his files from work, but he wrote a lot of the information in computer code, so I didn't understand it.

But from what I read, I figured he was developing some kind of neural network structure."

"So you remembered the basics from your high school physics class. I'm impressed."

"Don't be too impressed, because that's about all I understood."

"Sorry, Christina, I don't know anything about that project. Peter kept to himself these past few months. We were both in charge of developing the new microprocessor, but that wasn't anything unusual." He paused. "Not saying it was insignificant, I mean it's going to be the smallest, fastest and cheapest chip out there, but it wasn't a DOD project."

"Right, but you sat next to him, wouldn't you know if he was working on something top-secret for the Department of Defense?"

"Even if I did, I couldn't tell you." He went back to tapping on the keyboard. "And listen, Christina, I think you need to concentrate on pushing this IPO forward. If this deal craters, we'll all be out of a job. Stick to investment banking."

"We're on schedule," Christina said. "And by the way, since you're now the chief engineer on the project, you'll have to come along on the road shows with us."

"I have to tell ya, I'm dreading that big time."

No one looked forward to road shows. Usually three meetings per day, with at least seven cities piled into a five-day workweek.

"I know. They're exhausting, but when an investment manager puts a million dollars of his fund into the deal and he has a technical question, he needs to ask you, not me."

"I'll do it. Just don't count on me to be bright and cheery in the mornings." A beeper went off in the background. "I gotta go, Christina. Call me when you get back."

What a useless conversation that was. And then something else occurred to her. She had accepted a romantic dinner invitation and she didn't have a thing to wear!

She ran out of the hotel and sprinted to the beach, where she found Suzan and Brandy asleep on chaise lounges under an umbrella.

"Brandy! Suzan!" she cried out. "You've got to help me."

"What's wrong?" Suzan jolted up from her chair. "Are you all right?"

"Yes—I'm sorry. Franco asked me to dinner tonight and I didn't bring anything decent to wear."

"Wait a minute, back up," Brandy said. "Franco asked you out? How did this come about?"

"It's not important. I'm desperate."

"What restaurant is he taking you to?" Suzan asked.

"Il Castello."

"You're kidding."

"Well, we're in luck," Brandy said. "Today's Wednesday—it's market day."

Christina's shoulders fell. "I don't want to go to a *flea market*."

"Remember Dorothy, you're not in Kansas anymore. This is Fo*rrrrr*te dei Ma*rrrrr*mi." Brandy may have tried to roll the words off her tongue as aristocratically as the locals did, but instead she sounded like she was gargling mouthwash.

Christina grinned. "All right, I'll give it a try." She pulled Brandy up from her chair. "Let's go."

*

The dusty, open-air market in the town center crawled with people, and tented stalls showcased everything from leather belts to lacy lingerie. They walked by handbags, shoes and children's clothing, until Brandy stopped and picked up a black and red lace bra.

"I read in one of the tourist brochures that people from all over Tuscany come here to shop."

Christina remained skeptical. "So far, it doesn't look any different from the market in Florence."

They kept walking, looking for what they wanted.

Christina pointed to a stall selling cashmere sweaters and coats. "In the middle of summer! I feel hotter just looking at them."

At first, nothing else caught Christina's attention, but eventually she noticed a stall that sold evening clothes. A mink coat, fifties style—caped and with three-quarter length sleeves— hung about eye height. Several black satin evening bags were arranged in neat rows on a wooden table.

"May I help you find anything?" A well-dressed woman with silver hair addressed them in clear English.

"Your clothes are beautiful," Christina said. "Do you have anything I could wear to an elegant restaurant?"

"Of course, Madame." She pointed to a rail of black dresses.

The rack reminded Christina of a time in Paris when she'd shopped at Le Petit Robe Noire, a boutique in The Palais Royale that sold exquisite little black dresses. Perhaps she had come to the right place after all.

Christina walked around the table and stepped into the small enclosure, careful not to knock over the only chair, already covered with clothes and a handbag. She pulled several dresses from the rail and took them to the changing area, situated in the corner behind a tattered curtain. Only three feet in diameter, the space was claustrophobic and stifling hot. If not for the hundreds of people walking by outside, she would've left the curtain open. She tried on some sleeveless dresses, some backless, one with a halter-neck that accentuated her shoulders, and one with a neckline that plunged to her belly button. Each time, she emerged from behind the curtain to model the latest LBD—Little Black Dress.

"That one's stunning," Suzan said.

"Gorgeous!" Brandy said of another.

But each time they exclaimed over one, the woman who worked the stall pursed her lips and kept quiet. After seeing Christina in five dresses, she touched her cheek with a polished pale-pink fingernail. "I have an idea." She walked to where a gold garment bag hung, unzipped it and pulled out a dress.

At first glance, it looked no different from the other black sleeveless dresses Christina had tried, but she took the woman's advice and retreated behind the curtain.

Once she slipped it on, she felt the difference immediately. Despite the hot day, the smooth silk actually felt cool. The couturier might have designed this dress especially for her. The hemline fell just above her knees—short enough to show off her legs but not too short as to appear tarty. Subtle black lace trimmed the sweeping neckline and the satin around the waist squeezed her in, creating the illusion of an hourglass figure.

She pulled the curtain open, stepped into the stall and twirled in front of the women. The skirt swirled around her knees in the style of a ballroom dancer.

"What do you think?"

"It's fabulous," Suzan said.

"Yup," Brandy nodded. "That's the dress for you."

The woman smiled. "It's vintage Valentino, Madame."

Christina hadn't even bothered to look at the label before she tried it on. "I should've known. It's flawless."

"Made by Signoré Garavani himself," the woman added.

"Garavani?" Christina asked. "Who's that?"

"*Valentino* Garavani."

Christina couldn't believe she held a dress Valentino himself had sewn. But then her smiling face fell. "Okay, now for the bad news. How much does it cost?"

Without blinking, the woman said, "Two thousand Euros, Madame."

"Two thousand Euros for a used dress?" Brandy said.

"*Vintage*," Christina said. "Not used." Knowing a good investment when she saw one, she turned to the woman and smiled. "It's lovely, I'll take it."

The woman nodded her approval. "A true classic will never go out of style."

Christina handed the woman her credit card. "I'll treasure it forever."

The woman gently wrapped the dress in tissue and placed it in a plastic bag.

Christina wrinkled her forehead at the sight of such a work of art residing in an ordinary grocery bag, but then she shrugged. She didn't need the traditional shiny red Valentino bag to tell her that she had just purchased a masterpiece.

*

When they returned to their room, they popped open a bottle of Prosecco and dressed for the evening. Stefano had invited Suzan and Brandy to a party on his yacht, so they were also in a festive mood.

Unwilling to appear too eager, Christina waited until she heard the clock chime a quarter past nine before she left to meet Franco. "Don't wait up." She flashed a big grin and walked out the door.

Franco and Donatella talked together in the hotel lobby when Christina arrived. Handsome and regal in a blue blazer and tan khakis, Franco fell silent when he saw her at the top of the staircase. She didn't have to wait long for a reaction. Once his expression settled into a smile, the smile stayed.

"Christina, you look beautiful. What happened to my American girl in her shorts and ponytail?"

"I trust I should take that as a compliment." She almost tripped down the last stair, nearly destroying the graceful image she wanted to project.

"Of course it's a compliment. You're ravishing. Wait out front, I'll pull up the car."

Christina shivered as she waited for Franco to bring around the car. Across the street at one of the many sidewalk cafés, Stefano sat having a drink with the creepy bald guy. On another occasion, she might have run over to confront them, but tonight she wanted to enjoy her evening with Franco and not worry about stalkers. She rationalized that if Stefano and that man were legitimate business associates, it was perfectly normal for them to sit and have a drink. When they looked over at her and raised their glasses in a mocking manner, she turned away. She watched the street for Franco, and expecting the Jetta, she jumped back when a shiny Mercedes convertible stopped in front of her. Charcoal grey, it looked like a CL 500 or maybe even a 600, but the back fender was covertly devoid of any metal numbers or letters.

Franco slid out from behind the wheel and opened the passenger side door for her.

"New car?" she asked.

"Not at all, but I keep it in the back—the Jetta's for staff members who need to run hotel errands."

"I see." She hoped she didn't look as bewildered as she felt.

Christina settled comfortably into the soft leather seats, savored the fragrant night air and let the sea breeze blow her hair freely in the wind as they drove down the coast. She felt no need to talk. Instead, she leaned her head against the neck rest and gazed at the bright full moon and the glittering stars.

Chapter Seven

They approached Il Castello along a narrow dirt road lined with fruit and nut orchards, and drove about ten minutes up the winding road before Christina noticed the white restaurant, a renaissance-era palazzo illuminated against the midnight-blue sky. It sat majestically on a hilltop overlooking the surrounding valley.

After about a mile, the road widened into a tree-lined cobblestone boulevard. They continued driving until they reached the imposing façade, where two enormous marble posts flanked an ornate iron gate that opened automatically as they entered. Franco pulled into the property beyond the gate and stopped the car. Two men in white dinner jackets simultaneously opened their doors and then escorted them up the marble stairs.

The maitre d' showed Franco and Christina to a quiet, candlelit table. Smoky mirrors, framed in chipped gold leaf, and portraits like the one of his grandmother lined Bordeaux-red walls. The restaurant held only about ten tables, all covered with white linen and gleaming crystal glasses that reflected candlelight in such a way that each goblet looked as though it contained a twinkling yellow star. Christina didn't know a lot about antiques, but the ornately carved sideboards and chairs appeared to be from the Rococo period, and they contrasted nicely with the simple linens and glassware. The only reason she knew anything about Rococo was because one of her clients had decorated his home in that style. *Genuine* Rococo pieces, his wife had insisted numerous times at dinner, shipped over from Europe. Christina couldn't understand why anyone would decorate an entire house in this overstated fashion, but hey—it was their house, not hers.

Franco pulled Christina's chair and then sat across from her. His skin glowed in the soft light of the candles. The flame reflected in his eyes made her wish she sat next to him.

"This restaurant is lovely, Franco." She glanced at the emblem on his jacket. It appeared to have an elaborately scrolled letter *D* on it, the profile of an ancient warrior whose face is shielded by a steel helmet, and a black raven with outstretched wings. "May I ask about that insignia on your jacket?"

"Of course." He looked down and pointed to the embroidery on his lapel. "This is my family crest. The *D* stands for my last name—Doria."

He lit up a cigarette, at which point Christina gave him the eye.

He immediately stubbed it out. "No smoking tonight, right?"

"It's okay, Franco. If you need to smoke I can't stop you."

"I don't *need* to do anything, except make love to beautiful women."

Christina blushed. He really was a bit much, but she enjoyed being around a hot-blooded man who adored and appreciated women. She was sick of all those metrosexuals, so into themselves they wouldn't notice an attractive, available woman if she passed them on the street in a string bikini.

"No, please, Franco, if you'd like to smoke, that's fine. But really, you should quit. Have you never heard of lung cancer?"

"You Americans are so self-righteous about smoking. It's part of our culture. You run and play sports, we smoke."

Christina laughed. "You have a point there, but you can't deny the facts. Your lungs won't survive fifty years of inhaling tobacco."

Franco reached into his breast pocket and took out his red-and-white pack of Marlboros. "See these?" He handed them to one of the hovering waiters. "They're gone. Forever."

"You're saying that you quit?"

"Yes, for you, my beautiful Christina, I quit."

Christina couldn't take him seriously, but he sure had all the right one-liners. "I'm proud of you, Franco." She winked at him. "You'll thank me in forty years."

The waiters poured champagne and brought out a platter of grilled Portobello mushrooms and a plate of carpaccio smothered in capers, olive oil and shaved slices of Parmesan cheese.

Christina gestured toward his crest. "Tell me more."

Franco twirled his fork against the thin pink meat and placed it to her lips. "Try some. It's delicious."

She formed her lips over the fork and slowly sucked the meat—so tender she didn't even need to chew it. She pointed again.

"Oh yes, the Doria family crest. What can I say? We're an ancient shipping family." He raised one eyebrow, gave her a sly look and lowered his voice. "And a family of fighters."

"Oh really?"

"Andrea Doria, my great-great-great-great..." He tapped the fingers on his right hand with his left thumb. After he ran out of fingers, he put his hands down. "Too many greats to count. Anyway, he was responsible for liberating the Italians from French domination. In fact, I'm named after him." He sat up straighter and pronounced each word as if he were introducing the Queen of England, "Franco; Giovanni; Andrea; Doria."

"Did you say *Andrea Doria*?" Christina asked. "Wasn't that the name of an ocean liner that sank in the fifties?"

Franco laughed. "I'm sorry to laugh, Christina, but that is such a typical American response. But yes, that ship was named after my ancestor, the famous naval commander." He finished his champagne and the waiters immediately replenished it.

"Since the 1500s, my ancestors acquired much of the land here in Tuscany. In fact this palazzo"—he glanced around the restaurant—"where we're dining tonight, was at one time the home of my great-great-grandparents. And all the white marble you see on the floors was excavated from one of our quarries."

Christina raised her eyebrows.

"But now," he said, "we are all working people, just like the rest of the Italians."

For some reason she didn't believe he was just plain working folk like *the rest of the Italians*.

"So you're in the hotel business now?"

"Not exactly." The waiter poured them each a glass of Montepulciano, a red wine from Tuscany. "A century ago, before Forte dei Marmi was the resort town it is now, the Hotel della Luna was the summer villa of my family. We recently converted it to a hotel. I manage it for my father in the summer. It's more like a vacation from my real job."

"So what's your *real* job?" Christina sliced a piece of the grilled Portobello mushroom and took a bite. It melted in her mouth and tasted like a sirloin steak.

"Besides shipping, we've been in the marble business for generations. My family once owned most of the mountains in this region, and we still own the rights to the natural resources. We excavate the marble and granite from the mountainside, and then we cut it and sell it around the world."

"You seem so young to be running a worldwide business."

"Thank you for the compliment, but I'm actually thirty-six years old." Franco reached across the table and lightly touched Christina's fingertips.

Christina eased her hand forward so that their fingers intertwined. "Please tell me more about the marble business. All my clients are high-tech. I'd love to hear more about something that doesn't involve silicon."

He continued talking about his company, and told her that only last spring he had completed his most prestigious project to date. "I spent nearly an entire year with the Sultan of Brunei," he said. "We collaborated with his designers and architects and supplied the marble and granite for his family's compound."

"Do you and Stefano work together?" Christina asked, still curious about his connection with Stefano.

"Yes, somewhat." Franco placed his fork and knife down on the plate. "Stefano's father has been one of our project managers for as long as I can remember. Stefano used to work as a laborer, but just recently, he started his own business exporting granite."

They had talked incessantly for over an hour, and they hadn't yet ordered their main course. Franco spoke to the waiters in Italian, and turned his attention back to Christina. He gripped her hand more tightly and brought it to his lips. "Now Christina, I appreciate you listening to tales about my business affairs, but please, tell me more about yourself. All I know is that you have this wonderful sweet quality about you; one that I cannot describe properly in English."

"I'm not used to so many compliments," she said. She had always considered herself to be a bit plain and something of a bookworm. But in response to Franco's questions, she told him about her childhood in the suburbs of Philadelphia, which all seemed insignificant compared to his family history. She also spoke a bit about her travels, her education, her current job, her charity work at a homeless shelter, and her passion for outdoor sports.

After a while, she began to feel ridiculous talking about herself. Could he be for real? She had never felt a more intense attraction to anyone. Franco's respect and adoration was something she had only dreamed of discovering. Who would've thought she had to travel halfway around the world to find him.

He released his hand from hers and touched her cheek. "While you're here, I'd like to take you to one of our marble quarries. It's quite an amazing sight to see the stone in the raw form, before it is transformed into something as smooth as your skin."

Christina lowered her eyes so she wouldn't blush again. She turned away and gazed out the window at the orchards glowing in the moonlight, on the hillside his family had once owned. She sensed his pride in his heritage. How wonderful that he felt comfortable sharing that with her.

Franco looked down at his watch. "Excuse me, dolcina, I need to make a phone call." He got up from the table and left the room.

At first startled by his abrupt departure, but then grateful for the time it gave her to think. Christina wondered if she had gotten in over her head. With all the wealth that Silicon Valley created, she had become accustomed to new money, but she had never been in the company of European aristocracy. Were her table manners good enough? What about her choice of dress, or the fact that she didn't speak much Italian? Even her hair and make-up were suddenly suspect. But did he care about that sort of perfection? She hoped not.

"Is everything okay?" she asked when he returned. Though she wondered, she didn't ask whom he called at near-midnight.

He sat back down. "Yes, everything's fine." He reached over the table, held her hand and smiled. "Now, where were we?"

The waiters brought more wine, angel-hair pasta with a light pesto sauce, and grilled fish. By the time dinner ended, she could hardly wait to leave the restaurant to be alone with Franco. She hoped he felt the same, but she knew she had to be careful. She didn't know Franco well and she certainly had her doubts about his friend Stefano. Nor did she want history to repeat itself; every past relationship that had gotten this far had either fizzled out or ended up hurting her.

Franco leaned across the table and spoke quietly. "My darling, let us now leave Il Castello."

Christina lifted the napkin from her lap and let it crumple onto the table. She wanted to maintain her composure, yet her heart raced in anticipation.

As they descended the white marble steps, Franco placed an assuring hand on the small of her back, sending shivers up her spine. Christina slid into the waiting car and crossed her leg while Franco tipped the valet. When he got behind the wheel, he turned to Christina for several seconds; she met his penetrating gaze, but quickly averted her eyes. He thrust the car into first gear and sped down the winding road. With each gear change, her heart beat harder. Her hair flew in the wind, and city lights flickered on the hillside below, like a thousand candles lit just for them.

When they reached the sea, Christina felt the tires sink into the sand even before the car came to a rolling stop. The headlights beamed across the dark sea—a rumpled mass of black satin, trimmed in soft white silk. Undulating waves lapped against the beach like slow, rhythmic breathing. Christina instinctively slipped out of her sandals.

Franco got out of the car and walked over to the passenger side. Christina reached for her door handle, but Franco shook his head. He opened the door and extended his hand. Fingers entwined with hers, he led her toward the water's edge.

The sand felt cool and soft under her feet. Ten paces, twenty paces. She squeezed his hand. A private beach, a full moon, a million stars; what more could one ask for?

Franco broke their stride and pulled her to him. He brought his hands to her face, then his mouth to hers. He continued to kiss her hard while his hands explored first her ribcage, just below her breasts, and then her hips and upper thighs. Electricity surged through her body as he dropped to his knees and kissed her thighs, slowly working his way under the hem of her dress.

He pulled her down to him, slipped her dress over her head in one seamless motion, removed his blazer and spread it on the sand. The silk lining felt softly luxurious against Christina's back.

"Christina," he whispered, and then he gently rolled on top of her.

They kissed hard and passionately for several minutes. Christina could have continued like that for hours, but psychologically she wasn't ready for the rest. Also, she felt a bit guilty enjoying herself so much. She had come to Italy to find out who killed Peter, not to start a love affair with a man she barely knew.

She whispered to Franco, "I'm sorry, this is all a bit fast for me. I hope you understand."

He sighed loudly, rolled off her and flopped onto the sand. After a second or two, he cradled her in his arms. "It's all right, dolcina, we have many more nights together."

Chapter Eight

The three women had designated the breakfast room at the Hotel della Luna as the place to share their adventures from the night before. By the time Christina got down to the dining room, Brandy and Suzan had already devoured a basket of bread and finished the entire pot of coffee and steamed milk. Clearly, the Atkins diet was lost on this group.

"Thanks for waiting." Christina held up the empty breadbasket. She spotted a waiter and ordered both coffee and bread.

"We were famished," Suzan said. "We spent the whole night drinking and dancing on Stefano's yacht. All they had to eat was caviar and crackers."

"So the party platters didn't live up to your discerning palate?"

The waiter poured Christina a steaming cup of coffee while she transferred half a cup of hot frothy milk from a small silver pitcher into her cup.

"We're actually getting sick of caviar." Brandy pressed the pink flesh on her cheeks. "I think I'm bloated."

"Sooo…" Suzan said. "Tell us about your date with Franco. We've been dying to hear."

Christina took a sip of coffee and pushed her hair behind her ears. "Everything was perfect. The restaurant was magical, and the time we spent talking and getting to know each other was incredible. I should also add that the chemistry between us is dangerous. To sum it up, I've completely fallen for him."

"After one date?" Suzan teased.

"It wasn't difficult, let me tell you." Christina slathered her roll with strawberry jam. "Besides the fact that he's incredibly handsome, emotionally and physically sensuous, a wealthy businessman and a descendant of Italian nobility, he also thinks I'm great."

"What did you just say?" Brandy set down her coffee cup.

"He thinks I'm great," Christina repeated.

"No, not that part," Brandy said. "I'm talking about *wealthy businessman and Italian nobility*. He's just a kid."

"He's thirty-six years old."

"Why is he working at a hotel?" Brandy asked.

"It's not his full time job. The hotel used to be his family's summer home."

"How did his family get so rich running a hotel three months a year?" Brandy popped another piece of bread in her mouth.

"Their fortune comes from their marble and granite business. He and his father run it together."

"I want to hear more about that *dangerous chemistry* between the two of you," Suzan said.

"I'll leave that to your imagination." Christina winked. "Now, tell me more about the party on Stefano's yacht."

Suzan set her coffee cup down. "It was quite the scene. I've never seen so many glamorous people in one place. I can tell Stefano loves all the attention."

"He's a playboy." Brandy licked some residual jam off her fingertips.

"Well I think he's just a typical young guy with lots of money," Suzan said. "His world revolves around his yacht, ample cleavage and buckets of champagne and caviar."

Christina imitated a deejay spinning records. "If I didn't know better I would've thought you were slumming with P Diddy and Paris Hilton."

Brandy pulled out a shiny gold compact and checked her teeth for stray breadcrumbs. A diamond on the corner of the compact reflected the morning sun.

"Is that new?" Christina asked.

"Stefano gave it to me last night."

"He gave me one too," Suzan said.

"And *why,* may I ask?"

"Actually they were party favors. All the women on his yacht got one last night."

"Yeah, and most of them used it for coke."

"Are you joking? That's so 1980."

"Come on, Christina," Brandy said. "Get off your high horse. You have to expect drugs at a party like that."

"And if the Coast Guard stormed aboard you'd be sleeping in an Italian jail." Christina looked at the table covered with empty breadbaskets and coffee cups. "Trust me, you'd miss the espresso."

"Don't worry," Suzan said. "We're not stupid, but even I was amazed at how much was available." She smoothed her hair. "Anyway, I have to admit, Stefano is kind of fun. He invited us to sail to Sardinia. We're leaving this afternoon. Can you join us?"

"I don't think Franco can get away from the hotel," Christina said. "And besides, we're busy this afternoon. He's taking me to see one of his marble quarries."

"You would rather visit a stone pit than spend a few days on a Mediterranean island?" Brandy lit up a cigarette. "We're talking the Costa *Smeer-elda* here. The hot spot of Italian glitz."

"Not really my style," Christina said. "And besides, we won't be in Italy much longer. I'd like to spend as much time with him as possible."

Suzan came to her defense. "I guess if I was completely head-over-heels with a sexy Italian man, I'd stick around too. Especially if that chemistry is as dangerous as you say. But I'll give you Stefano's mobile number in case you need to reach us."

They had just finished the last morsel of bread when Christina saw a stunning Italian woman enter the hotel. She had long black hair and was the most stylish woman Christina had ever laid eyes on. She wore a pencil-slim linen skirt that accentuated lean, tan legs. A sheer white linen blouse with a white corset underneath, which would've looked trashy on anyone else, looked elegant on her. A colorful scarf, knotted loosely, swung from her handbag. She waved a slender dark hand at Donatella and walked toward Franco's office.

"I wonder who *that* was." Suzan's eyes followed the woman as she clicked in high heels across the marble floor.

Franco emerged from his office and gave the woman a kiss on both cheeks. They retreated into his room and he shut the door.

"Who's the super model?" asked Brandy.

Christina looked down at her t-shirt and khaki shorts and wished she could morph into the chair. "Knowing Franco, probably an Italian Princess."

Naturally, Franco would prefer someone like that woman over the daughter of a truck driver. She hated herself for thinking that; after all, both she and her family had accomplished so much, and she was proud of what her father had done with her grandfather's business, but sometimes her insecurities got the best of her. Investment banking was tough. Only the best and the brightest made it to the top, but there were a lot of smart people out there. She'd discovered that the more polished her veneer, the better her chances. For example, she always presented herself as Christina, not Chris or Christy. Only her parents and close childhood friends, like Peter, called her Christy. Thinking of Peter again, tears pooled in her eyes.

"Hey," Suzan said. "You've never been one to shy away from a little competition. I can't believe you're letting that woman get to you."

Christina dabbed her eyes with the linen napkin. "I wasn't crying over her, I was thinking about Peter." She bit her lip to check her emotions. "I really miss him."

Suzan leaned across the table and touched Christina's hand. "I know you do. And I also know you're going to find out who killed him."

"Thanks for your vote of confidence, but that still won't bring him back." She folded her napkin and placed it to the side of her plate. "I need to go back to sleep for a while."

She got up from the table and was part way across the foyer when Donatella called her name.

"Signorina Culhane." Donatella scurried over to Christina and handed her an envelope. "You have a message."

Christina took the envelope. "Thank you, Donatella."

She opened it on her way up the stairs and read the message: *We know why you're here, Culhane. Stay out of it.*

The hair on her arms stood up, but her tears stopped immediately. She quickly turned around and called downstairs. "Donatella, do you know who delivered this message?"

She shook her head. "I'm sorry, Signorina. I found it on the desk."

She bolted back down the stairs to show Suzan. The message wasn't signed, but Christina's best guess was that it came from that sleazy business associate of Stefano's.

Suzan put her coffee cup down when she saw her. "What's wrong?"

Christina threw the note on the table. "Read this."

Suzan read it and stood up. "That does it. We're leaving." She pushed the chair under the table. "Peter got himself killed messing with the wrong people, and I'm not going to let the same happen to you."

"There's no way in hell I'm leaving now," Christina said. "This note confirms that something's going on here, and I'm certain it has something to do with Peter's death." She looked at Suzan. "And didn't you just tell me that you know I'll figure it out?"

Suzan rolled her eyes. "Yeah, I guess I did."

"The only way I'm going to do that is by sticking around. Of course you two can leave, but I'm staying."

"C'mon Christina," Suzan said. "You know I'd never leave you swingin' on your own." She looked over at Brandy. "Brandy?"

"Of course I'm staying. I'm on vacation. Besides, I wouldn't miss this yacht party for thc world." She got up from the table. "In fact I have a one o'clock—oh excuse me—a *thirteen* o'clock hair appointment." She slung her handbag over her shoulder and sashayed away from the table. "I'll see you ladies tonight."

*

Franco rang Christina's room at five-thirty that evening. His sexy voice awakened her.

"I'm driving out to the quarry before the sun sets. Are you still interested in joining me?"

"Mmmm." She stretched her arms and rubbed her eyes. "Of course," she said, attempting to stifle an audible yawn. Christina was just coming out of a wonderful dream: Franco's luscious lips had been locked onto hers when the phone rang. Normally, she'd resent waking from such pleasure, but not this time. What she had dreamt about was waiting for her downstairs.

"I'll be down in a few minutes." She stripped out of her shorts and changed into a brightly colored sundress that showed off her suntanned skin. By the time she got downstairs, Franco already waited for her in the car.

The sun was still warm and the heat from the leather seats nearly burned her when she sat down, but a wicker basket nestled in the back seat caught her eye and distracted her. Visible inside was a fresh baguette, cut flowers and candles. A coolbox sat beside the basket, the cover hiding its contents.

They sped off in Franco's convertible and wound their way up to the top of the mountain. As they ascended, the air got cooler, so Christina wrapped her pashmina around her shoulders. The salty smell of the sea dissipated as they climbed, and the air smelled fresh and crisp, like an autumn day in Vermont. As they got closer to the mountain peaks, Christina saw that her snow-covered mountains were indeed rugged marble. Centuries of erosion had carved dark grey streaks into the jagged edges of the white stone.

At the quarry, droves of sweaty male workers were leaving for the day. Flatbed trucks loaded with slabs of marble rumbled down the mountain, while the large steel machines used to excavate the stone lay idle. Clouds of dust filled the air; the gritty particles adhered to Christina's contacts and made her eyes itch.

Franco suggested that Christina wait in the car while he discussed some business with the foreman. He came back as the last of the workers left and gave Christina a tour of the quarry. The caverns smelled musty and were cold as an ice cave. As they walked deeper into the mountain, where the stone excavation took place, Christina shivered. Franco put his arm around her and kissed her passionately.

"Now that'll make a girl forget the cold," she said.

He laughed and released her. "Let's go back outside. We don't want to miss the sunset."

Warm sunlight still beat down on the mountainside, creating a welcoming feel, and pink wispy clouds diffused the light. Franco walked back to the car and pulled out his picnic basket. They found a plateau that overlooked the sea, and Franco placed the basket on a white-and-red-checkered blanket he pulled from the trunk. He also produced a silver ice bucket, filled with ice from the coolbox, and placed a bottle of Greco di Tuffo in it. He poured them each a glass and dropped in a bright red strawberry. They clinked their glasses and took a sip of the cold white wine.

Franco removed one of the strawberries and brought it to Christina's lips. She took a bite, and then fed him the rest. He gave her a piece of sweet melon wrapped in thinly sliced, salty prosciutto, waited until she ate a bit and then kissed her. His lips, as smooth as the melon, tasted as luscious as an entire basket of strawberries.

Franco unwrapped silver-and-blue foil from a *Bacio de Perugina*, and placed the chocolate on Christina's tongue. As the creamy hazelnut-flavor melted in her mouth, he kissed her again, and this time his tongue explored her mouth. He stroked the top of her leg, and then he inched his hand under her dress. He drew back for a moment to remove his shirt and then brought his warm chest down on hers.

Christina's skin had become damp and hot. From the silver bucket by their side, she removed an ice cube, rolled it down Franco's chest and then brought it to her neck. Franco wrapped his mouth around the ice and guided it down her décolletage. It melted when it hit the flesh between her breasts, and Franco licked the liquid from her skin in slow, rhythmic strokes.

She wriggled away. "Franco, I need to ask you something."

He raised his head. "Now?"

"Who was that woman at your office this afternoon?"

"Just an old family friend."

"She seemed like more than that to me."

He tried kissing her again, but her guard was up. "No really, Franco. It seemed like you two are really close. I saw you kiss her and then invite her into your office."

Franco pulled away. "You're acting like a naïve American."

"That was a low blow." Christina straightened her skirt. "Maybe you don't understand me. I'm not a loose European who jumps into bed with just anyone."

"Now, *that* was a low blow. Not all Europeans are," he flicked his wrist, "as you say, *loose*."

"I really felt something with you last night. But I'm not going to let myself get hurt if you're involved with someone else. And I sure as hell won't play second best."

Franco pulled her closer to him. "Honestly, Christina, she's just an old family friend."

Christina wished he had been more precise in answering her question, but she didn't want to pry too much. Number one rule: don't appear jealous. Just as in business, never let the other side observe your weakness.

She wanted to mention the note, but her sixth sense told her to keep that information to herself until she knew who all the players in this dangerous game were. There was no question that she was extremely attracted to Franco, and she desperately wanted to trust him, but she needed time—and more information.

They drank their wine and remained silent a few minutes, watching the sun disappear behind the mountains and turn the sky from bluish pink to deep apricot. When the grey of dusk appeared, Franco lit the candles and held her in his arms. She looked at him and savored the visual feast: he had such a young, smooth visage, yet he represented generations of strength and power. As the shimmering moon peeked over the mountaintops, Christina continued to lose herself in thoughts. She had never intended to meet someone like him, but everyone said that love hits you the hardest when you least expect it. She resolved that while she remained in Italy she'd continue to enjoy his company. However, once she crossed the Atlantic, she needed to prepare for the romance to end.

Chapter Nine

The following morning, Franco knocked on her door with a hot breakfast, presented on a silver tray.

She sat on the end of the bed and poured herself a cup of coffee. "You even brought the *Wall Street Journal*. Are you trying to win me back?" She picked up the paper and glanced at the headlines.

The coffee cup dropped from her hand, and she shrieked as hot coffee spilled onto her leg. She scooted backward away from the mess and read the headline again: **Symex Engineer shot in Silicon Valley Burglary.**

"Christina, are you okay?" Franco wiped the coffee off her leg with a linen napkin.

Her hands shook as she skimmed the article. *Three truckloads of microchips taken from the Symex plant…packed and ready for shipping to their distributor…*Aloud, she continued, "Engineer Martin Denton, previously working with recently deceased Peter Carmaletti on top-secret Department of Defense projects, was shot and pronounced dead at the scene. Junior programmer Simon LeBlanc, also recovering from gunshot wounds, is expected to recover. The company declined to comment on the theft of proprietary designs."

Christina stared at Franco. "Oh my God. This is terrible." Her hands trembled and she suddenly felt very cold. *Another engineer dead.* No way was Peter's death a suicide. "I know this has something to do with Peter's death."

"Calm down, Christina." Franco put his hand on her shoulder. "There's nothing you can do."

She brushed his hand aside. "Right now I need to reach Suzan." Her heart pounded. "What did I do with Stefano's mobile number?"

She frantically dug through her handbag and found the scrap of paper with the number scratched on it. She phoned over to Sardinia and got through within seconds.

"*Pronto?*" Stefano answered.

"Stefano, it's Christina. I need to speak with Suzan."

"She's right here."

"Hey—what's up?" Suzan shouted into the phone. "It's great over here. I'm soaking in the morning sun, perched on the bow of Stefano's yacht. Are you two going to make it?"

She heard Stefano yelling in the background: "I'm king of the worrrrld!"

"No, we're not. Now, Suzan, listen to me. An engineer from Symex was shot. He's dead, and some proprietary designs were stolen. I just read about it in the European *Wall Street Journal*, which means the news is at least a day old." She paused to take a breath. "I think those stolen designs were the ones Peter was working on before he transferred to the subsidiary."

"The ones you were talking about on the beach in Nice?" Suzan's voice became lower and more somber.

"I'm not sure. But if they are, and they get into the wrong hands, Symex could be in a lot of trouble." Missing designs would be far more harmful than a billion-dollar chip robbery.

"Not only Symex—the Department of Defense will be jeopardized as well. I'll ask Stefano to power his yacht back to the mainland immediately."

Christina hung up the phone and got back into bed. She brought the blanket up to her chin. "I'm sorry, Franco, but I'm afraid we have to cut our trip short. The situation at home just got worse, much worse." She reached for him. "I only wish I didn't have to leave you so soon."

"Don't worry, dolcina, we'll see each other again." Franco looked in her eyes. "I do business all over the world. It's nothing for me to fly to San Francisco. What makes you think I would let you slip out of my life so easily?"

*

That afternoon, the three women congregated in Christina's bedroom.

"I asked Stefano about the bald guy," Brandy said, "and he told me he's just someone he supplies marble to in the US."

"I don't buy it," Christina said.

"I didn't either, but that's what he said." Brandy shrugged and disappeared into the bathroom just as Franco approached from the sitting room.

He knocked lightly on the doorframe. "When do you need to leave?"

Christina went to him. "As soon as we can change our tickets and catch the first plane out of here."

He brought Christina's hand to his lips. "Promise me one more night."

"My guess is that the next plane won't be until tomorrow morning."

"I have an idea that may help you with that." Franco cleared his throat and squared his shoulders. "I failed to mention that Doria Marble owns a jet."

Stefano joined them and interrupted. "And a fleet of tankers, but I'm presuming Franco's not going to ship you girls back on *The Doria*."

"The Doria?" Suzan questioned. "As in the *Andrea Doria*?"

Christina grinned at Franco.

He laughed and spread his hands, palms up. "I told you, Christina, this is all anyone remembers. But I have a business meeting in Toronto next week. I could fly over a few days early. We'll fly from here to Toronto, and then you can take a commercial flight to San Francisco. This should save you some time."

Christina jumped up and kissed him. "That would be fantastic. When do we leave?"

"We'll leave tomorrow morning." Franco cupped her face in his hands. "I just need to clear it with my father."

She clung to him for several seconds. "Thank you so much."

"My pleasure, dolcina." He kissed the top of her head. "My only regret is that a present for you, a small souvenir from your holiday, is not finished. It looks like I'll have to ship it to you later." He stepped away from her. "Also, every week my family and another old Tuscan family get together for a late lunch. It's not a formal affair, but my parents insist I attend. It's today."

Stefano patted Franco on the back. "You bet he attends. His future in the marble business depends on it."

Franco shot him a nasty look.

Christina quickly changed the subject. "I'd better tell Brandy about our travel plans." She was not yet out of earshot when she heard Stefano say gruffly to Franco: *"Perche non hai ditto a Christina la vera ragione perche devi incantranti con loro deni settimana?"*

Christina listened with alarm. Although she didn't understand what he had said, she certainly understood the word "Christina" and the harsh tone with which he had delivered the sentence. She walked back into the room and stared at Stefano.

"Oh, excuse me, Christina," Stefano said, sarcastically. "I was rude. Let me translate: why don't you ask your lover boy why he's obliged to meet with this other family once a week?"

Franco stabbed a finger at Stefano. "Stay out of this, Marani." He then turned and looked affectionately at Christina. "Dolcina, it's really not important, just a family matter." He clutched her hand. "I'll be back at six and we'll spend the rest of the evening together."

She smiled feebly. "Take your time." She had one more day in Italy, and as far as she was concerned, Franco had one more day to redeem himself.

Chapter Ten

Christina and Franco spent a quiet evening together at the beach, walking for hours, holding hands. The warm breeze and the smell of the salt water reminded Christina of the time they'd lain in each other's arms on the sand after their dinner at Il Castello. Yet, as much as she enjoyed living this fairy tale, she would leave tomorrow with a lot of unanswered questions regarding Franco. And with no new information on Peter's murder.

Christina stopped and unbuckled her sandals. The sand felt cold on her feet. "Just curious, Franco. How well do you know Stefano?"

"Why?"

"I think Suzan likes him, and I want to know what you think. Friends or not, I've seen the hostility between you."

"I'd be lying if I said I'd want my daughter to marry him."

"What do you mean?"

"He's had his problems." Reaching for her hand, he led her toward the water. "But haven't we all?"

Christina stopped and dropped his hand. "This is important, Franco. What kind of problems?"

"Mostly drugs, wrecking cars, that sort of thing." He bent over and took off his shoes. "To be honest, we're really not that close any more. He's changed a lot since he started his own business. He didn't grow up with much money, but now he's forking it in."

"You mean *raking* it in."

"I'm going to rake you." Franco picked Christina up and carried her out to the surf. "This is our last night together dolcina; let's not worry about Stefano and Suzan." He pretended to let her drop in the water.

She laughed and gripped him tighter.

"You don't trust me?"

How should she answer that? His dropping her in the water was one thing, but woman's intuition told her that he knew more than he had said.

Still holding her in his arms, he kissed her while the water swirled around his feet. He pulled away and smiled. "Why is it that whenever I kiss you, I taste strawberry *sorbetto*?"

"I'll tell you when I'm firmly planted on the sand."

Franco carried her back toward the beach and set her down.

Christina smoothed her sundress. "I got hooked on Bonne Bell Lip Smacker when I was a kid." She laughed. "Some things we never outgrow."

"Like my love to paint." Franco picked up her sandals and carried them for her. He wrapped his arm around her shoulders. "Except that I started with crayons, and now I use oils."

Christina elbowed him in the side. "Okay, you made your point. I can be a little childish."

"My point is simply that you are *carina*."

They continued walking for several minutes in silence, his arm around her shoulder, hers around his waist.

"So carina, when can I see you again?"

"Soon, I hope." She stopped walking and grasped both his hands.

Franco pulled Christina closer to him. He kissed the white area her skimpy bikini top had shielded from the sun. "I could never commit to marriage without these flames of passion."

Christina eased away. "Did you say *marriage*?"

"Don't you ever think about these things?" Franco pulled her back to his chest.

"Doesn't every woman?"

"I don't know. I'm not a woman."

Marriage. What would it be like to marry a foreigner? Where would they live? Would their children go to school in America or Europe? *Children?* What was she thinking?

Franco touched her freckled nose. "It's nothing to be afraid of, Christina."

She had never considered marriage with her previous boyfriends. But Franco was different; he was thoughtful, sensitive, affectionate and most obviously, scary sexy!

He lifted her off her feet again and carried her into the crashing waves. When a forceful surge of water nearly knocked them over, he eased her down and they ran back to the shore and fell onto the dry sand. The sun had just set on the empty beach. Franco rolled onto Christina and pinned her wrists above her head. They kissed as if nothing else mattered, and when he pushed her sundress over her waist, she stood, slipped the dress over her head and tossed it in the sand. This was her last night in Italy, and she could no longer resist Franco. She felt better knowing that he and Stefano weren't the best of friends, and as for the Italian supermodel, well, who cared? Franco was with her tonight, not with the glamorous Italian.

She dug her fingers into the muscles of his back and then reached around to release each of the five buttons on his jeans. When he crawled out of his trousers, the contrast between his silk boxer shorts and his hard body was too much for her. As he slid her panties down her legs, she tore his shorts off.

He explored her with his fingers for several minutes, and lightly kissed her neck. She held onto the last few seconds of this pleasurable crescendo as long as possible, and when he finally entered her, she felt a year's worth of tension flood from her body. Franco seemed to hold on, too, and then, when at last he relented to his own desire, he lay on top of her. He opened his mouth, but instead of saying anything, he closed his eyes and wrapped his arms around her until the balmy breeze lulled them to sleep.

Christina woke to a gold ring of sun peeking above the horizon. She rolled over and watched Franco as he slept, peacefully and still. In the midst of the black stubble on his chin, she noticed a light pink scar where hair no longer grew. She kissed her fingers and brought them to his chin, where she gently touched the pink line. She wanted to wake him and tell him that she wished she could watch every sunrise with him for the rest of her life, but instead she forced herself to stay in the moment and not get carried away with unrealistic expectations and emotions. She had been down this road before and she didn't need the heartache and disappointment again. Whatever happened in their future, the memory of last night and this morning would last forever. That had to be enough—for now.

*

They brushed the sand out of their hair and strolled back to the hotel as the sleepy town of Forte dei Marmi came alive. The air was warm and humid, and already merchants hosed off the sidewalks in front of their shops. The familiar aroma of freshly baking bread wafted onto the street. Christina would've liked to stop for a quick breakfast at one of the local *panettaries,* but she knew the others expected them.

As it was, when they reached the hotel, Suzan and Brandy stood in the lobby, Suzan with Christina's mobile phone to her ear. When she saw Christina, she covered the receiver. "I've been talking to George for the past half hour. They have no idea who killed Denton or who's responsible for the robbery. On top of this, their stock has dropped fifty percent."

Christina took the phone from Suzan. "Hi George, Christina here. I'm sorry to hear about Martin Denton, did you know him well?"

"Not that well, but I know he had a wife and two children. It's a tragedy."

"We'll be back in the Bay Area in about twelve hours. Now, let me ask you this. Did those stolen designs have anything to do with Symex's military division?"

"Yes. The situation here is urgent. Suzan said you may have some ideas?"

"Maybe," Christina said. "In the meantime, could you put me in contact with whoever's in charge of the investigation?"

"Of course, but if you and Suzan have any leads, you'll need to talk to the police and probably the FBI,"

"That's fine. Whatever we can do." The pit in Christina's stomach grew even bigger. She snapped the phone shut as their limousine pulled to the curb. She ran upstairs to get her luggage as the driver loaded the rest of the bags into the trunk.

*

Franco's plane proved far more luxurious than Christina had imagined. The main cabin was as comfortable as a living room, with a wide screen TV, stereo system, fully stocked bar at the front, and six leather chairs and a sofa to the rear.

The trip took less than seven hours. Franco explained that this particular model of Gulfstream, the GV, flew at 54,000 feet, and cut twenty-five percent off the time of a commercial flight. Franco mostly talked on the telephone, worked on his laptop computer and helped the women make their travel arrangements to San Francisco.

"Can I use that?" Christina asked, when Franco finished using his computer.

She connected to the Internet and brought up the Google website. She punched in Curtis Saunders' name, from the hotel guest list Franco had supplied. The first item that popped up was a piece on the latest board meeting for Silicon Valley Electronics. A few of Saunders' top executives had sold their stock before the holdback period had expired. They had subsequently left the country, but were still under investigation. She looked up from the computer.

"Suzan, do you have any idea who Curtis Saunders is?"

"I've heard of him." Suzan put down the glossy Formula One magazine she had found on the coffee table. "He's got a pretty sleazy reputation in the Valley, but I'm not sure why. When we get back to work, I'll run a LexisNexis search."

"It's important. I think Curtis Saunders may be the connection between Peter and Italy."

When she finished with the computer, Franco sought her out. "Now dolcina," he said, "that present I spoke about. It's almost finished. I'll send it to California on one of our container ships."

She loved it when he called her *dolcina*, which roughly translated as 'sweet thing' or 'sweetness'. "Is it that big?" she asked.

He laughed at her reaction. "No, of course not. Doria Marble sends container ships of marble nearly every month to the Port of Oakland. From there, we ship the marble throughout the West Coast and up to Vancouver. It will be no problem to enclose a private shipment."

He kissed her forehead. "To avoid problems with the customs officials, I'll call you when I know when it will arrive. And I'll make sure you get a visitor's pass. The port is enormous. It's not every day a young woman walks onto the docking area and picks up a package."

"I'm familiar with the port," she said. "I see it all the time when I drive over the Bay Bridge."

"Good, then you won't get lost."

The co-pilot emerged from the cockpit to tell them that they had started their descent. They would land in Toronto in twenty minutes.

*

Franco wondered how Christina would react when she received his package. Was he acting too hastily? He didn't normally wear his emotions on his sleeve, but Christina drove him to distraction, a diversion he didn't need. The pressure from his family was crushing enough.

Maybe a little distance between the two of them might help clear his head. She was such a welcome breath of fresh air, but on the other hand, he wasn't prepared for a tornado. She had come into his life at a very inconvenient time and he could certainly do without the added complication; but he wasn't willing to give her up either—not just yet.

Chapter Eleven

"What a whirlwind," Christina mused, as Air Canada flight 757 lifted off the runway en route to San Francisco. Franco had arranged a car to take them directly from the executive terminal to the international one, and now she watched out the window as square brown houses, green clumps of trees and long rectangular streets slowly diminished in size. "I can't believe everything that's happened this past week."

"I know," Suzan said. "I just hope that whoever stole those designs isn't smart enough to understand the full ramifications."

Christina released the air phone from the seat in front of her and punched George Stinson's direct line.

"Hi George. Christina here. We're landing on time. Do you want us to meet you anywhere?"

"That's not necessary," he said. "The FBI's planning to meet you at the airport as soon as you land. They'll drive you directly to their Northern California Headquarters. The shit's really hit the fan. I'll let them fill you in."

A wave of nausea swept over Christina. *The FBI?*

George's voice disappeared into the crackle of the airwaves, but just as he predicted, when the plane touched down at San Francisco International airport, the flight attendant told them that a government car waited for them on the tarmac. She escorted them down a side staircase at the front of the plane amidst the overpowering smell of aviation fuel. Two FBI agents greeted them, dressed in standard attire—dark suits and sunglasses.

"Good afternoon, ladies." The taller one flipped open his badge. "Please get in quickly. Your bags will be here in a few minutes."

Normally Christina would've appreciated the unexpected luxury of avoiding the customs line, but today's alternative only made her palms sweat, particularly when the agent in the passenger seat turned around and spoke to them.

"We've begun a thorough background check on each of you." He spoke through a bushy brown mustache that added to his grave demeanor. "Since Culhane and Anders work with Symex, they'll need to stay with us." He turned to Brandy. "It looks as if Ms. Jensen will not be essential to our investigation, so we'll be happy to give you door-to-door service." He looked down at his folder. "I see you live in Pacific Heights."

"That's right," Brandy said. "And I can hardly wait to get home."

Two airport officials arrived at the car carrying their luggage. Christina heard one of them mutter something about *one of these broads being way over the weight limit*, but after a few pushes and several grunts the trunk slammed shut and the driver took off.

As the car sped down the tarmac, the man with the mustache spoke again. "Now, for you two." He pointed a stubby finger at Suzan and then at Christina. "We're taking you to our office for some questions. A special agent from the Foreign Counter-intelligence division in D.C. flew in yesterday to oversee this investigation. You're meeting with him in an hour. Also an Air Force General and a technology advisor from DARPA will be on call to answer any questions pertaining to the Symex project."

Christina felt queasy. This was serious, but *a special agent from the Foreign Counter intelligence division? An Air Force General? An advisor from DARPA?* She was in way over her head.

When the car pulled into Brandy's driveway, the agents admonished her to not leave town without notifying them, nor to discuss the case with anyone. Christina wished she could hop out of the car with her. Instead, she accepted Brandy's quick hug goodbye, and promised to call her tomorrow.

When they reached the concrete building on Golden Gate Avenue, in San Francisco's Civic Center, the agents ushered Christina and Suzan into two separate offices for questioning. Christina found herself in the office of Special Agent Wilson, a middle-aged man with a military-style haircut, who sat behind an LSD—known in government circles as a large, steel desk—sipping a bottle of the hyper-oxygenated water Penta. No pictures hung on the walls, and the items on his desk consisted of a lamp, a phone, a computer monitor and a stack of folders. With his navy blazer off and his shirt sleeves rolled up, the veins on his biceps and forearms bulged like earthworms.

The FBI agent from the car handed Wilson a blue folder with the official seal of the US Government on it.

"Sit down, Ms Culhane," Wilson said gruffly. Heavy brown eyebrows, speckled with grey, framed his dark eyes. "I need a few minutes to scan this." He leaned back in his chair and began to read.

Christina settled into a stiff metal chair and waited. Wilson nodded several times and scribbled a few notes. Finally, he looked up from the folder. "It says here that five years ago we interviewed you when we screened Carmaletti."

"That's right." Christina nodded.

"So I take it you were close friends?"

"Very close. We've known each other since tenth grade."

Wilson closed the folder. "When did you last see Carmaletti, and what did you discuss?"

Christina's mouth felt dry. She eyed the water bottle on Wilson's desk and wished she could have a sip.

"Does someone finally believe me, that Peter's death wasn't a suicide?"

Wilson leaned forward over his desk and pointed a finger at her. "First, you didn't answer my question; and second, yes, given the Martin Denton case, we have reason to believe that

Carmaletti's death wasn't a suicide." He leaned back in his chair. "Now, answer my first question."

"May I have a glass of water, please?"

"Oh—sure."

He punched a button on his phone, and Christina heard a woman's voice on the speakerphone.

"Shirley, will you bring in a pitcher of water and some glasses, please?"

"I'll be right in."

"Thank you," Christina said. "I had lunch with Peter the day he died. He seemed very anxious, but he didn't say what was bothering him."

Wilson's secretary brought in the water and some plastic glasses. Judging from her hairstyle, she had a standing appointment for a weekly set and dry.

Christina thanked her and poured herself a glass. "It seemed likely that Peter was having some problems at work. He talked about wanting to go away for a long time, a really long time. He also asked how quickly he could liquidate his stock."

"What did you tell him?"

"That he couldn't sell anything for at least a year. He seemed disappointed, but certainly not suicidal."

"He didn't mention that he was in any type of danger?"

"None at all."

"The next thing I need to know is why you went to Italy, and in particular to this Hotel Luna, or whatever the name is."

Christina nodded. "Hotel della Luna. Peter had received several phone calls from that hotel, and I thought it was strange that he didn't place even one return call—almost like someone was harassing him."

Wilson pulled out a stack of photos from his folder and showed her the top one. "Do you know this man?"

Christina looked at the photo. "Stefano. I met him in Italy. What does he have to do with Peter's death?"

"Not sure." Wilson put the photo on the desk "Stefano Marani has been linked to a large Italian drug ring. He was never indicted, but we think there's more to the story. We have reason to believe he may have moved on to smuggling weapons technology."

"Jesus," Christina said. "He gave me a weird feeling, but I never would've guessed he was involved in arms trafficking." She shifted in her chair. "Something else strange happened while I was on my trip."

"What's that?" Wilson asked.

"I think a man may have been following me, and I think this same man broke into my hotel room and stole a file with Peter's personal notes in it."

Wilson held up his hand. "Let's back up a minute. Why did you have one of Carmaletti's files?"

"Mary—his wife—gave it to me."

"So what did this man look like?"

"He was a big bald guy. Probably American, but I'm not sure."

Wilson pulled out another photograph and slid it across the desk. "This man?"

"Yes. That's him." Christina straightened up in her chair. So she wasn't just imagining things. "Who is he?"

"His name is Arnold Hague. And, yes, he's a US citizen. He's a middle-man for Marani's granite business."

Christina thought he was involved in more than just granite. "How does all this tie into Peter?"

"Your friend Peter designed an anti-ballistic missile that no other country in the world has come close to designing." Wilson sipped his water leisurely, as if it were a glass of scotch. "I obviously can't go into the details, but it was so top-secret that the blueprints, which were formatted onto a coded disk, could only be read by inserting an encryption chip, also designed by Peter, into a specialized computer."

Christina finally realized the magnitude of what Peter had been working on.

"A day before Martin Denton was murdered," Wilson continued, "he reported that the coded disk, the one containing the blueprint for the missile, went missing."

Wilson leaned across his desk and stared at Christina, making her uneasy. "So you see, Ms. Culhane, this is very grave. If these designs were sold to a terrorist group, or to a rogue nation with advanced missile capabilities, such as China, Iran or North Korea, the security of the United States and our allies could be in serious jeopardy."

"I understand," Christina said, willing her voice not to quiver. "But didn't you say that the disk can't be read without a special encryption chip? Was that stolen also?"

Wilson leaned back in his chair and ran his hand over the top of his buzz-cut. "We're not sure yet. There were several prototypes of this chip manufactured, but since Carmaletti is dead, and he was the chief engineer, we don't know if anyone actually manufactured the real thing. The project was still in the preliminary stages."

"What about George Stinson? Wouldn't he know if Peter had finalized the chip?"

"He said he wasn't working on that particular project. But we need to investigate that further."

"And what about Curtis Saunders?" Christina asked.

"Saunders?" Wilson raised an eyebrow.

"Yeah, I think that's who called Peter from Italy."

Wilson jotted the name on his pad. "He's been under investigation for insider trading and securities fraud, but nothing that has to do with the Department of Defense."

"Well, I'm pretty sure he was in touch with Peter."

"We'll look into that. For now, let's get back to Italy." Wilson picked up the stack of photos again. "How did you meet Marani?"

"Stefano? I was introduced to him through Franco."

Wilson paused and then asked, "You mean Franco Doria?"

The pit in Christina's stomach grew larger. "How do you know about Franco? Is he involved too?"

"Dino Rossi, the brother of Doria's fiancée, ran in the same drug circles as Stefano."

Christina set her cup of water down so quickly some of it spilled over. "Did you just say Franco has a fiancée?"

"He's engaged to Alessandra Rossi of Rossi Quarries," Wilson said matter-of-factly. "Doria is a shrewd businessman. If his family and the Rossi family merge their companies, he'll control the lion's share of the international marble market."

Christina found it hard to breathe, almost as if she were drowning. How could this be? She had nearly admitted to herself, and to Franco, that she was falling in love. Had she really been so naïve as to believe they shared anything more than a summer fling?

"I need to know, Agent Wilson. Just how deeply is Franco involved?"

Wilson answered bluntly. "I'm not at liberty to discuss that part of the investigation with you."

Christina stared at him blankly. Why could he talk about Stefano and the bald guy, but not about Franco?

"You okay, Miss Culhane?"

Her head felt heavy, and Agent Wilson suddenly looked blurry.

"Miss Culhane, you okay?"

She lowered her head and took some deep breaths. When she felt better, she said, "I think I'm just tired from the flight. May I go home now?"

"First I need to see if your pal Anders is through." He buzzed Shirley and asked her to go next door and check on Suzan. "If Anders is finished, bring her in," he said into the speakerphone.

Christina still felt foggy when Suzan entered the office, escorted by another agent. "You look like you've just seen a ghost, girl," Suzan said. "What happened?"

"I'll tell you later."

Suzan sat down in the chair next to Christina, and Wilson resumed.

"Okay, ladies." He pressed his palms on his desk. "Let me tell you where we're at. All current employees, and anyone who's worked for Symex within the past ten years, are under investigation. The robbery of the chips is a financial setback for Symex, but not nearly as catastrophic as the missing ballistic-missile plans."

"Was the primary purpose of the robbery for the chips or for the designs?" Christina asked.

"Can't say. Before Denton died we got a few words out of him. He told us that a big guy wearing a ski mask came in, shot him and went directly to the securitized building. The set of disks that contain the designs were in a case marked BHAAD1. The perp probably had the sense to realize that whatever was in that case must be important."

"Bad One?" Suzan asked. "That sounds like the name of a rap group."

"No, Miss Anders." Agent Wilson didn't even smile. "BHAAD1 is not a rap group. It's an acronym that stands for Ballistic High Altitude Area Defense. The BHAAD system is the only core theater missile-defense system which, when completed, will be capable of engaging the full spectrum of theater-class ballistic-missile threats. We can only hope that whoever stole those designs does not understand the full ramifications of the project."

What Agent Wilson said began to gel in Christina's brain, and the bits from Peter's file, that she'd read in Italy, finally made sense. The BHAAD system would provide a defense against ballistic missiles that carry lethal hit-to-kill interceptors. The missiles would fly at higher levels and have longer ranges. But the designs were only the first step. Whoever stole the designs now had the power to manufacture missiles of their own and sell them to the highest bidder.

"Are we talking about something like the Patriot missiles from the Gulf War? The ones that were supposed to blow the Scuds out of the sky but missed?" Christina asked.

Wilson snapped his fingers at her. "You got it. China is neck and neck with us in the race to develop a long-range ballistic missile. Our intelligence officers spotted one on the Wuzhai Missile and Space Test Center. It's called the Dong Feng-31. Wilson leaned his bulky chest forward and spoke in a lower voice. "This missile has a five thousand-mile range and carries multiple warheads. It has the power to wipe out the entire West Coast of America."

Christina looked over at Suzan. Her face had lost its color and looked frozen.

Wilson settled back in his chair. "Whoever masterminded this robbery could take the Symex designs to any country engaged in warfare, or to one in the process of remilitarizing."

"But again, without that encryption chip," Christina said, "Peter's designs are useless?"

"Not exactly. A rough prototype, even with a few bugs in it, would provide enough information to crack the code."

He finished off his water and tossed the bottle into a metal waste paper basket. The clank made Christina jump. "All right, ladies, you're finished for now. Tomorrow you'll have to make a visit to the SFPD. For the time being, we're working with San Francisco's finest on this case."

Christina and Suzan got up from their chairs. Wilson also stood. "I'll have a car take you home. But I'm warning you"—his voice rose—"be careful. *No one* is to be trusted until we're in possession of that encryption chip, and until we know who killed Carmaletti and Denton."

Agent Wilson shook hands with each of them and walked them to the door. "Thank you for your time. I'll be in touch."

In the unmarked government car, Christina reflected upon the past week. Who would've thought that their vacation to Italy would end with them being driven home by a Federal Agent? As the car rolled away and the dreary FBI Headquarters faded into the distance, the mystical, romantic interlude between her and Franco faded with it.

She turned to Suzan. "Franco's engaged."

"What?" Suzan spoke so loudly that the agent driving the car swiveled his head toward them.

"You heard me. Engaged."

"How'd you find that out?"

Christina explained everything Wilson had told her, including the information on Stefano.

Suzan threw her hands in the air. "Go figure. The first fun guy I've met who halfway interested me is wanted by the FBI, and yours is engaged!"

Christina dropped the next bombshell. "And Franco may be caught up in all this."

Suzan turned to her. "Please don't tell me…"

"When I asked Wilson if Franco was involved, he basically said: no comment."

"Sorry, sister, but this doesn't sound good."

Christina shook her head. "I'm such an idiot. I go to Europe to find Peter's killer, and instead I fall for a guy who may be involved in his death. How could I be so stupid?"

Suzan put her arm around Christina and squeezed. "You'll bounce back. He's not the only guy out there."

"But we really connected." Christina swiped at her eyes. "You know my track record. When have you ever seen me this crazy about someone?"

"I'm not denying that you were, but the guy doesn't deserve you. You need to forget about him, and I'm going to help you."

"And just how will you do that?"

Suzan gave her an all-too-familiar grin. "Don't worry, I'll think of something."

Chapter Twelve

Christina didn't even check her messages. Tomorrow was Friday—she would try to sleep in, and later, she would go to her office and attempt to make a dent in her mail, log onto her computer and return e-mails. But jet lag woke her at three-thirty a.m.

It was still too dark to go running, so she listened to her messages. There were several from her friends and family, all wanting to hear about her trip. Then, to her astonishment, a message from someone at Senator Cartwright's office in Washington DC. She replayed it to make sure she heard it correctly. The Senator's secretary asked that she call his office. He would be attending a reception in San Francisco, in his honor, and the Senator would like her to be his guest.

Why Senator Cartwright would call her, she had no idea. She remembered meeting him at a fund-raiser she had attended a year ago, but the event was so crowded she had barely had a chance to exchange more than a few words with him. He was an extremely influential, handsome politician from California with enough political savvy to gain the support of both Silicon Valley in the North and the entertainment community in the South. Because of his immense popularity, many considered him the leading presidential contender. Still in his early forties, and after his divorce last year, he was one of the most eligible bachelors in the country. Since it was only seven a.m. in Washington DC, she'd call him in a few hours.

There was no word from Franco, and she wondered why he hadn't called to see if she had made it home safely. After all, he didn't know she knew about his fiancée.

She thought she'd come to the end of her messages when she heard static and an unrecognizable voice crackle from her machine.

Return what's not yours. It's not worth losing your life over.

The hairs on her arms and neck stood up. She played the message again. The voice sounded mechanically altered, so she couldn't recognize it. The threatening message in Italy had frightened her, but this one, on her home turf, left her feeling very exposed and vulnerable. She saved the message to play for Agent Wilson later. With the sun finally coming up, she really felt the need to run; it would be her first good one in over a week.

Her route along the Marina Green, the Saint Francis Yacht Club and out to the Golden Gate Bridge reminded Christina that in spite of her travels to fun, exciting places all over the world, it was great to be home.

As she jogged, she thought about Senator Cartwright. Why would he call *her*, a year later, and request that she accompany him to a party in his honor? Was he interested in her socially, or did this have something to do with her Silicon Valley connections? She picked up her pace. And why hadn't Franco called? She had tried to put a brave face on for Suzan, but she desperately wanted to speak to him.

*

Christina was not the only one awake early that morning.

The Chinese Consulate resided in the Cathedral Hill section of town. A large white building, with blue-trimmed windows, it bustled with activity this morning. Upstairs in the parlor room, the Consul hosted a breakfast meeting to discuss trade practices and the MFN status, while downstairs, in a room completely segregated from the main house, an entirely different type of business took place. The basement, which looked more like the command center for NASA, hummed with the sound of computers and powerful surveillance equipment.

A young aide watched a flashing computer screen. He took off his earphones and reached for one of the many telephones that sat on the table next to him. Late last night an anonymous caller had phoned regarding the sale of some valuable information. The aide gave him standard instructions—call back at precisely nine a.m.

He answered the phone on the first ring. The aide asked the caller to identify himself. Of course he did not, but he explained that he had something he knew would be of interest to the Chinese government, and he requested that someone meet him in the bar at Tadich Grill on California Street at two p.m. The aide agreed a split second before the phone went dead.

*

It was nearly seven a.m. when Christina heard her telephone ring. Why did it always ring as soon as she got in the shower? Her answering machine clicked on and she heard Franco's delicious accent, as smooth as ever. She grabbed a towel, ran to the phone and was about to pick up, but she hesitated. He had been in meetings and at job sites for the past twenty-four hours, he said.

Christina wanted to talk to him, but she knew that would only perpetuate the pain. Instead of answering the call, she continued listening. "I hope you got home safely, my darling, I'll call again soon."

The answering machine clicked off with a finality for which Christina was unprepared. She lifted the receiver and pressed star-six-nine. The automated voice told her that the number was not available. Though she knew Franco was in Canada, not Italy, she called the hotel. Perhaps they had a number for him.

"*Buon giorno,* Hotel della Luna et Stelli."

"Hello Donatella. It's me, Christina. How are you?"

"I'm fine *signorina*. Are you coming back to visit us?"

"Unfortunately, no. I was just wondering—do you know where Franco's staying in Toronto."

"I didn't know *Signoré* Doria was in Toronto. Did you try his mobile phone?"

"I don't have that number." She had never asked for it, because she had no need for it in Italy, and he had never offered it.

"I'm sorry *signorina*, but he instructed all of us to never give out his number."

Great. Donatella probably thought she was just another lovesick woman pining over Franco. But who was she fooling? She *was* a lovesick woman pining over Franco.

"I understand, Donatella. I'm sorry to have disturbed you. If he phones, will you ask him to call me?"

"Of course. We hope to see you again. *Arrivederci signorina.*"

"*Arrivederci*, Donatella." Christina slowly put the phone down. Maybe by the time Franco rang her back, she would be strong enough to confront him about his engagement and involvement with the FBI.

She walked back into the bathroom and wrapped herself in a towel. She made some coffee, and then she called Suzan to wake her and to see if she wanted to drive into the office together. Her machine answered.

"Suzan…wake up." First she spoke, and then she shouted into the machine. "It's Christina."

Suzan finally picked up the phone, sounding groggy. "I'm too tired to go to work this morning."

"We should at least make an appearance. Also, remember we have to stop in at the police department this morning."

"Oh—that's right." She yawned into the phone. "Pick me up in half an hour."

*

The meeting at the San Francisco Police Department intimidated Christina far less than the one at the FBI office. The department was such a zoo that they started nearly an hour late. While they waited, Suzan and Christina sat on worn wooden chairs in the waiting area, where they watched a disparate group of prostitutes, protesters, and homeless parade through the corridor.

Christina tried to sit patiently, but only managed to fidget. When she tapped her foot on the ground, she still felt the sand from Italy in her sandals. Finally, Sergeant Wong pushed her way through the glass doors. A petite Asian woman with short black hair, she wore trendy glasses with turquoise frames.

"Sorry to keep you waiting. The mayor's trying to clean up the streets by arresting the homeless and making us deal with the problem." She reached into the pocket of her uniform shirt and pulled out a tissue. She blew her nose. "Why don't you follow me back to my office?"

They sat on two wooden chairs opposite her clean and orderly desk. Unlike Wilson's office, this one had photos hanging on the walls—pictures of Sergeant Wong and some girlfriends hiking in Yosemite, river rafting, and skiing at Lake Tahoe. A plant that looked like a miniature palm tree sat on the windowsill behind her desk, and an overgrown ivy hung from the ceiling in the corner, its green leaves trailing down the wall.

"Can I offer you girls some coffee? Or how about some tea?"

"No thanks." Christina would've killed for the Italian espresso she'd been drinking the past week.

Sergeant Wong sat down and pushed away a half-eaten tofu and sprout sandwich. "I've been on the force nearly twenty years, and it's only been recently that we've had problems with stolen microchips. What's it going to be ten years from now—people stealing the AIDS vaccine to sell on the black market?"

She opened a folder. "So you think a man by the name of Arnold Hague, Stefano Marani *and* Curtis Saunders are behind this?" She took off her glasses and looked up at the women. "That's a lot of suspects."

"We're not certain," answered Christina, "but we have reason to believe that they're all involved in some way."

She told her the story she'd relayed to Agent Wilson. At the end of her recount, she pulled a microchip from her purse. "I also brought you this DSP chip from my message machine. Someone left me a threatening message. I was hoping you could have it analyzed for me."

"Sure, let me have it." She extended her French manicured hand across the desk. "You've answered everything I need to know for now. I'll get back to you if I have any more questions, and I'll let you know what turns up with your answering machine."

The two women got up from behind the desk. Sergeant Wong gave them each a business card. "Here, take this. It has my beeper number on it. Call me if you run into trouble."

*

They finally made it to their offices and found nearly a foot of mail on each of their desks. Christina logged onto her computer and found over five hundred e-mail messages, many of them spam, but still time-consuming to delete. And not one from Franco. At two-thirty, she wandered into Suzan's office.

Suzan stood by the side of her desk with a stack of mail. She threw a few letters onto her desk and the rest into her wastepaper basket. "I can't believe all this junk. Have you heard from George?"

Christina pulled an Abercrombie & Fitch catalogue out of the basket, flipped through it and tossed it back. "No, we better give him a call."

"Better now than never," Suzan said.

"Hi George," Christina said into the speakerphone. "Any news yet?"

"Unfortunately, nothing. How did everything go at the FBI?"

"Frightening." Christina sat down. "We also just got back from the police department. And last night, when I was going through my messages, I think I got one from someone who's trying to scare me. I gave the memory chip to the police to analyze the voice pattern."

"You'd better be careful. Let the authorities handle this."

Christina pulled her hair off her face. "It's impossible to sit still knowing Peter's killer is still out there, and that those missile designs could be auctioned off to the highest bidder. Do you know if the stolen chips have hit the market yet?"

"As far as we know, they haven't surfaced. Anyway, you'd better do something about this stock price. Our investors are screaming that we do something to push it back up."

"We're working on a press release, but let me tell you, it's hard to make this sound any different than it is."

George expelled a deep breath into the phone. "Did the FBI give you any idea who may be responsible for all this?"

"No, and to be honest, George, I'm not supposed to discuss it."

George didn't say anything.

"George—are you still there?"

"Sorry, I'm a bit distracted."

"Yeah, me too. I'll talk to you later."

Bart beeped through just as she hung up the phone.

"Jacobs is on line two for you, Christina."

Christina looked at Suzan. All she needed was heat from Jacobs.

Her hand shook as she picked up the receiver. "Mr. Jacobs? This is Christina."

"What's this I hear about you being involved in this Symex problem?" His voice came through loud and gruff.

"We're not involved, we were questioned by the FBI and police because I knew Peter well, and because we've been working with Symex on spinning off the new company." She tried to keep her voice from quivering.

"If Symex finds out that you jeopardized their financial condition in any way, you'll be looking for another job."

"Don't worry, sir, everything will be fine." She could barely eke out the words. Things were far from fine.

*

While Christina ate a sandwich at her desk, the last of the business lunch crowd finally cleared out of Tadich's and returned to work. Tadich's, known as the best fish joint in town, opened during the Gold Rush of 1849, and has been an institution ever since. It was the only place where the three-martini lunch had not sprinted into the sunset alongside the health craze.

At the end of the restaurant, in a dark corner, two men—one Asian, one Caucasian—sat at a small table, hunched over and whispering with their heads close together. The waiter approached their table and asked them if they would like something to drink. The Asian put up his hand, gesturing to leave them alone. The Caucasian man slid a single sheet of paper across the table. After the young Asian aide looked at it, he nodded his head, and the Caucasian swiftly left the restaurant. Sitting alone at the table, the Chinese man ordered a drink and walked over to the pay phone. When he hung up, he walked outside into the bright sun. They had a deal.

Chapter Thirteen

By Thursday morning, Christina had finally regained her momentum at work, and could concentrate on something other than the Symex fiasco. She was about to call George Stinson when Bart buzzed through.

"I've got Senator Cartwright on the line."

She picked up the receiver. "Hello Richard. It's been a long time. I was surprised to hear from you."

"Yes it *has* been a long time. Thanks for taking my call. I'm sure my secretary mentioned the fund-raiser next week, but if you're free, I'd like to take you to dinner tonight so we can catch up."

Well, that's short notice. If she were playing by today's dating rules, she would have flat-out declined, but since he *was* a US Senator and probably the next President, she'd make an exception.

"I just got back from Italy, so I'm beat. If we could make it early, I'd love to join you."

"I'm staying at the Fairmont. Why don't we meet there at six forty-five?"

*

Christina purposely wore a navy Armani suit, a pearl necklace and one-carat diamond stud earrings. She hoped the suit would convey the sense of business she'd wanted to maintain with Senator Cartwright. For a splash of color, she tied a Pucci scarf around her handbag, as the woman in Franco's hotel had, a woman she now assumed must have been Alessandra Rossi.

Since the Fairmont was just a short cable-car ride from the Financial District, she left her car parked in the lot beneath her office building. The fog had rolled back in and Christina shivered as she clung to the outside rail of the cable car. She couldn't tell if she trembled from the cold weather or with nerves at the thought of seeing the Senator again. She had run a bit late and hoped she would have time to slip into the powder room to comb her wind-blown hair, but no such luck.

As she walked into the hotel lobby, decorated with gilded mirrors and velvet curtains, Senator Cartwright sat in a brocade-upholstered chair by the entrance. He looked a bit older but even more distinguished than when she last saw him. His hair had gone nearly completely grey, but his face still retained its angularity and chiseled look. She could see why so many women doted on him.

"Hello, Christina." He rose, towering over her with his broad shoulders and six-foot-four frame. "I'm happy to see you again. You look stunning."

"Thank you. It's good to see you again, also." She would need to be careful not to let the evening stray from the intended purpose of catching up. He'd only become more handsome with age.

A tall, athletic looking man with blondish-white hair and bright blue eyes stood and walked over to them.

"Christina," Richard said. "This is Erich. Since 9/11 I've had a few death threats. I'm required to have twenty-four-hour security.'

Christina smiled at him. "Hello, Erich."

Erich nodded, but nothing more.

Richard and Christina walked from the Fairmont along Sacramento Street, while Erich stayed no more than ten feet behind them. They passed the Pacific Union Club and Grace Cathedral and talked about such innocuous subjects as the history of Nob Hill and the barons of industry—Stanford, Huntington, Hopkins and Crocker, known as the "Big Four"—who had built the city. Stanford founded a university, Crocker a bank and a shopping galleria, and Huntington and Hopkins each had a hotel that bore his name atop Nob Hill.

Heads turned as they entered Venticello, a rustic Italian restaurant with fairy lights dangling above leaded-glass windows. Christina had not considered that she would be in the presence of one of the most recognizable men in California, and because of the intimacy of the restaurant, none of the tables was private. The Senator, of course, didn't mind; after all, he would run for President one day.

"Christina," he said softly. "If this makes you uncomfortable, we could go somewhere else. How does a four-course meal back at the hotel sound?"

"I'm fine." She clutched her handbag firmly. "Let's stay here."

The hostess escorted them to a corner table covered with a red and white-checkered tablecloth. A single candle flickered in the center. Richard held her chair for her and ordered them a bottle of Chianti Classico, from the Villa Antinori, before the hostess left them to peruse the menus. Erich mumbled something into the cord dangling from his ear and sat at a table next to them.

As Christina's nervousness eased, she swept her hair behind her ear and crossed her legs. "So, what's keeping the Chairperson of the Senate Armed Services Committee busy these days?"

He sighed and shook his head. "It's been a tough ride. I'm working on a bill to raise funds to speed up the development of our theater missile defense arsenal. Those damn Democrats—oh, excuse me, I assume you're Republican."

"Don't worry." She dipped a piece of fresh focaccia into olive oil. "I am, a liberal one, but I still lean toward the right." For effect, she leaned her torso to the right, like the Leaning Tower of Pisa.

Senator Cartwright smiled and took a sip of wine, letting it linger in his mouth for a few seconds before responding. "The Democrats fight me every step of the way. We've been trying to kill the Anti-Ballistic Missile Treaty, and they've been putting up roadblocks."

"Are you afraid that a foreign power could launch an attack that would cripple us while we stood defenseless under the guidelines of the Anti-Ballistic Missile Treaty?"

"Yes, exactly." He reached over to pour Christina more wine, but she had only taken one sip. She covered her glass with her hand.

He put down his glass of wine and looked into her eyes. "I must say that I'm quite impressed that you're concerned with this issue, and for that matter, that you know the least bit about it. I need to have someone like you by my side—a woman who can hold her own with anyone from the pampered wife of a corporate CEO to the Chief Financial Officer of a major Silicon Valley company. And now, I learn, with one who understands our vulnerability to the anti-ballistic missile treaty. They're all supporters of mine and they will all be out in force next Tuesday."

"I'm honored that you'd ask me." She smiled. "But let me tell you, the last fundraiser I attended wasn't what I thought it would be."

Richard frowned. "What happened?"

"It's kind of funny actually." She took another sip of wine. "I was under the impression that for a thousand dollars a plate, the food would be fabulous. My date thought the same, and he didn't eat all day. For that kind of money, he assumed the dinner would be an all-you-can-eat buffet." She took another sip of wine, more comfortable with the Senator now. "The buffet consisted of three ham and cheese casserole dishes. They could have come from

Costco, and can you believe it—they were still in aluminum foil pans! We didn't eat much, and guess where we ended up?"

Richard's eyes smiled. "Please." He swirled his wine in the large round goblet. "Indulge me."

"A drive-thru McDonald's window. We ordered two Quarter Pounders and two vanilla shakes."

Richard laughed. "I think that experience is more typical than one would think. The food is always atrocious." He leaned across the table. "But what do you think? It couldn't hurt your business development efforts to attend. Plus it's only cocktails. You won't have to sit through a dinner of rubber chicken or runny casseroles."

"Of course I'll go." She winked at him. "I just won't expect much."

He held up his glass. "Here's to an evening of plastered smiles, plastic *hors d'oeuvres*, and pomp and ceremony."

A waiter stopped by and poured Richard another glass of wine. Christina still nursed her first.

"Now, Christina," Richard said. "Tell me what you have been working on this past year."

"You could say that I'm buried in a small crisis at the moment."

"Oh?" His brows arched. "What kind of crisis?"

"I really can't talk about it." She looked away. "When everything gets resolved, I'll tell you."

He held up his glass. "Promise?"

She clinked his glass to his. "Promise."

After dinner, Richard paid the bill and they walked outside into the cold foggy night, with Erich staying a few steps behind. Cable cars clanked in the distance.

"Would you like to walk back to the hotel with me and get a cab from there?"

She untied her scarf from her handbag and wrapped it around her neck. "I'll catch the cable car on California Street and ride it down to my office."

He extended his hand in a businesslike fashion. "Well then, I guess this is where we say good night. I'll call next week with details about the party." He shook her hand. Then, unexpectedly, he kissed her lightly on the cheek. "Thank you for joining me tonight."

Christina watched the Senator turn back toward the hotel. As handsome as he was, she yearned for Franco. Even now, she couldn't stop thinking about him.

Chapter Fourteen

As soon as Christina pushed her front door open, she heard the monotonous, high-pitched beeping of her telephone. She flicked on the light, and every nerve on her spine bristled. Furniture lay overturned on the floor, along with emptied dresser drawers and broken lamps. Her phone had been knocked across the room.

She listened for strange noises. Hearing none, she presumed that whoever had done this no longer lurked in her apartment, and she crept toward her living room. At first glance, nothing seemed to be missing, but the intruder had broken her back window. Silk curtains blew in the wind and cast eerie grey shadows; her skin prickled with fear and cold. She tried to call the police, but she couldn't get a dial tone. The shrill beeping continued until she unplugged the cord from the socket and plugged it back in. Only then did she remember Sergeant Wong's card. When she located it, she had her paged and then immediately placed a call to Suzan.

"I can't stay here alone," she said, as soon as she had explained what happened. "Can I stay with you tonight?"

"Of course. Should I come get you?"

Christina wrapped herself in a blanket. "I'll be okay if you'll stay on the phone until the police get here, and then I'll be right over."

Sergeant Wong and her partner got to her apartment in less than half an hour. Christina breathed a sigh of relief at the sight of her familiar face. "Thank God it's you," she said.

"We'll take a look around." The sergeant pulled a small notepad from her shirt pocket while the other officer checked the other rooms.

"It looks like I've been robbed, but I haven't noticed anything missing."

"Let's have a look." Sgt Wong surveyed the apartment and then went to the broken window. She poked her head outside and looked at the small garden two stories down. "This was no random break-in. Someone deliberately climbed this tree. It would have been much easier to hit one of the lower units. And look over there. Your next-door neighbor has all the lights off and the window is wide open."

In the kitchen, she nodded toward the refrigerator. "See this?" The door had been left wide open. And all of Christina's spices were pulled from the cabinets and dumped onto the floor. Sergeant Wong shook her head. "They think you have something of value to them—maybe something to do with that computer account you're working on. I know it's probably a great piece of business, but you need to remove yourself from it as much as possible. If this is the work of the same people who heisted the chips, they're not afraid to use a gun. Two men are already dead because of this."

Sgt Wong walked into Christina's bedroom, where the other officer dusted for fingerprints. "Have you checked your closets?"

"There's really nothing of value in them, except clothes and shoes, but I'll look."

Christina opened her closet door. The light automatically clicked on. "Oh my God!" She covered her mouth.

"What is it?"

Christina held up half of her Valentino dress. She bent down to pick up the other half. "My dress has been slit." The dress she had worn for her romantic dinner at Il Castello.

Sgt Wong examined it and whistled. "That was one sharp knife." She looked up at Christina. "These folks mean business. I'd advise you not to stay here tonight."

Christina sunk down on her bed. "I've arranged to stay with a friend."

"Can I give you a lift?"

"Please. I'd feel a lot safer."

Chapter Fifteen

Suzan lit a candle and popped in a CD from her Café del Mar collection. The ambient-style club music filled her living room and helped to calm her nerves. But the tranquil atmosphere she'd created wasn't enough to dull the anxiety caused by Christina's call. She reached into a ceramic vase she'd bought in South America, pulled out a half-smoked joint and lit it. She struggled into a lotus position and meditated—but in spite of the pot, the chill-out music and candles, her brain turned cartwheels. What if Christina ended up dead like Peter? These guys would stop at nothing until they got what they wanted, but what was it that they wanted from her? With luck, she could knock some sense into Christina and get her to back off and leave the detective work to the professionals.

*

Sergeant Wong pulled up to Suzan's flat just before midnight. "Be careful, Christina."

"I will. Thanks for the ride."

"Wait, I forgot to give this to you." Sgt Wong held a plastic zip-lock bag containing the memory chip from Christina's answering machine. "We couldn't pinpoint exactly whose voice it was, but whoever it is, he has a Southern accent."

When Suzan buzzed her in, Christina trudged up to the third floor apartment, where the odor of freshly smoked marijuana nearly knocked her over.

Suzan stood at the door with a pint of Ben & Jerry's in her hand. "C'mon in, girl." She put a hand on Christina's shoulder. "Are you going to be okay?'

"Probably, but I'd be lying if I said I weren't frightened. Whoever did this also sliced my beautiful Valentino dress in half."

"This is really scaring me"

"The police want me to resign the Symex account." Christina rifled through the freezer for some more ice cream. She had been so engrossed in conversation with the Senator at dinner that she had barely touched her osso bucco. The veal had been so tender it had fallen off the bone. Now, she would've killed for a bite. "Of course, I can't. I worked for over a year to bring it in. I don't get it—I'm basically just a salesperson. Why would I be a threat to anyone?"

"I don't know, but the account is in the door; someone else in the firm could take over from here." She licked her spoon.

Christina found a half-empty pint of Cherry Garcia. "It's not just about meeting my quota, Suzan. I want to find out who killed Peter."

Suzan scraped the last bit of ice cream from the container. "I understand that, but Peter wouldn't want you to get hurt. Whoever took those chips has to be afraid that you may lead the police to them." She waved her spoon in the air, her voice frantic. "The more you know about the company, the more the FBI wants to know, and the more they know, the more these guys want to cut you out of the loop. This time your dress, next time your throat. You need to get out while you still can." She threw her ice cream carton into the garbage can. "Why don't you tell George tomorrow that you're resigning? Someone else from the firm can take over."

"I'll think about it." Christina ate a spoonful of ice cream and set the carton aside. All the anxiety had made her stomach uneasy. "I still don't understand why anyone would be after me, but let me tell you—it pisses me off that they broke into my condo, and slit my dress." She rummaged through her duffle bag for her toothbrush and something to sleep in. She found a cotton t-shirt and pulled it out. "No matter what, Suzan, I'm going to get to the bottom of this."

"Oh, great. The last thing I wanted was to put a fire under you." Suzan opened the hall closet and pulled out a sheet, a pillow and a wool blanket and threw them onto her brown leather sofa. "Before we go to sleep, tell me about your dinner."

Christina fell onto the couch and lay her head on the pillow. She was in no mood to talk about dinner with the Senator.

But Suzan grabbed the pillow out from under Christina's head. "Sooo—how was dinner?"

"Okay, okay." Christina pulled the blanket up to her chin. "He's actually a decent guy. I think we'll have fun at the reception next week."

"How can I snag a ticket?"

"I'll see if Richard can comp you one. He's supposed to call early next week with more details. But I have a feeling he may call sooner."

*

Christina shot up from the sofa, unsure where she was for a moment, until she heard the message machine click on with Suzan's voice screeching from the speaker: "Christina, it's me. Pick up if you're awake."

She located the phone. "What happened? Why didn't you wake me?"

"I tried, but you were dead to the world. You needed the sleep. Take your time coming in."

"Don't worry, I will." Christina stretched her arms toward the ceiling. "My back is killing me. I appreciate the hospitality, but I think I'm going to have to see a chiropractor."

"Sorry about that. Come to think of it, a few men have said the same thing. Anyway, the coffee should still be hot."

"Thanks, I'm going to need a kick start this morning."

"So, what are you going to do about Symex?"

Christina massaged the back of her neck. "I'll give George a call when I get in. In the meantime, can you transfer me to Bart?"

The phone clicked. A few bars of classical music played in her ear.

"Hey Bart. Did a man named Franco Doria call last night and leave a message?"

"Sorry. Nothing."

"Thanks. I'll be there in an hour."

"Wait, Christina. You had a few other calls. Jacobs from New York wanted to know what's going on with Symex; Senator Cartwright asked you to call him at the Fairmont, and Brandy called—nothing important."

Christina hung up and dialed the Fairmont. The front desk operator said that the Senator wasn't in, but would she like to leave a message? Christina gave her name and number.

Before she had a chance to hang up, the operator said, "Hold one moment, please," and within seconds, she was connected directly to his room.

"Hello Christina," Richard said. "I called last night to see if you got home safely, but your phone was out of order."

"You don't know the half of it," she said. "My place was broken into last night."

"My God. Are you all right?"

"A little shaken, but I'm sure I'll get over it."

"I should've escorted you home. I will in the future."

"Please, Richard, don't worry about it. This wasn't your fault. I've been living alone for nearly ten years and have made it home safely every night except this one. The police think it has something to do with the account I'm working on."

"The one you won't tell me anything about?"

"How'd you guess? Anyway, let's talk later. I need to get into the office."

"Are you sure you're all right?" he asked.

"Not really."

*

When Christina finally made it to work, she found Suzan in her office, struggling over a spreadsheet on her computer. She looked up when Christina walked in.

"Hey—how are you feeling?"

"A bit better." Christina set her handbag on the chair. "Thanks for letting me sleep in."

"You should lie low for a while. You can stay at my place as long as you need to."

"I appreciate the offer, but my neck and back couldn't take another night on your couch." She rubbed the top of her shoulders. "I think I'll check into a hotel for a bit. Maybe the Sheraton Palace. I have that party there Tuesday night, so I won't have to worry about drinking and driving."

"Always the practical one." Suzan focused on her computer and gripped her mouse. "Now get outta here. This needs to be in New York before five o'clock their time."

From her office, Christina called Agent Wilson. She told him someone had broken into her apartment and had torn it apart.

"Listen, Culhane. Unless you're honest with me, I can't help you. You need to tell me what you have that they want."

"I *am* being honest with you. I don't have anything, and I don't know what they're looking for." Her voice rose. "And don't shoot the messenger. I'm the victim here!" She slammed down the phone.

Within seconds, Bart beeped through. "Senator Cartwright's on the line."

Her hand still shook as she picked up the phone.

"Christina. How are you holding up?"

"Fine—I guess. Whoever broke into my apartment last night has succeeded in scaring me enough that I won't go back."

"Don't take this the wrong way, but why don't you stay here at the Fairmont? I'm staying in a three-bedroom suite, and there's an empty bedroom. It's completely separate from my room—with its own lock and phone line."

Christina took off her glasses and bit the stem. "Thanks for the offer, but that's not such a good idea."

"Really, you shouldn't be alone. Erich may be a bit of a bore, but he's a trained federal agent, and you could use the added security. You could even check in under an assumed name."

Christina swiveled her chair around to look out toward the bay, where a giant cargo ship, stacked with brightly colored containers, inched toward Alcatraz. She liked the idea of the added security, and besides, the hotel was just up the hill from her office.

She swiveled back around. "All right, you sold me. Are you sure it's empty?"

"Positive. I'll call housekeeping and have them prepare it. I need to return to Washington today, but I'll be back Sunday night."

"Thanks, Richard. I appreciate your help." She hoped she wasn't getting herself into trouble. The last thing she needed was a rebound relationship.

Suzan popped her head in the doorway. "How about if I go home with you after work and help you throw some things together for next week?"

"Perfect. Let's meet around six."

*

Christina's apprehension increased when she returned to her condo and found the door already open a few inches.

"I remember closing the door last night," she told Suzan.

"Were the police still here when you left?"

"They left with me, and I swear, I closed it."

"Whoever broke in the first time may have come back," Suzan said. "Let's just get in and out as quickly as possible."

Christina's heart beat rapidly as she pushed the door open further. She listened carefully, and hearing nothing, she proceeded into the hallway. The white pillows from her couch lay strewn all over the living room, and broken glass and dead flowers littered the wool carpet.

"I've seen your place look worse than this," Suzan said, attempting levity. "Remember, last year when you went through your "I don't want to see anyone, or leave my house" phase? You didn't let Rosa in for over two weeks."

Christina picked up a few business suits that had been thrown from her closet onto the floor, and attempted to straighten the wrinkles before she put them into her hanging bag. She hadn't bothered to unpack everything when she returned home, so many of her things still remained in her suitcase.

"Remember this?" Christina held up the string bikini she'd bought in Nice. "It seems at least a year since we were at the beach." She brushed the sand off and threw it into her laundry basket. "I miss those days."

The Valentino dress still lay crumpled in two pieces on the floor. "Do you think it can be repaired?" She held half the dress in her hand.

Suzan shook her head. "Sorry, sister, it's a goner."

Christina folded both halves and placed them in a drawer. The dress and the memories it represented—she could part with neither just yet. "This place is giving me the creeps. Let's pack up and get out of here." She picked up a lamp and set it back on her dresser. "It's useless to organize this mess now."

"And besides, I'm starving," Suzan said. "Let's get something to eat."

They had to wait to cross the street in front of Christina's condo while a pack of men riding bikes flew through the intersection. They had more logos on their tight-fitting shirts than advertisements on a NASCAR.

While they waited in line at the local sushi place, Christina thought she saw George Stinson walk by on the other side of the street. She handed Suzan some money and asked her to order a California roll and some Ahi sashimi.

"George," Christina called.

He turned, clearly startled to see her.

"Hi," she said. "I didn't know you lived here."

"Ha! That's a joke." His eyes didn't smile and he didn't seem happy to see her. "I live in the Sunset. I don't manage my money as well as you must."

"I'd be happy to help you. That's what we do at Kingstone."

"No need." George shoved his hands in his pockets. "I'll be out from under my pile of debt in a few months."

"Time to sell your stock options?"

"Something like that." His glasses slid down his nose. He pushed them back up and averted his eyes.

She felt for him. He must be nervous about the investigation. She could hardly sleep or walk down the street without looking over her shoulder. "Anyway, George, I'm glad I ran into you. I planned to give you a call first thing Monday morning."

"Discovered something new?"

"I wondered if you'd heard from Agent Wilson recently."

"Why?" He looked directly at her this time.

"I'm curious about an encryption chip he mentioned during our interrogation. He said they needed to track down all the prototypes. I was wondering whether or not he'd talked to you about it."

George put his hands in his pockets and rattled some change. "Uh—yes, I just spoke to him. He said they were able to account for all of them. It's nothing you need worry about."

"That's good to hear—one less thing I'll need to do tomorrow." Across the street, Suzan waited on the sidewalk with her food. "Good seeing you, George."

"So?" Suzan handed Christina her food.

"He seemed a bit on edge, but I guess that's to be expected under the circumstances."

"I know how I felt after my time with the Feds. It's something I don't want to do again, and I'm barely involved."

"Let's head over to the Fairmont," Christina said.

*

By the time they reached the hotel, Christina could think of nothing more than checking in and going to sleep. A room in the Presidential Suite had been reserved for her, the front desk clerk said, and the bell captain escorted them up in the private elevator. On the eighth floor, they stepped into a marble foyer, where a dozen long-stem white roses stood in a vase on the hall table. Christina tipped the valet and opened a card addressed to Margaret Smith, the alias she would use during her stay.

"*Christina, enjoy your stay, Richard.*"

Suzan yanked the card from Christina. "Let me see that." She read the hand-written card.

"Let's take these back to my room." She picked up the vase with one hand and her suitcase with the other.

In the corridor, Christina turned the doorknob on one of the doors. Locked. "This must be Richard's room."

Suzan tried the next door. "This one's locked, too."

"Probably Erich's room," Christina said. "I wouldn't want to stay next to Richard anyway. Let's keep looking."

They entered an enormous living room, furnished with a baby grand piano, two round oak tables, and chintz-covered couches. Next to the marble fireplace sat an oversized writing desk, equipped with a fax machine, computer and telephone.

They retraced their steps to the foyer and explored the next room, most spectacular of all. Speechless, they entered a magnificent two-storey, circular library. Rows of books lined the walls behind an antique desk; across the room from that, a maroon leather sofa, tufted with brass buttons, sat atop plush hunter-green carpet. In the back of the room, a narrow winding staircase led upward. Unable to resist seeing where it would take them, they followed the stairs up to a walkway in front of more book-lined shelves. Above them a midnight-blue ceiling dome had been accented with constellations, painted in gold leaf.

"Look at this workmanship. I feel like I'm in a planetarium." Christina stared in awe for several minutes, and then they wound their way back downstairs.

In the lower portion of the library, on the other side of the book-lined walls, French doors opened to a rooftop terrace with views of downtown San Francisco and the Bay. In the other direction, the glittering lights of Treasure Island connected to Oakland by way of the Bay Bridge.

"Nice digs," Suzan said.

Christina stepped through another set of French doors into a formal dining room. Beneath an enormous crystal chandelier, a Chippendale dining table spread nearly fifty feet in length, flanked by twenty matching chairs. Adjacent to the dining room, they discovered a gourmet kitchen with all the amenities: a Jenn

Air barbecue, a Subzero refrigerator, and a six burner Wolf range.

Christina ran her fingers along the granite countertops. "I hadn't planned to do much cooking, but what the hell, maybe I'll throw a party one night."

They left the kitchen and continued looking for the third bedroom. Finally, they noticed another door across from the dining room. Christina opened it.

"Look at this. I'll definitely feel at home in here."

"No doubt!" Suzan said.

They grinned at each other and took the room in—a lovely four-poster bed, fluffy pillows, and a small couch for reading. A hand painted map of the world covered the walls, and French windows opened to a view of the many hills of San Francisco.

Christina noticed a separate deadbolt, the key still in the lock. She appreciated that it was a comfortable distance—clear at the other end of the suite—from the Senator's room.

Christina sank into the bed. "I can hardly wait to go to sleep."

*

The moment Christina arrived at work the next morning, Bart stopped her. "Franco's been trying to reach you. I wasn't sure if you wanted me to give him your cell-phone number, so I didn't, but let me tell you, that man has the sexiest voice on the planet. If he calls again, I won't let him hang up."

Christina smiled. "You did the right thing." She disliked discussing business, or anything for that matter, on her mobile. The connection was always poor, and traffic distracting. She used the phone strictly to make appointments, pick up messages or to leave a quick message. And texting? Forget about it! It took half an hour to text a single sentence. "But if he calls again, please let me know, and give him my cell number."

"And while I have him on the line, I'll give him mine too."

"Are you trying to steal my boyfriend, Bart?"

"So, now he's your *boyfriend*?"

"Well, not really." Christina bit her lip. "It's complicated." She enjoyed joking around with Bart, but preferred to keep their relationship on a professional level. "Also, I'll be staying at the Fairmont Hotel for the next week. The name I checked in under is Margaret Smith. Only you and Suzan know this, and I'd like to keep it that way. Unless Franco calls."

Wilson may have said to trust no one, but she *had* slept with Franco. He might have some explaining to do, but he was no killer.

"Is everything okay?"

"Not really, I need to sort a few things out."

Alone in her office, she opened her e-mail, and read the one from Suzan first. For a girl from Orinda, one of the wealthier suburbs, she could really put on the streetwise hip-hop:

```
hey girl, at meetings all day in san jose. made
some phone calls and got the 411 on Saunders, but
still need to run the lexy-nexy report. will get
the dirt on him soon. catch ya later, suzu.
```

Kingstone subscribed to LexixNexis, a search engine much more extensive than Google. As an analyst, Suzan had access to the terminal, which provided information on lawsuits, shareholder grievances and court records.

Later, after four straight hours at her desk, Christina shut down her computer and pushed a few files to the side of her desk. She beeped Bart. "That's it for today. I'm drained." Emotionally and physically. "Have a nice weekend, Bart, and call me at the hotel if you need me."

Chapter Sixteen

Christina had just finished reading the Sunday *New York Times* when the extension in her room rang. She jumped when she heard the phone—her nerves were on edge, and not many people knew she was staying at The Fairmont.

"Christina. I just got back from Washington and I wondered if you'd like to join me for dinner."

"Oh—Richard." She sat on the sofa and curled her bare feet under her. "Any other night that would sound great, but not tonight. I have an early presentation tomorrow and I have a lot of work to prepare. Thanks for the flowers, though."

"I'm glad you liked them, but I'm not taking *no* for an answer so easily. I don't plan to go out either. We'll order room service and have dinner in our dining room."

"In that case, I'll join you," she conceded. "At least I won't have a problem getting home."

"Very well then," he said. "Why don't you meet me in the library so we can have a drink before our dinner arrives?"

"I have a few things to organize for tomorrow; I'll meet you in an hour."

Christina sorted through the paperwork she'd brought home from her office, organized her PowerPoint presentation on her laptop, and finally put her clothes in the closet. She'd been living out of her suitcase all weekend, and the room had begun to look like her condo, without the help of Rosa. But she stayed here as a guest; it was time to straighten up a bit. Spotting the map of Forte dei Marmi, she smoothed its edges and pressed it into her leather day planner. Then, rather than change out of her faded Levis and cashmere v-neck, she slipped on a pair of worn leather loafers and walked into the next room.

Candles and fresh flowers surrounded two intimate place settings at the end of the long mahogany table. She found

Richard in the library, where he sat on the leather couch drinking a glass of red wine and reading *The Economist.* A raging orange and red fire crackled in the fireplace.

"Good evening, Richard." The smell of burning wood made her feel cozy and warm, as if she were at home with her family in Philadelphia.

"Please join me." He gestured for her to sit down on the couch and poured her a glass of wine. "I'm enjoying a fabulous bottle of '82 Bordeaux, Chateau Lafite. They have an incredible wine cellar here."

She took a sip of wine. "I'll say." It tasted rich and smooth, like a combination of blackberries and sweet peppers.

"Do you know any of the history behind this suite?"

"None at all, but I'd love to hear it."

"This library was where Secretary of State Stettinius, in 1945, drafted the Charter of the United Nations. In fact, he signed it right there on that desk." He pointed to the antique desk that sat in front of the book-lined walls.

"But the most scandalous story I heard was about John F. Kennedy," he continued. "When he visited San Francisco, he and Mrs. Kennedy would stay in the room where I'm sleeping, and it was rumored that Angie Dickinson would sneak into your room."

Richard replenished her glass. "Rumor has it that she came up a rarely used stairway off the kitchen, and then she and President Kennedy would meet in the middle of the night, right here in this library."

"From what I've heard about JFK, I believe it," Christina said.

"Dinner should be here any minute. I hope you don't mind, but I took the liberty of ordering for both of us. If I remember correctly, you're not a vegetarian."

"No way. I've been a carnivore all my life and proud of it." She appreciated Richard's effort. Admittedly, it felt comforting to be indulged. *But what was she getting herself into?* Her grandmother had been fond of saying that she liked to jump from the fire into the frying pan. Back then, she had broken up with her Italian boyfriend from the wrong side of the tracks, only to end up with an Irish boy from the wrong side of the river. If her grandmother were alive today, she'd probably say that she had run from the white marble palazzo in Italy to the White House on Pennsylvania Avenue.

Richard interrupted her thoughts. "Let's celebrate your move to your new home—temporary as it is."

They touched wine glasses. "I do feel safer here, and it's very convenient."

From where Christina and Richard sat, they could both enjoy the spectacular view of Berkeley Hills and of the Bay Bridge, where strands of white lights connected the peaks and slopes of the eight-mile span of steel. Streams of red taillights and white headlights flowed like molten metal across the engineering masterpiece.

When the door buzzer rang, Richard let the room service staff in. Christina watched the waiters lift silver serving tops from the plates. She smelled the filet mignon and roasted vegetables even before they had a chance to place the plates on silver chargers.

"This sure beats what I planned to have for dinner. At most, I thought I'd pop some popcorn and call it an early night."

"Well, I hope you enjoy it," Richard said. "I'm sure you've seen some incredible homes, but I thought you'd find this suite, especially with all the history, a nice change of pace."

"So, you think I'm manor born?" Christina smiled, amused at his observation. "I actually had a very middle-class childhood. But of course, I've worked with executives who've taken their companies public. They've opened my eyes to *The Lifestyles of the Rich and Famous*."

"Now I know why I like you so much. You're very down to earth. I can't tell you how many pretentious little rich-girls I've met over the years."

They enjoyed their steak, grilled medium rare, and nearly another bottle of wine, before the waiters returned with dessert: a flambé of cherries. Over bites of it, Christina presented Richard with a question she'd been dying to ask.

"I know you plan to run for President. I'm curious as to how you'll address the issue of your divorce."

"You're not the first person to bring that up." He wiped his lips with a linen napkin and leaned back in his chair. "Did you read about the escapades of my wife in Hollywood?"

Christina nodded.

"Frankly, that was too much for me to handle." Richard shook his head. "And, with fifty percent of all first marriages ending in divorce, my feeling is that at least twenty-five percent of the married population is unhappy. Maybe they're sticking it out for the sake of the children or for appearances. It happens all the time in Washington, and it's dishonest. I'd rather be forthright with the American people, admit my past mistakes and move on with my life."

"I like that answer."

He held up his wine glass. "I'm glad to hear I passed the first round of interrogations."

After the waiters left, Richard leaned across the table. "Christina, why don't we think about spending more time together? You're such a welcome change from all the stodginess back in Washington and the plastic phoniness down in LA." He paused and looked into her eyes. "I couldn't stop thinking of you when I was in Washington."

She hesitated. "That's kind of you to say, Richard, and I enjoy spending time with you, but I met a man in Italy. I'm actually quite fond of him." She wouldn't tell him the truth: that Franco was engaged and that she was stupid enough to hope they might one day pick up where they'd left off in Italy.

"Oh—I see," Richard backed away. "I didn't realize you were involved with someone."

"I can't say we're involved. I'm just not ready to complicate things right now."

"I can respect that." He reached over and touched her hand. "But, remember—long distance relationships rarely last."

She gently pulled her hand away. "I need to see how things progress. Anyway, we'll still spend time together. Remember we have your reception on Tuesday."

"You're very logical." He smiled warmly. "But you look tired. How about if I walk you home?"

She laughed and looked toward her bedroom door, just a few feet away. "Thanks, but I think this time I'll make it safely by myself."

Nevertheless, he stood up, pulled her chair back, and walked her to the door of her room.

She unlocked it, and opened it slightly.

Richard kissed her lightly on the cheek. "Goodnight."

"Goodnight, Richard," she whispered.

She watched him walk back to the other wing. Although memories of herself and Franco remained vivid, she could feel herself softening to the Senator. After all, what woman wouldn't? He was handsome, successful, charming and powerful—a potent aphrodisiac cocktail by anyone's standards. And besides, Franco wasn't exactly beating down her door to win her back. But as far as the Senator's mélange of intoxicating ingredients were concerned, she needed to limit herself. As enticing as Richard was, she shut the door, turned the deadbolt and poured herself a safe cold glass of water.

Chapter Seventeen

When Senator Cartwright heard the extension ring in the dining room, he excused himself from the lunch meeting he conducted.

"Is Ms. Culhane available?"

The man had such a pronounced accent Richard almost didn't understand him. She's not here right now," the Senator said. "May I give her a message?"

When the caller didn't immediately respond, Richard supposed this must be the man Christina had mentioned. Perhaps he had been taken off-guard to hear a man answer the phone in Christina's hotel suite.

At last the caller answered, brusquely. "Tell her Franco Doria called."

"I'll make certain she gets the message."

The Senator hung up the phone and returned to his meeting. A hint of a smile played at the corners of his mouth.

*

"Christina," Bart called through the intercom, "Brandy's on the phone. Can you take the call? By the way, did Franco reach you?"

Christina went still. "He called?"

"I gave him your cell number and the number of the hotel."

"I can't believe I missed him," she said. "Did you get a number?"

"Sorry, I didn't. He hung up pretty fast. But believe me honey, I'd *luh-ove* his number."

Christina's phone beeped, indicating that she had a call on hold.

"Shoot, I forgot about Brandy." She picked up the receiver.

151

"Hi Christina," Brandy said. "I just got my pictures back. How 'bout if the three of us get together tonight?"

"I'd love to see them, and you. A lot has happened since we got back. In fact, I'm not even living in my apartment anymore."

"What are you talking about?"

"I'll fill you in tonight. I'm staying in the Presidential Suite at the Fairmont. I told the man who invited me to stay there that I'd cook dinner for him and a few of his friends tonight. Do you want to join us?"

"Would love to."

"Great. Sevenish. I'll see you then."

*

Christina left the office in time to run to one of the local markets and got back to the hotel a few minutes before seven, carrying several bags of groceries. She almost collided with Richard, who had also just stepped in.

"Can I give you a hand?" He reached out to prevent Christina from dropping a head of lettuce and an eggplant.

"I never seem to have enough hands to carry everything."

"It looks like you're planning a party for twenty of your closest friends." He laughed at her as she tried to keep the tomatoes, fresh basil and a bottle of olive oil from spilling onto the floor. "I thought we talked about a small dinner party."

"I only invited two people, but I thought I should buy extra in case you invited sixteen of *your* friends."

"Actually, only one. A friend of mine from Stanford."

She gestured at the kitchen counter, covered with grocery bags. "We'll have leftovers for a week." She took a loaf of Italian bread from the bag. "I should have everything under control by around seven."

"I'll change clothes, and then help with dinner."

Christina heard the doorbell. She rinsed her hands and went to the foyer.

"Hi guys. Suzan, why don't you show Brandy around while Richard and I get everything organized?"

"Who's Richard?" Brandy asked. She followed Suzan down the hallway.

"Long story. I'll fill you in while I'm giving you the tour."

Richard returned to the kitchen wearing a long-sleeved burgundy Polo shirt and khaki trousers. He and Christina finished unloading the groceries, opened a few bottles of Barolo, played some Puccini on the home theater system and began to cook an easily prepared Italian meal: pasta, salad and grilled vegetables. Eventually Suzan and Brandy made their way over to the kitchen, and Christina poured them a glass of wine.

"Can we help?" Brandy asked, her eyes fixated on Richard.

Christina took the lid off the large pot and checked to see if the water boiled yet. Richard chopped tomatoes.

"Brandy, I'd like to introduce you to Senator Richard Cartwright."

Richard wiped tomato juice off his hands with the blue and white-checkered towel attached to his belt. "Pleased to meet you, Brandy."

"The pleasure is mine, Senator." She let the rim of her wineglass rest against her lips for a full minute before she sipped.

Suzan extended her hand. "Hi, I'm Suzan."

"Nice to meet you." He shook her hand. "I've heard a lot about you."

"Why don't you two sit in the library and enjoy your glass of wine?" Christina scraped the tomatoes off the cutting board and slid them into a skillet that sizzled with olive oil. "We have everything under control, but if you hear the door ring, go ahead and answer it. One of Richard's friends is joining us."

*

As they walked to the library, Brandy turned to Suzan. "So that's *Richard?* Senator Cartwright? One of the most eligible men in the country? When did this start?"

Suzan and Brandy sat down on the leather couch in the library.

"Christina claims it's not a big deal. She says they're just friends."

"I don't believe for a minute that there isn't anything romantic between them," Brandy said. "Did you see them in the kitchen cooking together? They look like happy newlyweds!"

"I know, but I think she left her heart in Italy—with Franco."

A ring at the front door interrupted them, and Suzan jumped up to answer it. The man in the doorway appeared to be about forty years old. He had short, wavy blond hair and a tan face. He exuded an East Coast preppy aura and wore a light-blue oxford shirt with a pale yellow sweater tied around his shoulders.

"Hi," he said in a slightly effeminate voice, "I'm Curtis Saunders."

Suzan flinched when she heard the name, and immediately turned around to look for Christina.

*

"CJ,", Richard said. "I see you've met Suzan." He put his hand on Christina's shoulder. "Christina, meet Curtis Saunders."

Christina dropped the knife she held. In a million years, she never would've guessed that Richard's guest would be Curtis Saunders.

"I apologize," CJ said, "I guess I should have brought flowers instead." He set a bottle of Jack Daniels on the counter. "How about a few glasses? Let's get this party started."

"I'll get them, Richard." Christina went into the library and from the cherry wood drinks bar she removed two finely cut crystal glasses. She splashed some whisky into each of their glasses and poured herself a glass of wine. After a large therapeutic sip, she whispered to Suzan, "We need to talk."

Suzan nodded her head. "Absolutely."

Christina scooped the chopped garlic and fresh basil up with her knife and placed them into the simmering tomato sauce. "Richard, you'll have to excuse me. I'll be right back."

Suzan led Christina by the elbow out to the terrace. "Curtis Saunders is a *friend* of Richard's?"

"I know. I can't believe it. They went to Stanford together." She hoped that was their only connection. "What did you find out about Saunders?"

"I don't want you to think less of Richard, but Saunders is bad news."

"I know. Agent Wilson said he's been under investigation for insider trading. But why do you think he made those calls to Peter from Italy?"

"I have no idea, but if I'd known Saunders was having dinner with us, I would've tried to tell you sooner."

"Tell me what?" Christina tried to check her impatience. "What did you find out?"

"The SEC is currently investigating Saunders, and his company. The feds have reason to believe he may have cooked the books to make the stock price higher than it should be."

"How'd he do that?"

"Apparently Saunders set up a bogus company to buy his custom chips—you know, those gate arrays that have been keeping the company alive."

Christina nodded. Actually, Silicon Valley Electronics manufactured semi-custom chips. Gate array chips were put together from the company's design library in order to optimize each chip for a specific application. The application, anything from an airplane autopilot device to a missile-guidance control system, would depend on the particular needs of the customer's engineering department.

Suzan glanced into the dining room. No one was there, but she lowered her voice anyway. "Invoices revealed that the company delivered chips, but nothing's legitimate. The bills sit in a PO Box and are never paid. Meanwhile, the earnings look great, because the product has gone out, so the stock price goes up. By the time the auditors catch up with them, most of the insiders have sold their stock and fled the country to a tax-friendly island in the Caribbean or the Netherlands Antilles. According to my friend, Saunders' accountants are really sweating it. This has gone unchecked for over a year, and the stock price has more than tripled."

"Sounds like a good short-sell to me."

"You're probably right." Suzan rested her hand on the iron railing and stared out toward Treasure Island. "Not only that, but there's a rumor—and I'm not saying it's substantiated—but there's a rumor that he may have been bribing government officials."

"Richard?"

"I logged onto LexisNexis and Richard's name never came up; only lower level officials were implicated. But I wouldn't trust CJ as far as I could spit him."

"Do you think we should ask him how he knows Peter?"

Suzan shook her head. "I wouldn't. It's better that he doesn't know we're aware of anything."

Brandy poked her head out the terrace door. "Dinner's ready."

It was nearly eight-thirty and the bright lights on the East Bay hills flickered against the darkening sky. The massive military building on Treasure Island reflected light like the White House.

"This reminds me," Brandy said, looking at Treasure Island, "I've got to call Rob. Remember meeting him at Bix?"

"*Hell-lo?*" Christina pointed to her head. "How could we forget meeting Cary Grant?"

"I think he's back in town filming his movie on Treasure Island. Do you want to go over and check it out next week?"

"I'd love to," Suzan said.

"Yeah, me too." But Christina spoke without enthusiasm. She couldn't get beyond the fact that she'd be sitting down to dinner with Curtis Saunders.

The pasta was perfectly al denté, the vegetables grilled just right and the Italian wine Christina had chosen, a 1997 Brunello, tasted smooth and delicious. It also numbed Christina to CJ's rude behavior. As if it wasn't enough that he sopped up marinara sauce with bread, licked his fingers and chased down good wine with a shot of whisky, he spoke only to Richard and never bothered to engage the women in conversation. Christina could hardly wait to shove the guy out the door.

But after dinner, they all retired to the library to look at Brandy's photos while the hotel staff cleaned up the colossal mess they had made in the kitchen. All the while, Curtis Saunders incessantly name-dropped and boasted about how profitable his company had become since he'd founded it ten years earlier.

When Christina could stand it no longer, she got up from the sofa. "Sorry to miss the rest of these fascinating stories, but I have an early-morning meeting and should probably get some sleep."

By now, CJ slurred his words. In a Southern drawl that had escaped her when he was sober, he said: "Yeah—likewise. Thanks for cookin'."

Suzan excused herself after Christina made the move to break up the evening, and Richard stood to shake hands with her. But Brandy remained in the library, clinging to CJ's every word.

"We've got to clue Brandy in about her new friend," Christina whispered to Suzan as they walked to the foyer. "I can't believe she's actually impressed by that guy."

"I'll give her a call tomorrow."

"Thanks, I'll barely have time to brush my hair." Christina gave Suzan a friendly hug goodnight. "I won't be in until ten-thirty or eleven tomorrow. I have a meeting in the East Bay at eight."

*

At twelve-thirty the next afternoon, Christina opened the door to the office foyer and collided with Bart.

"I'm sorry, Bart." She helped pick up his magazines, which had fallen to the floor. "Are you okay?"

"I'm fine. But you look flustered. What happened? I've been telling people you'd be back mid-morning."

"Traffic couldn't have been worse." Christina put down her stack of papers on the receptionist's desk and smoothed her skirt. "An accident on the Bay Bridge backed up traffic for nearly two hours."

Bart shook his finger at her. "You could have called."

"I would've, but I forgot to charge my cell phone. But hey, at least I remembered to take it."

"A lot of good it did you. Anyway, I left your messages on your desk. Also, Suzan's been looking for you. I think she's in her office."

She scooped up her papers and walked back to Suzan's office, where she collapsed into a chair.

Suzan looked up from her computer screen. "Good thing you're sitting down."

"Why? What happened?"

Suzan twirled her hair around her index finger. "I started calling Brandy at seven this morning. No answer, so at first I figured she'd turned the phone off. I called an hour later, and still no answer, but this time I left a message for her to call me."

Christina leaned forward. "Don't tell me—"

"You got it." Suzan pounded her desk. "She didn't get home until ten this morning."

Christina let out a low whistle. "I hope you set her straight."

"I was honest." Suzan leaned back in her chair. "After all she's a friend, and I don't want her fed a pack of lies."

"Did you tell her that CJ might be the subject of a criminal investigation?"

"Not initially. I asked what in God's name attracted her to him."

"Suzan!"

"Well, he's such a phony. Could you believe that sweater tied around his shoulders? Puh-lease. The guy grew up on a tobacco farm in North Carolina, not some mansion in Newport. Anyway, I think his supposed success and alleged connections impressed her. I told her what I knew, but she defended him."

"Will she see him again?"

"They'll be at Richard's reception tonight." Suzan leaned back in her chair and propped her feet on the desk.

"Maybe I should call her."

"She said she'd be out all day, showing property."

"Oh well, she's a big girl." Christina gathered her papers and stood.

Suzan held up her hand. "I just got word from Symex that they let George go."

"That's terrible." Christina sat back down. "Why'd they do that?"

"I don't know. But they're giving the pink slip to a lot of middle managers. After a billion dollar robbery it'd be difficult for any company to bounce back."

"But he's one of the last senior engineers left."

"Well, as I said, I don't know the full story."

*

In his room at the Fairmont, Richard struggled with his bow tie. He'd been trying to tie the perfect knot for several minutes when he heard the telephone ring.

"Richard Cartwright," he answered, irritated at an interruption just as he almost finished the last loop.

"So what have you done for me lately?" Curtis Saunders slurred into the phone.

"What's that supposed to mean?"

"You know what I'm talking about."

Richard heard ice cubes clink in a glass, and then the sound of CJ taking a big gulp. "Listen, CJ, I've got to play this one carefully. But mark my words, by the end of tonight I'll have something for you."

"I'm getting impatient. I hope you haven't forgotten who funneled all that money into your last campaign."

"Tell me something I haven't already heard." Richard slammed down the phone. That was one bastard he wished he'd never met.

Chapter Eighteen

Christina rushed back to the hotel from her meeting with only a few minutes to spare before she was to meet Richard. She stepped into a floor-length, black strapless dress and checked her appearance in the full-length mirror. The soft velvet clung to her slender figure. She turned sideways and ran her hands along her waist to smooth out the wrinkles and sucked in her stomach. Luckily, she hadn't had time to eat lunch.

She clipped on a delicate pair of crystal and black onyx drop earrings and pulled her hair back into a French twist, a style she knew accentuated her long neck and prominent collarbones. Finally, she slipped into a pair of black gloves and pulled them up past her elbows. She took a few deep breaths to calm her nerves, clasped her silk evening bag and walked into the library to meet Richard. She found him out on the terrace, gazing at the Bay.

He turned as she opened the French doors. "Christina. You're breathtaking." He wore a traditional Savile Row black dinner jacket.

"Why thank you, Senator." She curtsied playfully. "You look quite dignified yourself."

He extended his hand. "Please, come share this incredible view with me."

She reached for his hand and he led her to the balcony. Standing side by side, they soaked in the tranquil sight of white sailboats gliding across the bay at dusk. They refrained from talking, but she felt warm and comfortable standing next to him. After a few moments, he wrapped his arm around her waist and pulled her closer to him. The gesture seemed natural, and she did not pull away, but when he turned and placed his other arm around her, she was torn. He had become difficult to resist.

"Please Christina," he whispered. "Allow me to kiss you. I think I'm falling in love with you. I can't help myself."

Despite her misgivings, she relented, and they kissed passionately for a few seconds before she backed away.

"I'm sorry. I'm not ready for this." She stepped several feet away from him. "Let's forget this ever happened."

"I should apologize, Christina. You made it very clear to me that you had feelings for someone else." He moved closer to her. "But don't tell me you didn't respond as I did."

Christina turned away to re-apply her lipstick. Erich stood in the dining room; he cleared his throat and pointed to his watch.

*

The ride in the limousine to the Sheraton Palace was quiet, yet not uncomfortable. With Erich sitting up front in the passenger's seat, Richard closed the privacy window. He placed his hand on Christina's knee and again apologized for putting her in such a compromising position.

She put her hand over his and said softly, "Thank you, it's fine. It wasn't a big deal, and it's not necessary to apologize again."

They pulled into the front entrance area, and white-gloved attendants opened their door and escorted them out of the car. They stepped onto the red carpet and ascended marble steps to the hotel lobby. Flash bulbs from a herd of paparazzi exploded as they entered the building. Reporters from all the major newspapers and television stations struggled to get the Senator's attention, and Erich did his best to keep them away.

One aggressive reporter from KGO shoved her microphone to Richard's mouth. "Senator," she yelled. "What do you think about the recently uncovered irregularities linked with certain defense contracts?"

Before he had a chance to comment, a brash, bearded photographer plowed the woman over and flashed a picture. "Who's the babe?" he shouted. "Another Hollywood actress?"

Richard turned to Christina. "Don't let any of this bother you. They'll do anything to sell a story."

He held her hand and pulled her through the crowd, with Erich in front to clear a path.

"Does this happen every time you attend a cocktail party?" Christina asked, just as they made it safely into the lobby of the hotel.

"Not usually." He took a deep breath, and Christina sensed his relief. He had made it into the hotel without another character attack. "Normally, I don't get crushed by reporters and photographers, but because of all the celebrities expected tonight, they're out in full force."

Hundreds of elegantly dressed supporters of Senator Cartwright filled the massive hotel lobby. Above them soared a five-story atrium, with its original plate-glass ceiling. Christina had forgotten what an impression this historic hotel could make. More than a hundred years old, a recent renovation had preserved rather than destroyed its elegance. Three-foot high Ming Dynasty vases, filled with willow branches, fresh lilies, and cherry blossoms, sat on marble pedestals placed throughout the room, and all fifty tables in the Garden Court Restaurant were decorated with gold candles and tropical flowers for the reception. Two ice sculptures, one of a unicorn, one of an elephant, sat on either end of a fifty-foot banquet table. Silver platters filled with fresh lobster, caviar and white and black truffles covered the white tablecloth. A carving station sat at the end of the table, alongside a pink juicy prime rib under a heat lamp. All of it was a definite upgrade from the last benefit she had attended.

Richard squeezed her hand. "Are you ready?"

She nodded and released his hand. They walked into a swarm of black tuxedos and sequined dresses. Christina couldn't keep track of everyone she recognized. In particular, she noticed ex-President Ford with his wife Betty, talking with a few of her "clients"—people Christina knew had been in and out of the Betty Ford Clinic in Palm Springs several times. She also spotted Arnold Shwarzenegger and his wife Maria Shriver, probably the only Democrat in the room. And was that George Stinson? Wearing an elegant black suit? She was about to walk over to him when Curtis Saunders and Brandy approached him. So those two knew each other. What did that mean, if anything? She watched for a few moments, until Curtis put his hand on Brandy's shoulder and whispered something in her ear. Brandy shot him a dirty look and stomped away.

Christina finally located Suzan, who looked playful and sexy in a gorgeous aubergine lace dress with a pair of matching leather pumps. That's Suzan, Christina thought, leather and lace.

Suzan spotted Christina, waved and walked over to her. "Aren't you Miss Glamorous tonight?"

"You look fantastic too. You should wear your hair down more often, the men can't keep their eyes off you."

"Enough of the mutual admiration stuff." Suzan pulled Christina away from the Senator and the small gathering of people clustered around him. "You need to hear this."

They joined Brandy at the bar.

"I could be one of Charlie's Angels." Brandy settled onto a bar stool. "First of all, you were right," she said to Suzan. "CJ's a real jerk. He ordered me to fetch him a double-shot of whisky without even introducing me to the man he was talking to. When I returned with his drink, like a devoted Stepford wife, he was squeezing some other woman's ass. Anyway, I told him not to bother looking for me at the end of the evening. I'm leaving without him."

"Good for you," Suzan said.

Brandy ordered a Cosmopolitan from the barely-legal bartender. "Now, listen to this," she said to Christina. "I asked CJ how he liked Forte Dei Marmi. He said he'd never heard of the place, but I knew he was lying, so I wanted to see how deep a hole he'd dig for himself. I said I knew he was there, and I asked him why he said he wasn't."

"What did he say to that?" asked Christina.

"He said that his and Dick's business is none of mine."

"Dick?"

Suzan interjected. "I think she means Richard."

Christina felt ill, like she had when Agent Wilson told her about Franco's fiancée. "You think Richard has something to do with Peter's death?"

Suzan ordered two watermelon vodka shots, handed one to Christina and turned to Brandy. "Brandy, give up your barstool. I think Christina needs to sit down."

Christina sat on Brandy's warm barstool and threw back the shot.

Suzan downed hers as well and motioned to the bartender for another. "Before we try, convict and hang Richard, let's be reasonable here. All we know is that they're friends who went to school together."

"My instinct is telling me otherwise." Christina put her elbow on the bar and rested her head on her hand. "Why do you think Richard popped into my life the minute I got back from Italy? Someone sent him to spy on me. Why is it that where men are concerned, I'm such a lousy judge of character?"

"You're not the only one," Brandy said. "My high school sweetheart's in jail, and my boyfriend from college had a sex change operation."

Suzan held up her shot and toasted Brandy. "You win." And then, "How's George holding up?"

"George? Who's that?"

"The man talking to CJ."

"That's George Stinson?" Brandy asked. "*The* George Stinson, from that Symex company of yours?"

"Yeah, that's him."

"He didn't strike me as someone who'd be working on your Symex deal. It seemed to me that George worked for CJ."

"Why would you think that?" Christina asked.

"I wasn't part of the conversation, but CJ seemed to be bossing him around."

"Did you catch anything they said?"

"I told you, I heard their tone, but that was about all."

"Brandy," Christina pleaded, "this is important. Think hard. Did you pick up anything?"

"I don't know." Brandy sighed. "I heard a few words, but they made no sense out of context."

"What did you hear? Do your best, and repeat everything you can remember."

Brandy held up her hand to the bartender and ordered another Cosmopolitan. "I heard him say something about "Chinks," and no deal without a ship."

Christina looked puzzled. She repeated what Brandy said to her. "Chinks, no deal without a ship."

Suzan jumped back into the conversation. "With that loser, *Chinks* probably means Chinese."

"Right," Christina said, "but why would he be talking about ships with George? Do you think he could have said *chip* instead of ship?"

"He could have," Brandy said.

"That's it." Christina slid off her barstool. "They must think I have the encryption chip. The one Peter designed."

"Well, do you?" Suzan asked.

"Of course not. But I can make them believe I do."

"How will you do that, and more importantly, why would you want to mess with them?"

"I'm not sure what's going on here, but if Saunders, George, or for that matter Richard, thinks I have the chip, maybe I can bait them into taking it from me."

"But if you don't have it, they can't take it," Suzan said.

"I realize that," Christina said. "I need to fool them into thinking that what they're taking is Peter's chip. And don't ask me how, because I don't know myself, yet."

Brandy finished her Cosmopolitan. "I hope Richard's clean, because he sure is handsome."

"To tell you the truth," Christina said, "I can't get my mind off Franco."

"Well, you need to." Suzan looked at Christina sternly. "He's engaged."

"Don't remind me."

"Plus, you don't know for sure how deep he's in with Stefano."

Christina held up her hand. "Enough already. I get the point. I can't help feeling something's not quite right with all of that, and until I speak to him myself, I'm giving him the benefit of the doubt."

Suzan looked beyond Christina's shoulder. "Time to forget Franco and put on your party face. Richard's on his way over."

Richard smiled at Suzan. "Excuse me ladies. I need to steal Christina away from you. It's time for her to make me look good." Richard extended his hand to Christina.

She forced a smile and walked back to the crowd of people. He wrapped his arm around her, but it no longer felt warm and comfortable, more like a boa constrictor about to squeeze its prey.

A reporter from ABC and her camera crew set up in front of the Senator. When the bright studio light went on, the reporter asked the Senator questions while Christina stood graciously by his side. Like a pro, he answered her questions without committing himself too heavily to one issue or another.

When the reporter thanked him and the TV crew started dismantling their equipment, Richard whispered into Christina's ear. "How about escaping as soon as possible?"

"My thoughts exactly. But you're the guest of honor. We can't be the first ones to leave."

"As soon as I make my obligatory toast, and thank everyone for coming, the reception will start to break up."

Richard picked up a silver coffee spoon and tapped his crystal champagne glass several times. The low roar silenced and the crowd turned toward the front of the room.

He held his glass high in the air. "Thank you all for coming tonight. I am overwhelmed by the success of this evening and flattered by all your support. Exciting and challenging times lay ahead for this country, and I'm honored to represent the State of California."

Listening to him talk, Christina experienced a collision of emotions. Her date for the evening—someone who had just confessed that he was falling in love with her—could possibly be the next President of the United States. On the other hand, he could be a criminal of the worst kind—a murderer.

Richard answered a few questions relevant to politics and his campaign. Flash bulbs ignited around the room as he posed for pictures with several of his supporters, friends and colleagues. He motioned for Christina to stand next to him, wrapped his arm around her waist and pulled her close. More flash bulbs exploded, blinding them both. He waved goodbye to the crowd and again thanked them for attending the night's fundraiser.

Erich moved to shepherd them out of the room, but Christina resisted. She hadn't talked to George all evening and she had some questions for him. For one, she wanted to know how he knew Curtis Saunders. And had he really been laid off, or was he fired?

"Ms. Culhane," Erich said sternly, "we really must go."

She stood firm. "I need to find someone. If you must leave, please go without me."

Richard gripped her elbow. "What's this about Christina?"

"I need to talk to a client of mine, actually an ex-client. I'll meet you back at the hotel, Richard."

Richard turned to Erich and held his hands together as if in prayer. "Give us a few minutes."

Christina scanned the room for George. The crowd had started to thin, but the faces all blurred together. After a minute or two of squinting, she spotted George by the buffet table, where he dipped a plump pink prawn into red cocktail sauce. She broke herself free from Richard's grip and walked over to him. When George saw her, he ducked behind a waiter and lost himself in the crowd.

Richard caught up with Christina and grabbed her hand. "Christina, this is ridiculous. Why don't you just give the guy a call tomorrow? Erich's breathing down my neck to get out of here. Let's go back to the hotel and relax."

Oh, she'd give George a call—that was certain.

Chapter Nineteen

All Christina wanted was sleep, but Richard suggested that they have a drink and relax in the library, where a fireplace stacked with logs and crumpled newspaper awaited them. Richard struck a match, and within minutes a roaring fire blazed.

He poured them each a splash of brandy, took a sip and poured himself some more. Christina sat on the leather sofa and kicked off her stilettos. Her feet ached. Richard took one foot into his lap and massaged it expertly, but Christina pulled away. She knew where this would lead.

"Richard, I need to tell you something."

He leaned over and tried to kiss her. "Whatever it is, it can wait until tomorrow morning," he whispered.

"I don't think it can." She curled her feet under her. "You need to know that I'm a marked woman. I'm involved in something that could seriously damage your career."

He attempted to kiss her again. "You're worth the risk."

"No Richard." She pushed him back with her hand. "Peter, my friend from Symex, died a couple of weeks ago. I believe he was murdered, because before he died, he gave me a top-secret microchip. He said to keep it safe until everything sorted itself out."

Richard sat up. "What did he mean by that?"

"I'm not certain, but now someone wants to take it from me. That's why they ripped my place apart."

"Is this chip of his in a safe place?"

"Yes. I hid it in an antique gold locket my mother gave me. They haven't found it yet."

"Good thinking." He pulled her foot back onto his lap and began to massage it again. He ran his hand up her dress to the top of her stocking.

170

Christina put her hand on his, stopping him. "Richard, I'm sorry. You need to give me some time."

Richard nodded and gulped down the rest of his brandy.

*

Later that night, Christina lay in bed, unable to asleep. When Richard opened the door and whispered her name a few times, her heart beat so loudly she thought he would hear it.

He crept over to her dresser, where she kept her small jewelry box, and from the corner of her eye, she saw that he used a tiny penlight as he rummaged around in the box. Next, she heard him click her locket shut and leave the room.

Christina jumped out of bed and pulled on a pair of jeans. In the dark, she quickly threw a few things into a bag and then sneaked through the kitchen and down the secret passageway that Angie Dickinson had supposedly used.

From the lobby, she walked outside with as much dignity as she could muster, and spoke quickly to the doorman. "A cab, please."

The wind whipped brightly colored flags overhead while she waited. In only a light t-shirt and jeans, she shivered with fear and cold until the cab pulled forward. She slid into it.

"Where to, lady?"

She sat silent. She had not given this any thought. When the driver glanced back impatiently, she gave him Suzan's address and hoped that she'd be home. Out the window, the muted glow of a street lamp in the fog cast dim light on two lovers huddled together. At least they had each other. She felt like such a fool for nearly falling for Richard. First Franco, and then Richard. That was two strikes. She was on her way out when it came to the man game.

When the cab pulled up to Suzan's apartment building, Christina asked the driver to wait. She pressed Suzan's buzzer and kept her finger on it for several seconds.

"Damn." Suzan's buzzer was loud enough to wake the dead, but after several minutes, she still hadn't answered.

"Hey lady!" The driver yelled from the cab. "Do you want me to sit out here all night?"

She trudged back to the cab and crawled into the back seat. Her body felt like lead—all she wanted was to crawl into a warm bed.

The driver turned his head around. "Okay, where to?"

"Honestly, I don't know." Even to her own ears, her voice sounded strained and near panic. "Take me back to Italy," she mumbled.

"What did you say?"

"I need a minute." She sat slumped in the back seat, until a large Mercedes sedan pulled up next to the building. Could Richard have found her already? But Suzan stepped out of the passenger side and blew Brandy a kiss.

"I'm staying here," she said. "What do I owe you?"

The cabbie shook his head. "Eighteen fifty."

She handed him two twenty-dollar bills. "Keep the change."

Suzan jumped when she heard her name. "Christina, my God. You nearly scared me to death. What happened?"

"Long story." Inside, she fell onto the couch.

Suzan disappeared into the bedroom and reappeared in a flannel shirt and baggy gray sweatpants. "You look awful." She tossed an extra large blue sweatshirt at Christina. White letters across the front spelled out NAVY. "One of my ex-boyfriend's, but don't worry, I washed it." She also handed her a pair of cotton yoga trousers. "Come into the kitchen. I'll make some hot chocolate."

Christina put on the sweatshirt, which came down to her knees. "Just like I predicted, Richard fell for the bait."

"You're kidding."

Christina told her what had happened at the Fairmont.

"What did Richard actually take from your locket?"

"The memory chip from my answering machine." Christina stirred the hot chocolate and wrapped her hands around the warm cup. "I need to tell Agent Wilson about this first thing tomorrow morning."

"But you still don't know who killed Peter. Does this clear Franco?"

"I don't know. Maybe I need to eliminate him all together. I certainly don't need any more drama."

*

Suzan had left the paper opened to the Bay Area section. It took a moment for Christina to recognize herself as the smiling woman on the arm of Senator Cartwright.

"Oh my God." She picked up the paper and read the caption: "Senator Cartwright with his date, Miss Christina Culhane, at his $2500 per person fund-raiser."

"Just what I need." She crumpled up the paper and threw it in the garbage can.

She pulled on a pair of shorts and a t-shirt and headed out the door for a run. She needed to clear her head. She couldn't find her Swatch so she strapped on the watch Peter had given her. She'd run for twenty minutes and then turn around. But her mind raced and she couldn't concentrate on her stride. Who had killed Peter? She leaned toward Curtis Saunders, because he seemed to be the common denominator. Since he had registered at Franco's hotel, it made sense that he had made those calls to Peter from Forte dei Marmi, where the creepy bald guy, Arnold Hague, kept showing up. Plus, Saunders was a friend of Richard's, though how close she didn't know. Also, Brandy had thought that George was taking orders from Saunders. That, combined with his blatant avoidance of her last night at the reception, made him a suspect, too. Of course, Richard damned himself when he took the fake microchip. Given the evidence, wasn't it possible that they were all, to some degree, involved in Peter's death? She hoped Agent Wilson could help her sort it out.

She glanced at her watch, hoping it was time to turn around. Five minutes. It felt like at least fifteen. She ran a few more minutes and then checked again. The hands hadn't moved. She held the watch to her ear but didn't hear it ticking. Damn. The battery must be dead. She turned around and headed back to Suzan's.

In the shower, she remembered that Peter had included a new battery, and as soon as she dressed, she dug to the bottom of her handbag and pulled out the velvet bag the watch had come in. She popped open the back of the watch with a nail file and removed the old battery. Something fell out with it, something metal, and not more than a quarter inch square. *Peter you devil,* she whispered to herself.

Chapter Twenty

"You're shittin' me!" Agent Wilson bellowed into the phone.

"No, I'm not." Christina poured a cup of coffee. "I just found it this morning. Peter gave it to me the day before he was killed."

"And you've been carrying it around with you ever since?"

Christina pictured his face turning red.

"I didn't know I had it until my watch died."

"Until your watch died? What the hell's that supposed to mean?" She was sure that at this point a vein on his neck was ready to pop.

She poured some milk into her coffee and took a sip. "I'll explain everything when I see you."

"I'm sending a car over for you now. Where are you?"

"At my girlfriend's apartment." She gave him the address, and then called Bart. When she had finished giving him instructions for the morning, she asked him to transfer her to Suzan.

"Hey girl. How did you like that picture of yourself in *The Chronicle*?"

"If things had turned out differently last night, I would've thought it was terrific."

"You two look like the perfect couple. Too bad the rest of the San Francisco Bay Area doesn't know the real story."

"Tell me about it, but I called to tell you that I found that chip everyone's been looking for."

"Oh my God, Christina. Where was it?"

Christina briefly explained. She felt the coffee turning in her stomach. "At least the plans are useless without this chip."

"Jesus, girlfriend. Be careful. You're playing with the big boys now."

*

The same unmarked car that had met Christina at the airport two weeks ago arrived at Suzan's apartment in less than half an hour. Christina walked out to find the same type of driver: a no-nonsense suit with dark sunglasses and short brown hair.

The agent showed her his badge and opened the back door for her. She slid in and suddenly felt ill again; the vinyl seats and the new-car smell didn't help her already troubled stomach.

After they had driven only a few blocks, Christina tapped her driver on the shoulder. "Excuse me, but do you mind if I sit up front? I'm feeling a little queasy, and sitting in the back seat doesn't help."

"No problem, Miss Culhane, I'll pull right over."

"Please call me Christina." He didn't look a day over thirty. "By the way, what's your name? I didn't catch it when you flashed your badge for that full half-second."

He laughed and shrugged his shoulders. "Sorry about that. I get so caught up in procedure I forget the personal side of things."

He pulled the car to the curb and Christina moved into the front seat. He took off his aviator style Ray Bans and extended his hand. "Dan Stevenson."

"Pleased to meet you, Dan." His deep blue eyes startled her. What a shame he wore those dark glasses.

When they reached the FBI headquarters, he escorted her to Agent Wilson's office.

Wilson stood up from behind his desk. He motioned for her to sit and sunk back down himself. "Let's get right to business. Show me the chip."

She reached into her handbag and turned it over, along with an explanation of how she had tricked Senator Cartwright into believing he had taken the real thing.

Wilson turned the piece of metal between his thumb and index finger. "This sure looks like what we've been searching for." He placed the chip in a zip-lock bag and attached a red-and-white evidence tag.

"So, now what do we do?" Christina asked.

"We?" Wilson said.

"Won't this nail Hague or Saunders? One of them must've killed Peter, or had him killed; and probably Martin Denton too."

"Hold on a minute, Christina." Wilson held up his hand. "The chip doesn't prove that Saunders or Hague killed Peter."

"Do you think it was Richard Cartwright then?"

"No, of course not. He'd never risk his career by killing someone. And to be honest, I'm not sure if this is Saunders' style either." Before Christina could blurt out a rebuttal, he held up his hand. "But don't worry; I'm not ruling him out."

"He's the one who owns a computer company; and in my opinion, the one who's capable of putting those plans to use."

Wilson took a sip from a canned protein drink. "My bet is that whoever wanted that chip from Peter, and subsequently you, doesn't plan to blow up the world. They're in it for the money. Any terrorist group would pay top dollar for this."

Christina snapped her fingers. 'I think I have the answer."

"The answer?" Wilson set his protein drink on his desk. "What do you think this is—a game show?"

"Hear me out." Christina stood up. "Saunders is going to find out soon enough that the chip Richard gave him is a fake, and it's obvious he wants the real one."

Wilson looked unimpressed.

"What if I was able to set Saunders up? The way I set up Richard?"

"It's not Saunders we're after. He doesn't have the expertise to decipher the plans alone. Sit back down, Christina. We'll take it from here."

She sat, but she wasn't about to give up. She took off her glasses and bit the stem. "The more I think about this, the more it makes sense to me. I saw George Stinson talking to Curtis Saunders at Richard's fundraiser."

"Big deal," Wilson said. "Do you think we don't know that Stinson and Saunders have been in contact? They're in the same industry. Not a crime in my book."

"But," Christina held up her finger. "He also told me that his financial situation would be changing soon. For the better," she emphasized.

"Well, good for him, but that doesn't make him a murderer."

"No." She pointed her finger at Wilson. "That's because *you* can't prove anything. But I think I can. As far as he knows, I still have the chip." She pushed her hair behind her ears. "I could tell him I want a cut of whatever he's getting."

"Now calm down, Nancy Drew. These are dangerous criminals."

"I understand that." She brushed off the reference to her favorite childhood heroine. "But the plans are useless without the chip I just gave you, and you can't prove anything until he admits that this chip is his only means to a pay off."

Wilson uncrossed his arms.

"First, I'll call George at home and tell him I'm sorry to hear about Symex laying him off. Maybe we'll small talk for a few minutes. Then I'll go for the jugular." She picked up a pencil from Wilson's desk and clenched her fist around it. "I'll come right out and say it. I'll tell him I have what he wants, and I want a million bucks for it—or whatever you think." She pointed her pencil at the wall behind Wilson, as if she were giving a presentation at work. "He'll know exactly what I'm talking about. Next, I'll set a place for us to meet. Somewhere bright and safe."

Agent Wilson interrupted. "Christina, you're getting carried away. None of this works so easily in real life. First of all, a real extortionist wouldn't offer to hand over such a valuable piece of information without truly expecting to be paid. How do you expect George to pay you?"

"I'm sure he's been in touch with the ultimate buyer. And whoever it is, they'll have a few million lying around from the proceeds of the warehouse heist. I'm sure those chips hit the open market the next day."

Wilson pounded his fist on his desk. "You'll stay out of it, or I'll put you in custody."

Christina stood up. "They still think I have the chip, and for all I know, they'll kill me for it." She could feel her face and neck becoming red, and losing her cool would ruin her credibility. She settled back in her chair, took a deep breath and continued.

'How about if we just throw it out there and see what they do? After all, who cares whether they cough up the money or not? It's not as if I'm giving him the real code chip. If it's important enough to George, and it sounds as if it is, he'll think of something."

Agent Wilson cracked a faint smile. "Christina, you're incorrigible."

*

When Christina and Dan left the FBI building, she asked to stop at the Fairmont before they returned to Suzan's apartment. She needed to retrieve the remainder of her personal belongings, and she didn't want to do it alone.

When they arrived at the Presidential Suite, Dan told her to wait outside while he checked to make sure Cartwright wasn't inside.

"Looks good," he said moments later, and then whistled. "This is some place."

"Isn't it?" She walked through the library and back to her bedroom. "This will just take a minute."

When she returned, Dan had taken off his blue blazer and waited on the leather couch in the library. She hefted her duffel bag. "Let's get out of here."

"Where do you plan to go?" He put his coat and Ray Bans back on. "It's still not safe to return to your apartment."

"I'll stay at my girlfriend's house until everything's cleared up."

"Is there any security there?"

"Not even a doorman."

"We'll arrange around-the-clock protection. You shouldn't be staying anywhere without it. And I'll need to go back to your friend's apartment and check it out for you."

"Sure," Christina said. "I'll just call her."

Before she got in the car, she used her mobile and dialed Suzan's direct line. She got right through. "Hi, Suzan. Listen, there's this adorable FBI Agent that wants to check out your place."

"What are you talking about?"

"Is it okay if he looks around? He wants to make sure no one has planted any bugs or tapped the phones. He also wants to arrange around-the-clock protection for us. What do you think?"

"Well, uh…I don't know."

"Suzan, he's gorgeous. Leave work early, so you can meet him."

Suzan lowered her voice into the phone. "What about the pot?"

"Where do you have it stashed?"

"In my bathroom. Top drawer on the left. An old diaphragm holder."

Christina laughed. "I think it's safe. But don't worry, I'll make sure he doesn't find it. It's not like he's bringing drug-sniffing beagles."

*

Dan took off his coat and threw it over a stool in the kitchen. "This will take about half an hour."

"I'll make some coffee," Christina said.

Dan pulled a small metal device from his pocket. When he turned it on, static crackled. He got down on his hands and knees and dragged the device across the floorboards in Suzan's front hallway. After several minutes on all fours, he got up, and did the same along the crown molding on the ceiling. He walked into the living room, where he felt the mud in each of the plants, pointed the metal sensor under the sofa, the chairs and the coffee table.

Christina stepped into the bathroom before Dan began his search there. She found the stash, slipped it into her pocket and returned to the kitchen.

Dan joined her and swiped his hands together. "Everything's come up clean."

Christina was about to hand him his coffee when she noticed it was almost six. "It's after hours, would you like something a little stiffer to drink?" She held the coffee pot over the sink in a tipped position, ready to spill it down the drain.

"Sure, do you have any chocolate?"

*

Suzan breezed into her kitchen shortly after six-thirty, and stopped short at the sight of Dan's gun harnessed around his solid back. She smiled and gave Christina the thumbs up.

"Can we *please* get out of my kitchen," Suzan said. "If I knew I was having a party in here, I would've at least swept the floor."

Christina stood. "Suzan, meet Dan. Dan, Suzan."

As they moved to the living room, Suzan's front doorbell rang. Suzan reached for the button to answer it, but Dan put his hand over hers and answered it himself. The security officers. He buzzed them in, and then Christina and Suzan went with him to meet the officers in the lobby.

"Is upstairs secure?" one of them asked.

"Tight as a drum. She has a middle unit, with a window that opens to a small courtyard. The only access is through an inside stairwell."

"All right then, we'll plant ourselves here in the lobby."

The two agents shook hands with Suzan and Christina, and instructed them to forget they existed.

Dan escorted the two women back upstairs to brief Christina. "You know what you have to do tomorrow. Make the initial contact, set your time and place, but don't say anything else. We're going to be up all night finalizing the security."

"Don't worry, I'll play by the rules."

He stood up and patted his gun and then turned to Suzan. "It was good to meet you." His voice was firm. "I'm sure I'll see you again soon."

Suzan watched Dan's backside disappear down her hallway. "He's a hottie, all right, but could the guy be any stiffer? He spent an hour with us and he barely cracked a smile."

"Let's cut him some slack," Christina said. "I wouldn't want his job."

Suzan lit some incense. "Maybe there's some rule in their operations manual that prevents them from getting too close to those they protect."

"I don't know, but I wouldn't be in the mood to drink and chit-chat with two giddy women if I knew I had to work all night. I'm sure he's different on the weekend."

Suzan finished her glass of wine while Christina called home to check her messages. She smiled as she listened to the last one, and then she hung up and grinned at Suzan. "So—guess who left me a message?"

"Who?"

"Franco. He's said he's worried sick about me, and he's wondering why I haven't called."

"Why haven't you?"

"There's the little matter of his engagement. Plus, I still don't know what his involvement with Stefano is, or for that matter, Peter."

Suzan frowned. "It's time you two talked."

"He asked me to call him at the hotel in the morning." Christina placed her wineglass on the wicker trunk that sat in front of the sofa. "I better switch to coffee if I want to stay up until midnight to make that call."

"Want to make a Starbucks run?"

When they reached the lobby, one of the FBI men stood up. "Where are you two going?"

"We're just gonna grab an espresso," Suzan said.

"Sorry, not tonight. It's too dangerous, even if we accompany you."

"All right." Christina said. Then to Suzan. "That's just as well. If I'm going to manage everything tomorrow, I probably need to sleep anyway, not force myself to stay awake." She'd pass on the coffee—and on the call to Franco.

*

At seven-thirty the next morning, the first time she'd been to work early in over a month, she handed Bart a steaming hot latté and an almond biscotti.

"Great to see the old Christina back." Bart smiled as he took the top off his latte and licked the foam. "Listen; there are some FBI guys in your office. They said you knew they were coming. Is everything all right?"

"Don't worry, everything's under control."

She walked into her office and greeted the men. One of them wore tinted glasses, the other a blue blazer that didn't quite cover his belly. She extended her hand to each of them. "I hope I haven't kept you waiting long."

"No problem," the heavier one said. "Are you ready to make your call to Stinson?"

"Yes, I'd planned to do it first thing."

Tinted glasses said, "We have to take you off site. Given the proprietary information your firm deals with, we're not authorized to tape any conversations within the company walls."

"I understand." She pushed her glasses onto her head. "So where are we off to? Some inconspicuous white van with ACME Plumbing painted on the outside, equipped with the latest in surveillance equipment?"

"Very funny. We have an office suite for situations like this."

Remarkably, the office they used looked like an executive suite, unlike the stark government vestibules she'd become accustomed to seeing recently. Hardwood floors replaced the typical slab flooring, and they had even added oriental carpets. No metal furniture or beat-up wooden chairs crowded the room, only an antique mahogany partner's desk and several armchairs.

They led her into a second next room, which looked more like what she'd expected—a large metal table, telephones, cables, and sophisticated recording equipment. Dusty metal blinds covered the windows.

"Place the call whenever you're ready," the agent said.

"Is there a chair or something I could sit on?"

"No problem." They dragged one of the heavy, upholstered chairs in from the reception area.

She took a deep breath. "Okay, here I go." She lifted the cold metal receiver and asked, "Do I just dial, like a normal phone?"

"Yup. You don't even have to dial nine."

She punched the number, and took another deep breath. One ring…two rings…three rings. Her palms got clammy. She didn't want to leave a message, and she certainly didn't want to remain camped out in this makeshift office all morning.

He answered groggily on the fourth ring.

"Hi George, it's Christina."

"Christina? You're the last person I expected to hear from."

"Especially after the way you ran away from me at Cartwright's reception."

"I wasn't in the mood to socialize."

"I heard you got laid-off at Symex. Sorry to hear that."

"Don't feel sorry for me, I'm enjoying myself. They gave me a great comp package— in other words they're paying me to sleep in for the next several months."

"Well, I'm glad to hear you're not hurting."

She looked up at the agents. They eyed her intently. She had better get to the point.

"Anyway, George, I should probably cut through the bullshit. I'm pretty sure I have something you want."

"And what would that be?" His tone changed dramatically.

"Well, how about if we play a little guessing game? What's worth a ton of money, but weighs less than an ounce?" She waved her hand dismissively in front of her face. "No—that's too obvious, how about this? What has the power, when used in conjunction with something that was recently stolen, to wipe out the entire population of a large metropolitan area?"

The agents glared at her.

"Okay, Christina, cut the crap. What do you have?"

"You have to guess. I'm sure that engineering degree from MIT is worth something."

"So, you have the chip."

"I'm sorry George, I couldn't quite hear you. I thought you said something about a chip, but you need to be more precise."

"You know exactly which chip I'm referring to, you smart ass. You've had the code chip all along haven't you?"

She looked up at the agents and gave them a thumbs-up. "You're right, and I want two million dollars for it."

"You're crazy. I couldn't even give you half that. And by the way, congratulations on tricking Dick with that fake."

"Right, Richard. Well, he meant nothing to me, just another pawn in my game."

"Unlike Doria," George said.

So Arnold Hague must have been reporting back to him. "Doria's out of my life too. After you pay me, I'm leaving the country, *without* excess baggage. So, how 'bout it George? Two million or I take it to someone else."

George breathed heavily into the phone. "The most I can do is one million."

The agents both nodded vigorously at Christina. She needed to wrap this up.

"No," Christina said firmly. "You killed a dear friend of mine, and you're going to pay."

"Listen, Christina, I didn't kill Peter. He was a friend of mine, too. I only got involved because I needed the money. Engineers don't make much, and I was sick of seeing my inventions make billions for everyone else."

"Two million or no deal."

Christina saw the two agents stand up, furious with her.

"Okay," she said, "a million-and-a-half."

There was a long pause. The agents shook their heads.

"A million-and-a-half it is."

Both agents exhaled and sat back down. "Meet me at the Palace of Fine Arts in the Marina. Tomorrow morning at eight."

"Make it Friday," George said. "I have some things to take care of before then."

She looked to the agents for their approval. They nodded.

"Fine." She slammed down the phone and slumped back into her chair.

"Well done, Miss Culhane," the portly one said. "But let me tell you," he pointed a finger at her, "Friday, you do exactly as we say. The stakes are much higher."

"I needed to convince George that I was for real. I didn't want him to suspect a set-up."

"You got away with it today," the agent said, "but no more games. And another thing, until Friday you'll need increased personal security. In addition to the officers in the lobby of your girlfriend's apartment building, we're assigning Dan Stevenson to guard you.'

"What do you mean *guard me*?"

"Stevenson will drive you to and from work, sit outside your office—basically follow you everywhere."

"And while I'm sleeping?"

"We'll have you moved to a hotel. A female agent will accompany you. And don't worry; it's not going to be the Fairmont."

"I'm so tired of moving around." She picked up her handbag. "It would be heaven to sleep in my own bed for a solid week."

"This'll be over soon." The agent with the dark glasses closed his briefcase. "Then you'll be free to move back home."

When she returned to her office, Dan Stevenson waited in the lobby. Instead of his standard blue blazer, he wore a brown leather bomber jacket and a pair of Levis.

He smiled when he saw her. "I guess you know we're going to be glued at the hip for the next twenty-four hours. I'll try to stay out of your hair." They rode the elevator up to her office.

Christina put her glasses on and pulled out a stack of papers from her bag. "I planned to grab Suzan and go for lunch later. You're welcome to join us."

"I'm sorry, Christina, but you won't be going outside today. We'll leave the building after work together, and then I'll drive you directly to your hotel."

"What do you mean? I'll suffocate in here." She pointed to the large glass windows behind her desk. "These windows don't open."

He promptly snapped the draperies shut. "It's only until Friday. You'll manage."

Within minutes, Suzan poked her head into Christina's office. "Hi guys," she said, "how did your morning go with the FBI agents?"

"Pretty well, I guess. Everything's set for Friday morning. I can hardly wait to see the look on George's face when he gets arrested."

Dan gave her a stern look.

"Don't worry, Suzan can be trusted."

"Right," Suzan said. "Unless you think I'm some Soviet double agent, posing as a high tech analyst during the day."

"Hardly."

Christina looked up from her desk. "I was going to ask you to join us for lunch, but Dan has informed me that I can't go outside."

"Then I'll run down and get us some sandwiches. How 'bout it Dan, will that be safe enough for you?"

"Dan?" Christina asked.

He didn't bother to make eye contact, but spoke as if to an annoying child. "That'll be fine."

"Thanks, Suzan, you know where to find us." Christina said. "I need to get to work." She turned to Dan. "I hope you have something to occupy yourself. I'll be on the phone non-stop for the next several hours."

*

The next time Christina surfaced from her desk, she and Dan joined Suzan in the conference room, where Suzan had assembled a small feast of deli meats, assorted breads and salads.

"Actually," Suzan said, "This isn't all that bad."

"I'll say." Dan pulled from his coat pocket his metal bug detector. He walked around the room, the device crackling in his hand.

Suzan piled pasta salad onto her plate. "What's this I heard about you having to move into another hotel tonight?"

"It's only for one night." Christina poured herself some iced tea. "It doesn't sound all that bad. It's also for your protection. We're down to the wire now, and we don't want anything to go wrong before tomorrow."

"Where are you staying?"

"I'm sure it'll be somewhere in the Marina, because the sting is—"

Dan whirled around, his face flooded with color.

Christina looked at him with alarm. "You should loosen up. Suzan's not going to say anything to anyone."

Suzan walked over to the bar in the conference room, quartered a lime and shoved one of the wedges into a bottle of Corona. She held up the bottle. "Want one, Dan?"

"Not while I'm working. You're a bright woman, you should know that." He finished debugging and helped himself to a pile of potato salad.

"What is it with you two?" Christina finished her last forkful of salad. "I feel like the mother of two bickering children." She wiped her lips with a linen napkin and rose from the table. "I need to get back to my office and call our lawyers. You two can stay here and duke it out."

"Nope, duty calls," Dan said. "Thanks for lunch, Suzan."

*

Dan was still camped out on Christina's sofa when Bart beeped through on the intercom. "Franco's on the phone."

"Dan," she said. "May I have some privacy?"

He put down his magazine. "I should be here. Doria's name is in our files."

"Please, this is personal, very personal. If he mentions anything about Saunders or Stinson, I'll tell you."

"Okay, but I need to know. This is for your protection as well."

She smiled her thanks and waited until he left the room. Her hand shook as she picked up the receiver, and then she used her coolest, calmest voice. "Hello, Franco. I've been meaning to call you."

"Christina, I've been worried about you." She had never heard Franco sound so distressed. "You go back to California, and I never hear from you."

"That's because you lied to me, Franco. You're engaged. Do you have any idea how cheap I felt when I learned that?"

"Christina, my darling, first of all, I'm sorry you learned of my engagement." He sounded genuinely remorseful, even a bit desperate. "But it's not what you think."

"So tell me, what am I supposed to think?"

"Alessandra is like a sister to me. Our engagement was only a show, to please her dying father. He passed away last week. The funeral was yesterday."

"So—you're not engaged anymore?"

"I was never engaged. But now even the charade is over." He lowered his voice. "Who told you I was engaged? Stefano?"

"No, even better, the FBI."

"The FBI?" He sounded surprised.

"Yes, the FBI. They've been investigating your friend, Stefano, for years; and your brother-in-law, excuse me, soon-to-be brother-in-law, Dino Rossi, is also under investigation."

"Yes I know. Please let me explain."

He sounded so contrite. Could her instincts have been that far off the mark? He had been so patient with her when she wasn't ready to get intimate. That wasn't the behavior of someone who only wanted to use her. Also, what about that lovely, thoughtful picnic he prepared for the two of them? No man had ever done that for her before.

But Agent Wilson had warned her not to trust anyone, and after all, how did she know that Franco had truly broken off the engagement with Alessandra? "I heard that if you two married you'd control the largest marble company in the world."

"Yes, that is true, but we don't have to marry to accomplish that. This isn't ancient Rome. We can merge, just like any two companies."

"I need to ask you something else, Franco. What's your involvement with the FBI?"

After a silence, she heard him take a deep breath.

"I can explain everything, Christina, but not over the phone. I'm in Los Angeles now. I need to see you as soon as possible. I'll fly to you tomorrow."

"You're in LA!" Christina couldn't believe he was only an hour's flight away. But tomorrow wouldn't work. "I need to see you too, Franco. We have so much to talk about." She bit her lip. "But I'm not available until the weekend."

"Does this have something to do with the man who answered your phone at the hotel?"

Was that jealousy she detected in his voice? Luckily, he couldn't see her smile in response. "Richard? God, no. I'll explain everything to you on Saturday. I'm trusting you, Franco, so you need to trust me."

"I will, dolcina. I'll see you Saturday."

"And Franco...thank you for calling. I thought I'd lost you forever."

"That's my fault. But I promise to make it to you."

She giggled. She loved the way he could never get American clichés right and always screwed up the use of prepositions. "You mean, make it *up* to me."

"Yes, up to you. I must go now. Ciao, dolcina."

"Ciao, Franco."

Christina put down the phone, and sat dreamlike, until Dan walked back into her office and checked her back into reality.

"Anything I need to know about?" he asked.

"Not yet," Christina said. "He's coming to visit me on Saturday."

"Are you sure you trust him, Christina?"

"I'll let you know on Monday."

Chapter Twenty-one

After a tediously long day at Christina's office, Dan pulled up to a pink Victorian bed-and-breakfast in Pacific Heights.

"This isn't at all what I expected," Christina said.

"Exactly." Dan walked her to the front door and opened it for her. "We need to be as inconspicuous as possible."

The female agent waited in the lobby and stood as they entered. Compact and unsmiling, she extended her hand and shook Christina's firmly. "Agent Cheryl Smith. I'll be staying with you tonight and through tomorrow morning.'

She turned to Dan. "The room's clean. Powell's upstairs, standing by. I'll take it from here."

Christina thanked Dan. "I'll guess I'll see you tomorrow morning, then. Have a good night."

"I'll do my best." He smiled slightly. "Suzan's meeting me on Chestnut Street for drinks. She claims I owe her a few."

She waved goodbye. "Have fun, and remember, tomorrow morning—seven sharp."

When the two women approached Agent Powell, he motioned them to stand outside the door while he did another quick check inside, and then he returned. "All yours," he said to Cheryl. "Have a good night."

Christina entered the room. "It's pretty," she said. White and yellow wallpaper covered most of the walls, offset by lace curtains, and a large window seat, piled with fluffy pillows, overlooked a garden.

"I despise yellow," Cheryl said. "Not that it matters. In the morning, we won't be sitting around sipping tea. We'll have a few things to take care of."

Christina sat on a comfortable slipper chair. "Like what?"

"For one thing, I'll need to help you put this on." Cheryl placed a small recording device and some wires on the bed. "We need to tape these wires to your skin. And this is the antenna." She displayed a round metal object, the size of a quarter with a four-inch antenna. "We'll secure this along your backbone. It'll work better if you wear a bulky jacket or sweatshirt. If you don't have one, I brought one."

"That's all right; I packed a sweatshirt."

*

Christina tried to remain motionless while Cheryl applied the wires with white tape. The tape stretched her skin and pulled small hairs every time the device needed readjustment, but finally the cold metal receiver was in place. In less than an hour, she'd meet George. Her stomach growled, but all she could manage to eat was a bite of a bagel and a sip of orange juice.

At seven a.m., the telephone rang. Dan waited downstairs.

In the lobby, Cheryl touched Christina's arm. "Good luck. And don't worry, everything will be fine."

"I hope you're right." Christina watched Cheryl get in her car and drive away and wished she could do the same. Instead, to take her mind off her impending assignment, she nudged Dan. "Did you have fun last night?"

"I'll let Suzan answer that one," he said, deadpan.

He wore his Ray Bans, but Christina noticed a few faint lines wrinkling on the sides of his eyes, and his lips curved into the most minuscule smile. She knew it! They'd had a great time.

*

The Palace of Fine Arts resembled a sand-colored Roman ruin. Built in 1915 for the Pan-Pacific games, the site was a popular yet not overcrowded tourist attraction. Christina often came here on sunny Sunday afternoons to read the paper and enjoy the exquisite setting—a swan-filled lagoon, the rotunda with its massive Corinthian columns and sculptured weeping maidens.

They approached by car, and at Beach Street, Dan slowed and pointed out a white van stenciled with the company name J&J Painting. Several paint-splattered ladders were secured to its roof.

"Wilson and the rest of your back-up are in there. They'll see and hear everything from inside."

Dan pulled out a microphone, and confirmed with the men in the van that everything was in order, and then he steered the car back toward one of the side streets. At the next stop sign, he turned to face Christina. "It's all yours now."

Christina shivered as perspiration trickled down her back. "Do I look as scared as I feel?"

Dan put his hand on her shoulder. "Don't worry; I'll be stationed only half a block away."

"What if he guns me down before I make it to the rotunda?"

"Christina," Dan squeezed her shoulder. "We have you covered. SWAT specialists have this place surrounded. If anyone pulls a gun and poises it to shoot, he'll get taken out before he has a chance to pull the trigger."

"So, where are these guys and their guns?"

"You can't see the sharp shooters, but they're placed strategically around the structure, hidden behind the columns and pillars."

"Good, that's a relief. Anyway, I can't picture George as an expert marksman."

Christina checked her wire and recording device, and then strolled down Beach Street toward the ruins. Unusually, for a San Francisco summer morning, the sun shone brightly and dew glistened on the grass. The terra cotta columns and giant octagonal rotunda reflected brightly in the lagoon, where a gaggle of swans paddled gracefully and completed the peaceful scene.

Christina crept through the lengthy peristyle. As she passed each column, she hoped to spot one of the sharp shooters, but she noticed no one. At least they knew how to remain invisible.

A noisy splash erupted from the pond, and startled, she jumped nearly a foot backwards. What had happened? Quaking, she looked around. *Oh God, please don't let anything go wrong.*

It was only the swans. Five or six of them had flapped their wings and had taken off for a short flight across the pond. She had to get a hold on herself.

Her footsteps echoed on the cold stone floor of the rotunda, and she rubbed her chilled arms for warmth. Where was George?

She glanced at her watch. Ten minutes after eight. She positioned herself directly under the dome of the thirteen-story stone ceiling and waited. Again, she checked her watch. Twelve minutes past eight. It felt like an hour had elapsed. The silence, the chilly atmosphere and the musty dank smell enveloped her.

"Christina!" A voice reverberated throughout the rotunda.

She jumped, but didn't see anyone. Her eyes darted from pillar to pillar. She searched for a shadow—for any clue as to where he hid—but everything remained still. She heard nothing and saw no one.

"Okay George, you can come out now." Her voice rang out, stable and clear. "Your game of hide-and-seek is over."

No answer.

"Listen, George. Don't waste my time, I have what you need."

"It's not George." A deep, vaguely recognizable voice came from behind one of the pillars.

"Did George call in sick this morning?"

"You shouldn't try to be funny first thing in the morning, Miss Culhane. It's not becoming."

Perfect. If she kept him talking, the sharpshooters would place him. She also wanted to nail down the voice.

"Personally, I don't care who George sent, as long as you have my money." She paused for several seconds. "Do *not* play games with me."

"How do I know you brought the chip?"

"Trust me. My desk is already packed up. I want to cash out, just like George." She kept looking for some sign as to where he hid. "How do I know you have the money?"

"Walk over here, and I'll show you."

Christina walked in the general direction of the voice.

"Wrong way," he shouted. A bone-chilling laugh sounded from the other side of the rotunda.

She snapped her head around and looked in the other direction. She felt like Dorothy, listening to the mysterious Wizard's voice booming from behind a velvet curtain.

He laughed again. "We're in an echo chamber."

A shadow crept out from behind one of the pillars.

"Okay, here I go," she whispered.

As she moved closer, a large body lurched from behind the pillar. Arnold Hague.

She tried to remain calm and in control, but her entire body trembled. From the first time she had seen him on the plane, she knew he was trouble. "Let me see the money."

He lifted up a black leather bag, unzipped it and reached in. But instead of grabbing stacks of bills, he pulled out a gun.

Christina wanted to scream, but she couldn't make a sound.

He pointed the black metal pistol at Christina. "Now, why don't you hand over the chip, and we'll both walk away quietly."

"Oh, a *gun*." Christina emphasized the word, so the FBI agents could hear her loud and clear. "How courageous of you. You didn't think you could overpower me without one?"

"Okay, Culhane, you've gone far enough." He edged toward her.

She would've felt better if she'd seen his hand quiver, but he held the gun straight and steady. Why didn't someone come to her defense?

He stopped less than five feet away from her. "Give me the chip."

She stared directly into the black metal barrel, paralyzed by fear. He reached out his other hand. "The chip."

Suddenly a shot rang out. Blood splattered onto Christina's face, neck and clothes, and Hague let out a loud, low scream and fell to the ground, clasping his shoulder. Two men in uniform appeared and pinned him down. The high-pitched wail of an ambulance shrieked in the distance.

At the sight of the blood, Christina's knees buckled and she collapsed.

"You never should've gotten involved, Culhane," Hague shouted. "It's not over."

Dazed, she looked around for Dan, or at least for one of the agents from inside the van. Why didn't someone come for her?

Tires screeched from the other side of The Palace. A late model Camry skidded around the corner, headed for the Golden Gate Bridge.

George?

Dan's sedan and two police cars squealed out after the car. Finally, Agent Wilson joined her in the middle of the rotunda.

"Well, you did it Miss Culhane." Wilson shook her hand.

"I'm still shaking. I can't believe it's finally over."

"Well, it's not over yet. We still need to recover the encoded plans, but we're pretty certain Stinson or Saunders will supply us with those."

"Well, I'm looking forward to moving back into my own house and getting on with my life."

"I bet you are." He patted her on the back. "Come on, we'll drive you home."

Chapter Twenty-two

Miraculously, Christina's plants were still alive. And thank goodness for Rosa—between her and the insurance company, the apartment looked almost normal, the window repaired, carpets cleaned and most items back in their rightful place. Life was looking up. Already, she had managed a luxurious and much needed nap in her own bed; Andrew Jacobs, from New York, had personally left a message instructing her to take Monday and Tuesday off if she wished to; and Franco would arrive tomorrow. Tonight she would join Suzan and Dan for a party at his place.

Suzan rang her bell at exactly 8:05.

"Hurry," she said, "I've parked the pony illegally on the sidewalk, so I'll wait here." By *pony*, she meant her 64 ½ Mustang convertible, complete with its original 190 horse engine.

Christina waited until Suzan veered onto the street. "So, you and Dan?"

"I know. Something really clicked when we went out for drinks last night. He acted like a normal, free-spirited young guy." Her long, curly hair blew in the wind. "In fact, we're going camping this weekend."

Suzan circled Dan's apartment building on Telegraph Hill for the third time. At this time of night, even the illegal spots were taken. They finally found a place in a red zone. At most, a ticket would cost thirty dollars.

They trudged up four flights of stairs to Dan's apartment. The door stood wide open and music blasted into the hallway. The odor of stale beer reminded Christina of a frat party back in college. She was tired and didn't want to stay long, but she wanted to thank Dan for all his help.

A keg of beer leaked onto the linoleum floor in the kitchen. Dan offered them each a plastic cup filled with Budweiser.

"Did you ever catch up with George?" Christina asked.

"Yeah, it took a total of ten seconds. He barely made it to the Golden Gate Bridge before he spun out of control. We brought him in and asked about the disk containing the blueprint for the missile. He claimed he didn't have it, but that Saunders did, and sure enough, when we searched Saunders' house, we found it stashed under a pile of books, sitting idle until he got his hands on your code chip. We caught up with him at his corporate headquarters. He's under arrest and looking at twenty-to-life."

"I'm so glad this is finally over." Christina set her half-finished beer on a milk crate in the hallway. "But we still don't know who killed Peter."

"Both Stinson and Saunders are pointing the finger at each other, but they're trying to pin the actual murder on Arnold Hague." Dan took a sip of beer. "The good news is that Hague is talking. He's named Stefano Marani as Saunders' Italian connection. George was only the middleman. Marani planned to buy the chip from Saunders and sell it to a Chinese concern for an enormous sum."

"Have you arrested Stefano yet?"

"We don't have enough evidence, and plus, we can't find him. But Saunders, Stinson and Hague have all sold Marani out. Our intelligence has revealed that he's still scrambling to find the code chip to sell to the Chinese. What he doesn't know is that it's safe with us."

"What about Franco?" Christina couldn't help herself.

Dan shook his head. "I'm sorry, Christina, I can't talk about that part of our investigation."

She looked down the hallway and saw two preppies making out. "I should get going, anyway, I have a busy weekend."

"I'll drive you." Suzan blew Dan a kiss good-bye. "I'll be back in a half-hour."

Suzan peeled a parking ticket off her windshield. "Here, file this in my glove compartment." She handed Christina the ticket. "Some of your mail is in there. I picked it up from work. There's one letter in particular I thought you'd want to see."

Christina rifled through a stack of tickets and found her mail smashed in between them—a stack of bills, some invitations and an envelope with the official seal of the United States Senate.

"Aren't you going to open it?" Suzan asked.

"I can't read it in the car. It's too dark. I'll wait until I get home."

"I'll stop under this street light." Passing cars honked as Suzan abruptly pulled over to the curb.

Christina unfolded a neatly hand written letter from the envelope. At most, she had expected a terse note, typed by his secretary, on cheap paper. Instead, she read aloud:

Dear Christina,

I'm on my way back to Washington D.C. I can assure you that my obligation to a certain campaign supporter was only to confirm that you were in possession of something of interest to him.

I asked too few questions up front, and I certainly did not expect to fall in love with you in the process. You can't fault me for that. In fact, I nearly forgot my original intention after our first dinner together. Please find it in your heart to forgive me.

Always,
Richard

"Wow, that's pretty serious." Suzan cranked the car into first gear and sped away from the curb. "He really fell for you. What Senator, especially one who's running for President, would write something like that in his own handwriting? What are you going to do?"

"Nothing," Christina responded. "All I really care about is seeing Franco tomorrow." She folded the letter and put it back in its envelope. "But you're right; he knew what he was risking when he wrote this. I guess he trusts me not to sell it to the *National Enquirer.*"

Suzan slowed to a roll in front of Christina's building. "You know what they say: Never underestimate the power of *looove.*"

Chapter Twenty-three

Christina maneuvered her way through the various exit ramps and pulled up to the security gate at the Executive Aviation Terminal. The guard directed her to the parking lot, where she brushed her hair, put on some lip-gloss and adjusted her sunglasses. She looked up as she heard the loud noise of a powerful jet engine. She shaded her eyes and watched the sleek Gulfstream glide to a smooth landing.

After a strong blast, the engines hummed for a short time while they cooled off, and then they abruptly shut down. A heavy door swung open at the front of the plane and the mechanical stairway eased down. Franco emerged first. She had almost forgotten how gorgeous he was. The wind blew his black waves across his face and copper-rimmed sunglasses. He wore a knee-length, brown suede coat, faded jeans and leather boots.

She hoped he would think she looked pretty hot herself, in snug low-riding Seven jeans and a black knit top, just short enough to show off a bit of trim tummy.

He raised his hand when he saw her and she ran out to meet him. He dropped his leather duffel bag, and pulled her into him. They kissed passionately for a full minute, and then they walked back to her car with their arms around each other's waist.

"What do you want to see first?" Christina asked.

"The inside of your bedroom, of course."

Christina felt the same, but she hesitated. She threw out the ultimate deal breaker. "Before the bedroom, I need to know if you've been working with the FBI."

Franco's chest expanded and contracted. "Let's sit down."

They sat in her car, and Franco placed his hand on her leg. "Christina, you must believe me. My involvement with the FBI had nothing to do with your friend Peter. The FBI approached me because they wanted me to watch Dino Rossi. My father and I needed to keep him out of our business, and the American FBI wanted to arrest him for international drug trafficking. It worked out well for both of us. He's not behind bars, but he will be soon. If our two companies merge, we don't want anything to do with scum like Dino Rossi."

Christina nodded her head and smiled at him. "I'm sure there's a bit more to the story than that, but I'll accept that for now."

She started the car and sped back to the city. When at last they were alone in the privacy of Christina's apartment, they fell onto the couch in her living room and then onto the floor. A bellowing foghorn provided the background music for their lovemaking.

Hours later, she shook him gently. "Franco, are you hungry?"

He stretched his arms. "Only for you my darling."

"You're impossible!" She kissed him on his lips and then worked her way downward.

*

Only a few markets opened early on Sunday morning, and Lucca's Delicatessen on Chestnut Street was one of them. She chose an assortment of fruit and vegetable salads, plump olives, several varieties of cheese, some Italian pastries, chocolate biscotti and freshly baked bread. She added a quart of whole milk to steam for their coffee.

At the checkout counter, she almost dropped the container of milk when she saw the newspaper the clerk read. Christina caught two pictures on the front page: Arnold Hague being taken away from the Palace of Fine Arts on a stretcher, and Curtis Saunders being escorted from his office in handcuffs.

She grabbed her own edition of the San Francisco Chronicle, paid for her groceries and ran back to her apartment to share the excitement with Franco. She could hardly wait to get copies of the article to send to her parents and friends. At least this would help explain why she'd been *incommunicado* for the past several weeks.

Franco had just stepped out of the shower when Christina walked through the front door. The white towel around his waist contrasted superbly with his tanned, muscular chest.

"You're right, I'm starving." He greeted her with outstretched arms.

"Good, me too!" She gave him a quick kiss and handed him a pastry. "Here, while you're eating, I'll read you this article. It'll give you some idea of what I've been going through these past few weeks."

They crawled back into bed. A tourist from Nebraska had snapped the picture and sold it to the Chronicle. The article explained that while the FBI could not comment on all points, Saunders and Stinson were clearly implicated. The story briefly covered the chip heist and touched on the proprietary designs Symex had developed.

She turned to page A14 for the remainder of the story.

A blown-up picture of her face stared out at her, with her name in bold letters underneath. She recognized the photo from the one taken at the Sheraton Palace last week; except Richard Cartwright had been cut out. Her cheeks grew hot when she saw the picture and thought back to that night, but she kept reading. The rest of the details were sketchy. Again, the FBI could not comment on everything, but they did confirm that Christina Culhane had played a crucial role in arresting the men involved and in averting a disaster of global proportion.

Franco pulled her closer to him. "I had no idea how serious this was."

She hated to broach the next subject. "Franco, I need to tell you that Interpol, in conjunction with the FBI, is on the verge of arresting Stefano."

Franco sat up. "I'm not surprised. I knew he'd get in trouble eventually."

"Apparently he's involved in illegal arms dealings. It's very serious. Curtis Saunders, the man you just read about in the newspaper, was negotiating with Stefano to sell US weapons technology to the Chinese."

Franco shook his head. "He was always in trouble when he was younger, but I never expected something like this."

"Did you know about any of this?"

"I honestly had no idea." He pushed a strand of her hair off her face. "Stefano's always been very concerned with money and his image, but I never thought it would go so far."

"I've been through a lot, Franco, and I'm still a bit shaken. When I thought that the FBI was investigating you, you can't even begin to imagine how I felt."

"It sounds worse than it is. I was working *with* the FBI long before this American, Curtis Saunders, came to stay at my hotel. As I told you before, I needed to watch Dino Rossi because of his relationship to Alessandra. The FBI suspected he had a connection to Stefano but they needed proof in order to bring them both in. They suggested that I tell Stefano that he could use my hotel for his out-of-town guests, this way I could keep an ear on them and then feed the FBI information."

Christina giggled and interrupted him. "You mean keep an *eye* on them."

"Dolcina, you must believe me, I'm only guilty of protecting my marble business, nothing more."

What he said corroborated the bits of information she had gleaned from Agent Wilson. "I needed to hear that, but no matter what, *you* can't trust Stefano. He thinks I have something very important and he may try to manipulate you in order to get it."

"I'm not afraid of Stefano." He wrestled her under the covers, moved on top of her and whispered, "Fly back to Italy with me."

"Franco, that's the best offer I've heard in a long time. But—"

He pressed his finger to her lips. "No *buts* until you take more than two seconds to think about what I said."

The room had gotten brighter and warmer. The sun had finally broken through the dense morning fog.

"Franco, I promise I'll think about it, but now I want to do something for you. You showed me your beautiful city by the sea, and now I want to show you mine."

"Where will you take me?"

"You'll see."

Christina found her wicker picnic basket buried under several boxes of old shoes. She carried the basket into the kitchen and arranged everything she had bought that morning inside its checked cloth lining. Then, with Franco in the passenger seat, they cruised past the Saint Francis Yacht Club and up through the Presidio.

"The Presidio is an abandoned military base." She pulled over at one of the scenic overlooks so Franco could admire the view of the sailboats on the bay and the grandeur of the Golden Gate Bridge. They got out of the car to lean against the hood and breathe in the clean air.

"Next, I'm going to take you to the Palace of the Legion Honor." She drove near the cliffs above the bay. The fresh smell of the eucalyptus trees and the salty ocean air stung her nostrils. "It's an art museum. I thought you'd like seeing the paintings."

She parked near the white, pillared building, designed in French Classical style. The museum sat on the edge of a golf course and overlooked the Bay and the Golden Gate Bridge.

They strode through the circular cobblestone courtyard, past the Rodin sculpture, *The Thinker*, and into the building, where Christina watched Franco admire the paintings. He breathed in every detail, and did not speak for nearly an hour. He was a true artist, reverent, paying homage to the great masters of his trade.

They held hands as they left the museum and walked to the car for the picnic basket. Her basket of goodies was not as elaborate as the one Franco had surprised her with nearly a month ago—no candles, no fresh flowers, and no chocolate. Nonetheless, they had each other and the spectacular view of the Bay, the ships and sailboats crossing under the Golden Gate Bridge, and the light brown hills of the Marin Headlands in the distance.

Franco squeezed her hand. "I've been doing some thinking since you left Italy. Now that Alessandra's father has died, my father is pressuring me to merge our companies. Of course the easiest way to do this is for Alessandra and me to marry."

Christina felt her heart beating against her chest.

"But of course I don't want to do that."

"You'd better not."

"I'd like to expand the company and open an office here on the West Coast of America." He leaned back on his elbows and stretched his legs along the blanket. "Instead of flying back to Italy tomorrow morning, I'm going to look for warehouse space for Doria Marble. We could use an office on the West Coast, and San Francisco is just as good as Los Angeles. Even better, because you're here."

Christina rested her head on his chest. "You really scared me when you said that your father wanted you to marry Alessandra. All the uncertainty about your family business makes me nervous."

"No need to be nervous, dolcina." He touched her nose. "I'm taking charge now."

"Now that you're in charge, when will we see each other again?"

"I leave tomorrow night, but I'll be back soon." He smiled and wrapped his arms around her.

She felt as though she could conquer the world, as long as she had him to come home to every night.

*

"Do you want to borrow my car today while you look for office space?" Christina asked.

"I hired a driver. I don't know my way around this town, and it's better that I not waste time getting lost."

"Will I see you this evening?"

"I'm afraid not, my darling. I have meetings back in Italy tomorrow afternoon that I cannot miss. Remember, I lose nine hours on the trip home."

Her throat choked up, and she couldn't respond for a few seconds. "I can't believe you have to leave so soon. It seems as though you just arrived last night."

"It was a short trip, but two days is better than nothing." He kissed the top of her head and hugged her for several seconds. "Listen, my darling, we must say goodbye now. I'm sure my driver is downstairs already. Why don't you walk me down?"

She picked up her handbag and locked the door behind her. She had determined to focus all her energy on work until he returned.

A black, Lincoln Town Car sat parked in the driveway, blocking access to her garage. Franco put his fingers under her chin and forced her to lift her eyes. "Dolcina," he said softly, "The sooner I get into that car over there, the sooner I'll find myself an office."

"All right then," she said. "I hate long good-byes anyway. But please call me before you take off."

*

Later in the morning, Christina made it to Suzan's office for a quick chat. "How was your weekend with Dan? You haven't had a chance to tell me about it."

Suzan pointed to her reddened cheeks. "Let me just say this—it's a full body tan. We pitched a tent next to a crystal clear, mountain lake. Between skinny dipping and baking our naked bodies in the sun all day, we managed to enjoy a fantastic weekend together."

"Does he look as great in the buff as I imagine he does?"

"Better." Suzan flashed a naughty grin. "Anyway, get out of here." She waved her hand toward the door. "We both have a ton of work to do."

A ton of work was right. Christina had almost forgotten what it was like to concentrate on her job for a full ten hours. At least New York wasn't giving her a hard time. The favorable press she'd been getting hadn't hurt as far as business development went.

She returned calls, both personal and business, for five hours straight. It seemed as if everyone had called to hear about what had happened at the Palace of Fine Arts and to ask how the hell she'd become involved. Also, because her picture had appeared with Senator Cartwright less than a week ago, more than a few people wanted to know about that story. Is he as handsome in real life as in all the pictures? Does his power intimidate you? What's he really like?

Most of her calls resulted in appointments for the current week and the next. Business poured in; she was back in her element, once again on a natural high.

Around two, she ran downstairs to the deli located on the first floor and bought a container of yogurt and an apple. She ate the apple in the elevator and finished the yogurt in her office in less than a minute. This would hold her off until the end of the day, which at this point, seemed nowhere in sight.

Her phone beeped.

"*Furr-ahnco's* on the phone," Bart said, trying to imitate Franco's accent.

"Thanks Bart."

"Hi Franco," Christina said. "I miss you already. Any luck finding an office?"

"I've narrowed the options to the East Bay, somewhere closer to the Port of Oakland."

"Office space is more reasonable there." She had forgotten how easily she could slip into her business mode and remove her heart from the situation at hand.

"The Port of Oakland reminded me of something, dolcina. I need to complete one last detail on your present. I plan to send it tomorrow with a marble shipment we have going out. You'll be able to pick it up this Saturday. I sent a pass to the port office so just show them your ID."

She heard loud surging noises in the background.

"We just pulled up next to the plane. I need to confirm the flight plan with my pilot, so I better say good-bye."

"Ciao, Franco. Have a safe flight. I love you." And then silently, *Oh my god. What did I just say?*

"I love you too, dolcina."

So, it was official. She was in love, and she had admitted it.

Her mind raced ahead to Saturday. She had plans. What were they?

Treasure Island, that's right. The movie set. Brandy's friend, Rob, would be in town. Perfect. Treasure Island was on the way to Oakland.

She called Brandy's mobile phone. The static was terrible, but Brandy picked up. "It's Christina. I'm glad I caught you. What time do we go to Treasure Island next Saturday?"

"Rob asked me to pick him up at nine. But I can't do it. I'm showing property first thing."

"I'll be happy to pick him up. But you'll need to drive him back to the city. I have to run an errand at the Port of Oakland."

"An errand? At the Port of Oakland?" Brandy's voice rose.

"I have a million phone calls to return, so we'll leave that one until there's less static."

*

Christina finished all her paperwork and phone calls by seven, and ducked out of the office without saying goodbye to anyone. She could hardly wait to get home, put on a soft sweatshirt, and order a pizza.

As she phoned the local pizzeria, she noticed Richard's letter next to the phone. It had been recently opened. She remembered tucking the envelope under the phone, not next to it. Did that mean Franco had read it? And what if he had?

*

Her week flew by with meetings and scheduled appointments. Even Andrew Jacobs called from New York to congratulate her on all the business she had brought in that week.

"It's just the beginning," she told him. "I'm back in full force and nothing's going to get in my way now."

"That's what we like to hear, Culhane. You're a fighter—keep up the good work and enjoy your weekend."

"I will, sir. Thank you very much." She hung up the phone and walked into Suzan's office. "So, are you seeing Dan tonight?"

"Of course. How 'bout you, what are your plans?"

"I feel like renting old movies and going to sleep early. I want to get up and go for a run, and then I'll pick you up." She gave her a naughty grin. "Your house or Dan's?"

"Well, you saw his apartment, and since I'm not too keen on sharing a bathroom with three guys, it's safe to say I'll meet you at my house."

"I'll pick you up at quarter to nine, and then we'll get Rob."

"Enjoy your peaceful evening."

Her only stop on the way home was at Blockbuster. She rented *To Catch a Thief* and *Roman Holiday*, both of which would remind her of her own holiday in Italy.

Chapter Twenty-four

The next morning, Christina flipped on her television, always tuned to the business channel, CNBC. A commercial about some fat-burning tablet flashed on the screen. The ads on the weekend were even worse than the ones they ran during the week. She walked into the kitchen to pour herself more coffee. She wasn't entirely listening, but she could still hear the broadcast. "And in international business news, Rossi Quarries and Doria Marble announce a multi-billion Euro merger."

Christina sprinted back to her living room. In the upper right hand corner of her television screen, behind the head of the newscaster, hung a picture of a stunning dark-haired woman. The same woman she had seen in Franco's hotel.

The report continued: "After the death of GianCarlo Rossi, Mr Rossi named his daughter, Miss Alessandra Rossi, sole heir to the Rossi fortune. Miss Rossi announced today her plan to merge her late father's company with Doria Marble."

Christina had known this merger would occur, but it was a shock to see a full-color picture of Alessandra on her television screen. And of course, it didn't help that she was so photogenic. She had only seen her for a brief moment back at the hotel, but the screen accentuated her high cheekbones, full lips and thin nose.

She turned off the television and shuffled into her bedroom. Suzan expected her in fifteen minutes. This was not the time to let her insecurities get the best of her. There was nothing she could do about Franco's business affairs. She pulled her hair back into a ponytail and drove to Suzan's with her convertible top down and the radio on.

When she pulled up front of Suzan's apartment building, she reached for her mobile to call upstairs—the lazy person's doorbell—but she had forgotten it. With nowhere to park, she backed into a neighbor's driveway, blocking another car.

A minute later, Suzan came bouncing down the stairs, holding hands with Dan, who kissed her goodbye passionately.

Christina had planned to mention the CNBC report, but Suzan looked so content she changed her mind.

They pulled into the circular drive in front of Rob's co-op twenty minutes later. Built atop one of the highest hills in San Francisco, the ten-story building resembled a French chateau, with a stone facade, faux turrets and large plate-glass windows. The views from his penthouse must be spectacular. Suzan waited in the car while Christina ran in and asked the doorman to ring him.

Rob emerged from the elevator in jeans and a cotton button-down shirt. He smiled warmly and shook her hand.

At the car, Christina paused. "You remember Suzan, don't you?"

"Of course. I understand you're Christina's partner-in-crime these days. Brandy's been filling me in, but I'm keen to hear the details."

"How much do you know?" Christina asked.

"Only that your picture has been all over the paper this week."

"Even in LA?"

"Yes. First with Senator Cartwright, and then hailed as a heroine in an FBI sting. I'm thinking it might make a movie."

Christina screeched around the ramp that led to Treasure Island, and raised her eyebrows at Suzan.

Rob pointed to the small gatehouse. "Pull over at this security check point."

"There's Brandy," Suzan said. "She beat us here."

Rob gestured for Brandy to jump in back with him, and they proceeded to the gatehouse, where Rob showed the guard his identification. The guard scrutinized his credentials, and then waved them through.

They passed at least twenty fifty-foot trailers. "Some of those are for catering," Rob said. "The rest are makeup and costumes."

"Can I really get up close and personal with Brad Pitt?" Brandy asked.

"Brad's stunt double is doing all the work today. Brad may be around the set, but I can't promise anything."

They got out of the car and walked over to the water, where an action scene was being filmed. As they watched, stunt men jumped from speeding jet skis onto a speedboat, driven by Sandra Bullock's stunt double. Christina noticed the name Chris Rogers on the director's chair and recalled that he had directed several films set in the Bay Area. She'd read somewhere that he lived in Pacific Heights.

"Cut!" the director yelled through a bullhorn. "Cut!"

After the stuntmen and women heard the second command, they killed the engines.

The director rubbed his throat and continued yelling. "Remember, the boat has to look like it's spinning out of control. You're driving it in a straight line. Sandra could've done that herself, for God's sake." He paused and then yelled, "Take Four!" As he turned to sit down, he saw Rob and held up his hand to acknowledge him.

"They should be finished in a minute," Rob said.

This time the boat careened in circles.

"Cut!" the director yelled again. He took a sip of water. "Good job, that's a wrap. Bring the equipment to shore."

He put his bullhorn down and walked over to Rob and the three women.

"Nice boat," Rob said. The cigarette-style boat had just pulled to the shore and stunt people climbed out of it.

"We picked it up at a Treasury auction. It was confiscated from some drug runners in Panama."

Rob laughed. "I always like to hear we're budget minded." He introduced the women, and then reassured Chris. "We'll stay out of your way."

"Not a problem. Have fun touring the set. I've got another scene to finish before the noon sun blows the scene."

"See that huge building that looks like an airplane hangar?" Rob pointed it out in the distance. "Back in the forties, it used to be one, but now it's a state-of-the-art sound stage."

"Can we see it?" Suzan asked. Then noting the mid-morning spread the caterers had laid out on long tables, she added, "No one's going hungry on this set, are they?"

"Oh my god!" Brandy squealed. "I think I just saw Brad Pitt."

"Where?" Suzan whirled around.

"Over there." Brandy pointed to the large custom-built mobile home on the side of the road.

The back of his faded Diesel jeans disappeared into his air-conditioned mobile home.

"At least I saw him," Brandy said. "And from less than fifty feet away. Maybe I could knock on his door and ask him for a glass of ice water."

"Probably not a good idea." Rob picked three small bottles of Evian from a cooler and handed one to each of the women.

Inside the sound stage, the arena bustled with people fixing wires, checking lights and moving cameras along built-in tracks that resembled a miniature railroad.

"There isn't much going on right now," Rob said. "Let's check out the other side of the building."

"This is amazing." Christina watched a crew assemble a massive set that looked exactly like the inside of City Hall. "I feel as though I'm actually in the building. The detail work is phenomenal."

"That's the idea," Rob said. "It's too disruptive to film at City Hall day-after-day, so this is what they do instead. They'll probably only spend one day in the actual building, but most of the scene will be shot here."

Christina looked at her watch. "It's almost eleven-thirty. I should get going, Rob. I have to drive over to the Port of Oakland to pick up a package."

Brandy approached to listen, and Christina explained to both of them about the gift. She shook Rob's hand. "Thanks for showing me around—it's fun to know what goes on behind the scenes."

"My pleasure. Don't forget to call when you want to write your script."

"Let's do lunch," Christina said, laughing. "I'll have my people call your people."

Chapter Twenty-five

Just a few minutes after Christina left for the port, Suzan's mobile phone rang. She expected Dan to call, but the number on her phone displayed *anonymous* instead of *c-pie*, otherwise known as Dan, FBI, cutie pie.

"Franco?" she said, on hearing his voice. "This is a surprise. I thought you were in Italy."

"I was." He sounded frantic. "But I'm in the States now and I desperately need to reach Christina."

"She just left the Island a few minutes ago to pick up your present."

"What island?"

"Treasure Island, we're here watching a movie being filmed. Is everything okay?"

"No, not at all. I need to tell Christina not to go near *The Doria*. Stefano's on the ship. He conned the captain into letting him aboard."

Suzan could barely understand him. He spoke rapidly, and over the phone his accent was more pronounced. "Franco, please calm down and try to speak more clearly."

Franco only sounded more frustrated. He shouted into the phone. "Suzan, listen to me. Christina's in a great deal of danger. Stefano said that he wanted to deliver Christina's present personally. We must stop her before she gets on my ship."

"Don't worry. I'll call her."

"I just tried, she's not answering." He sounded out of breath. "A while back her assistant gave me your number. I had hoped you were together."

"She must have left her cell phone at home. Where are you?"

"I just landed at SFO. I'm running through the terminal to the taxi line."

No wonder he sounded out of breath. Visions of him hurdling through the airport, *á la* OJ Simpson, flashed into her mind.

"My father has the jet, so I had to fly commercial, and there were no direct flights to Oakland."

"We'll head over to the Port," Suzan said. "Don't worry, Franco; we'll catch her in time."

"I can't stress how urgent this is," Franco said. "I'll meet you at the port as soon as I can get there, but if you arrive before me, stop her."

"Will do." Suzan snapped her phone shut. She turned to Brandy who still lingered near Brad Pitt's trailer. "Brandy, I need to borrow your car. Christina's in trouble at the port."

Brandy tossed her water bottle into a large metal bin. "I'm going with you. Rob?"

"Let's go."

The earth rumbled and shook as they ran back to Brandy's car.

Brandy fell to the ground and covered her head. "Earthquake!"

Rob placed his hand on her shoulder. "Don't worry. It's a minor one."

"Not that minor." Brandy still crouched on the ground with her hands over her head.

Nearly twenty people ran from the sound stage. One of the women had blood on her forehead.

"I guess it was worse than I thought," Rob conceded.

One of the actors stuck his head out of his trailer. "Is everyone okay out here?"

"We have it under control," a man with CREW written on his shirt said, "Go back to sleep. We'll let you know when we're gonna shoot your next scene."

*

Christina had just exited the bridge when she felt the jolt. At first, she thought that one of her tires had blown, but when she noticed several cars swerve over to the roadside shoulder, the earthquake registered. She steered the car to the shoulder and waited. Across the water, a plume of smoke rose from a building in Oakland. Her hands shook as she turned on the radio. The all-news radio station, KGO, reported that a tumbler of 5.7 had just registered on the Richter scale. Several power outages had already swept the city.

Whatever else, she had to remain calm. She waited until other cars began to drive again, and then she continued driving toward the port.

*

Suzan, Brandy and Rob made it to the ramp that led to the bridge, and then Brandy slammed on the brakes, just missing the truck in front of her. Cars were backed up for nearly a quarter of a mile.

"What the hell," she screamed. "There must have been an accident on the bridge. We can't get anywhere near it. What are we going to do?"

"Turn around." Rob spoke in a calm, cool tone of voice.

"What are you talking about?" Brandy pounded her hands against the steering wheel. "This is the only way off the island."

"Trust me. Drive back to the beach."

Brandy squealed into a u-turn and floored it back to Treasure Island. She raced through the guard station and pulled up to the sand. Rob jumped out and ran over to where Chris was talking with a cameraman.

"Chris, don't ask any questions. We have an emergency and I need to use the boat."

Chris took off his cap, put it back on, and then handed him the keys. "Just bring it back in one piece."

*

From the back of a foul smelling cab, Franco furiously punched Suzan's number into his cell phone, but the earthquake had disrupted service. Bumper-to-bumper traffic on the Bay Bridge had the car paralyzed.

"Is there any other way to the Port of Oakland?"

"Fraid not, and it looks like we'll be stuck here for a while." The driver, also tuned to KGO, held up his hand. "Hold on, they're just coming on with the traffic report." The cabbie listened for a moment and then turned around. "There's been an accident, about a mile up. We're outta luck, buddy."

Franco slammed his hands against the front seat. "We need to get off the Bridge. I can't do anything sitting here."

"We're stuck. There's no way off unless you want to go to Treasure Island."

"Yes, I do. And do it now."

"Whatever you say." The driver inched along until he made it to the exit lane leading to Treasure Island. When they reached the gated entrance, Franco instructed the driver to go through without stopping.

"I can't do that, buddy. I'd lose my license."

"Okay, then I'll do it." Franco crawled from the back seat into the front passenger seat and told the driver to get out. The driver didn't budge. Franco leaned over, opened the door and pushed him out.

He floored it past the guard and the gatehouse, and kept going until he recognized Suzan and Brandy standing at the beach. With a cloud of dust blowing around the car, he got out and joined the group.

"Franco!" Suzan said. "My God. What are you doing here?" It took a second or two for the incongruous image to register— Franco the handsome aristocrat driving a beat-up taxi.

"Trying to get to the port. As fast as possible." Franco eyed the speedboat lying idle and a key on a white plastic float dangling from Rob's hand. "Are those the keys to that boat over there?"

"We were just headed over—"

Franco threw all his well-bred manners out the window, grabbed the keys from Rob and jumped into the speedboat. As the crow flew, he estimated it was two miles to the port, and to Christina.

Chapter Twenty-six

Christina pulled into the massive concrete area surrounding the Port of Oakland. She parked her car, walked toward a low-rise building and presented her identification to the man sitting behind a desk in the entryway. He gave her directions, and she walked toward the water. At the end of a pier, she saw a ship the size of an apartment building. Large white letters on the side spelled out DORIA. She smiled and walked faster.

At *The Doria*, a dark, bearded man in a navy uniform stopped her. She introduced herself, displayed her identification and told him that Franco had sent her to retrieve a package. He nodded and gestured for her to follow him.

They walked along a windowless metal corridor that instantly made her feel claustrophobic, and then the man opened the door to the bridge above deck, a large window-filled room with computer panels and nautical navigation devices. Christina knew nothing about boats, but she recognized the control room immediately.

She looked for the captain in his white uniform, and saw him slumped in the chair next to the helm. A tingling sensation on the back of her neck alerted her, and then a palpable sense of fear overtook her entire body. She ran back toward the door to escape, but the bearded man blocked it.

Stefano emerged from the other side of the bridge. He looked scruffier than he had in Italy. His black hair had grown several inches and his goatee was now a full beard.

"*Buon giorno*, Christina." His thick Italian accent sounded much rougher than when she first met him in Italy, and dripped with sarcasm. "What a pleasure to see you again."

"What's going on here, Stefano?" Christina knew she had just stepped onto a minefield.

"We've been waiting for you. You have something I need, and you're not getting off my ship until you give it to me."

"Your ship?"

He pointed a sweaty finger at her. "I commandeered her in Los Angeles. She's mine now, and so are you."

He moved toward her, but she blocked him by kick boxing him hard in the stomach, which sent him reeling backwards. Her leg ached from the impact, so she knew she had hit him hard enough to hurt him. He let out a loud grunt, clutched his stomach and fell. His face hit the sharp edge of the counter on the way down, but he groaned again and stumbled back on his feet. He dabbed at his cheek with a finger and found blood.

"So we're going to play rough?" He pointed to a swivel chair. "Tie her down."

The bearded man shoved her into the chair and wrapped duct tape around her waist, securing her.

Christina wasn't going to let a little tape stop her. She stood up with the chair still attached to her back. "If you lay one finger on me, Franco will kill you."

"That's where you're wrong—again." Stefano pushed her back down with a force so great it sent the chair sliding across the floor, slamming it and Christina against the wall and thrusting her neck forward as if she'd just been rear-ended on the freeway. "I'll kill you as easily as I killed your pal Peter."

"*You* killed Peter?"

"My man Hague did. I couldn't be bothered to fly to California. If Carmaletti had just handed over the chip, he wouldn't have ended up face down on a slab of concrete."

Christina tried to run away from him with the chair still on her back. "The FBI knows everything; you won't be able to leave the country."

Stefano overpowered her and bound her hands and feet to the chair with more duct tape. Her skin pinched and stung as he wrapped the sticky silver tape around her wrists and ankles.

"Turino," Stefano shouted to the bearded man, "guard the door and make sure no one bothers us."

Now she was alone with Stefano the pirate and barbarian, not the smooth charmer she'd met in Italy.

Stefano put his face in front of hers. He smelled disgusting, and sweat from his forehead dripped into her eyes. She blinked it away, but her eyes still stung.

He pulled a knife from the side of his belt. "Where's the chip, Christina?"

She spat in his face.

He slapped her cheek hard. "Do that again and I'll slash your pretty face."

Christina's cheek burned, but she didn't cry. She refused to give Stefano the satisfaction.

He raised the knife to her face. "Tell me where the chip is."

"I don't have the chip anymore. I promise."

"Your word means nothing to me. Saunders told me that you were going to sell it to him, but we both know that never happened."

Christina swallowed hard. "That was a set-up. I don't know where the chip is, I swear."

He pulled her ponytail, nearly pulling the hair from its roots. She screamed as he pulled it harder. "My bullshit detector's telling me that Miss Perfect is a liar." With one swift slice, he cut off her ponytail. Christina cringed when she saw her hair fall in a golden heap on the floor, but at least the pain had ceased. She screamed.

Stefano covered her mouth with his hand, but Christina bit it hard. Stefano shrieked when her teeth ruptured his skin and he whacked her in the face with the back of his hand.

The impact sent a dull throbbing pain along the side of her face. Had he broken her jaw?

"If brutalizing a defenseless woman is the best you can do, you're a coward."

Stefano's eyes turned to slits and he raised his fist. She braced herself for the blow, certain it would shatter her cheekbone. But he lowered his fist to his side and reached for his knife. Stefano touched the sharp blade tip to her mouth and held it there for a second.

"I'm in charge, Christina. Don't disobey me." He tapped the knife against her lip. She tasted her own blood and pressed her tongue to the corner of her lip to try to stop the bleeding. "Next time you bite, I'll remove your lips."

Stefano sliced the bottom of her shirt off, balled it up and shoved it into her mouth. "Try biting now, you bitch!"

Chapter Twenty-seven

Franco sped full throttle toward the port. The wind blew his hair and waves jolted his body as he raced under the Bay Bridge. When he saw the port, he throttled back. He squinted into the sun until he spotted *The Doria* a half-mile away. Since the port was commercial, there were no docking accommodations for a small boat.

He came up to *The Doria,* cut the engine and glided alongside the hull of the massive tanker. He was now adjacent to a fifty-foot wall of steel, and with no obvious way onto the ship, he powered the boat over to the wooden pier. Huge algae encrusted collision fenders swung from thick, weathered sea ropes attached to the steel pilings that supported the pier.

Franco killed the engine and tied the boat to one of the fenders. His only option was to scale the slimy rope and pull himself onto the pier. The smell of rotting sea life and gasoline swirled around him. He gripped the rope, the rough fibers scratching into his skin, and fist over fist he pulled his body up toward the pier. After about three feet, he lost his grasp and fell back down.

He wiped his wet hands on his shirt and started over. Sweat dripped into his eyes, making it nearly impossible to see, but wiping his eyes would cost him his grip and the precious few feet he had recovered from his fall. This time he made it halfway up before he felt his arms weaken. His heart pounded so hard he feared it might explode. To give his arms a rest, he pushed more with his legs and pulled less with his arms. He willed his muscles to give him just a few more minutes; he had the top of the pier in sight. With a final grunt, he heaved his body onto the walkway and fell down onto the wood, where sharp splinters dug into his hands and elbows. He caught his breath for a few seconds and then lifted himself up and ran down the pier to the ship.

He sprinted about fifty yards and reached the gangplank before years of smoking caught up with him; he was ready to collapse from the physical exertion, but he bent over, breathed in as much oxygen as his lungs could handle and then stormed the ship. He had to reach Christina before that savage Marani got his hands on her.

Franco immediately spotted Arturo Turino standing guard in front of the bridge. Once a second Captain with Doria Shipping, Franco had fired him years ago. He stopped dead in his tracks and hid behind a metal post. When Turino turned his back, Franco crept along the companion walkway to the tool locker, opened it and pulled out a heavy wrench.

At the first opportunity, Franco rushed at Turino and hit him in the head with the wrench. Turino crumpled to the floor, unconscious, and Franco searched him quickly for a weapon. He seized a switchblade from his pocket and silently entered the control room. When he saw Christina bound and gagged, with Stefano holding a knife to her face, he sprinted toward Stefano.

Franco attacked with the wrench raised, but Stefano saw him coming and ducked out of the way. He charged like a linebacker, and broke Franco's grip. He knocked the wrench out of his hand, and made a desperate slash to Franco's arm before Franco stabbed him in the shoulder with Turino's switchblade.

Stefano clutched his shoulder and cursed as blood seeped through his shirt. But with a loud grunt, he kicked Franco's wrist. The blow sent Franco's knife sliding across the floor. Franco fell, powerless as his weapon escaped him, but giving up wasn't an option.

He reached up and gripped Stefano's wrist so tight he forced him to drop his knife. Franco grabbed it and rolled on top of Stefano. He held the weapon to his face.

"Move and I'll kill you," he said.

Christina struggled to free herself. Even with a filthy face, torn clothing, bloody arms and greasy hair, she had never seen Franco look so sexy.

Suddenly, Turino appeared unsteadily at the doorway and aimed a gun at Franco's head. "Drop the knife and get up," he said.

Franco slowly put down the knife and stood.

"Hands up!" Turino ordered.

Franco put his hands up. "Take the gag off Christina, Stefano."

"I'm giving the orders now, *mio fratello*," Stefano said.

He swaggered over to Christina and took the fabric out of her mouth. "Now, beautiful Christina, see that gun pointed at Franco's head? It will go off in ten seconds if you don't tell me where I can find the chip."

"It's in my condo, in my jewelry box."

"We ripped your place apart two weeks ago," Stefano said. "I know you're lying." He brought his face closer to hers. "But maybe we missed something. How about if I escort you home to have another look? If it's not there, Turino will shoot Franco immediately. I'm sure he'll take great pleasure in doing that."

Turino nodded his head and smiled. He spoke in a working class Italian accent. "*Vendetta finale.*"

"Christina," Franco said. "Don't say anything more."

Christina couldn't bear to lose Franco. "The chip's in my watch. I've been hiding it there for weeks."

Stefano cut the watch off Christina's wrist and put it in his pocket. He looked over at Turino. "Take them to the engine room."

"Listen, Stefano," Franco pleaded. "Just let us go. You have the chip now; we won't tell anyone what happened."

Stefano leered at Franco. "You think I'm *stupido*?"

Turino led Christina and Franco to the engine room by gunpoint with Stefano staggering behind them.

In the stifling hot engine room, Stefano held a gun on Christina and Franco while Turino tied them back-to-back to a large metal pole.

When Turino finished, Stefano gave Franco a kiss on the cheek. *"Ciao, mio fratello."* He turned to Christina. "Forgive me for not kissing you goodbye, but I'm not fond of women who bite."

Turino and Stefano left the engine room and latched shut the heavy metal door behind them.

Christina felt doomed, but at least she was with Franco. "I don't want to die," she said, "especially not being able to look at you."

"I assure you, we're not going to die. I have a plan, but you must forgive me first. I broke a promise."

"What promise?"

"I've started smoking again."

"Okay, you started smoking again. I forgive you. Do you feel the need to say the Rosary to repent?"

"In my back pocket is my lighter. If you can reach in and get it, we can use it to burn off our ropes."

She reached back toward Franco but couldn't extend her fingers far enough to touch his pocket. She squirmed into the pole as much as possible and tried again. She could feel Franco's trousers and stretched her hand toward his back pocket. She felt the stitching around the pocket and extended her fingers inside. Now she felt the plastic lighter but couldn't get a grip on it.

"I'm nearly there, Franco. If you can just scoot back an inch or so, I think I'll be able to get a better grip."

Franco moved back a bit and Christina tried again. This time she pulled the lighter out, but with her sweaty hand she couldn't light it. She rubbed her fingers on the remaining bits of her cotton t-shirt to absorb the sweat. On her second attempt, she flicked the lighter and got a flame.

"Ouch!" Christina yelled.

"What happened?"

"I'm burning my thumb, not the rope."

"Be careful, dolcina. Take your time."

She tried again, this time positioning the flame closer to the rope, but this maneuver didn't work. The flame burnt the skin on the inside of her wrist. She moved her hand a few inches, and did her best to ignore the excruciating pain.

"I smell burning flesh. Are you hurt?"

"Not really," she lied. She flicked the lighter one more time and placed the flame directly under the rope.

"Well done, Christina, I can feel the ropes loosening."

Their hands finally broke free. They stood up, embraced each other and kissed until Franco eased away. He brought her burnt hand to his mouth. He kissed it and wrapped it in his shirt.

"Our troubles aren't over yet," Christina said. "We're still trapped in this furnace. We'll die of heat prostration if we don't get out of here soon." She walked to the door, only to confirm that Stefano had locked it from the outside.

"If we turn the generator off," Franco said, "Stefano's bound to come down when the lights and air-conditioning go off upstairs."

"Good idea. Any clue where the generator is?"

Franco shook his head. "No idea."

"All right, then, let's twist and turn everything we can find. Something's bound to happen." Christina spotted a large metal knob, and reached for it. "Jesus Christ!" She pulled her hand away. "It's burning hot." She took off her t-shirt and covered the knob with her shirt. It was too tight to budge. She spotted a large steel wheel and turned that. Hot steam sprayed out. She ducked so it wouldn't burn her face.

Franco yelled over the roar of the engines. "Help me with this lever."

Christina put her shirt back on. She saw Franco pushing down on a long black lever. She joined him and used all her weight as leverage, but they couldn't budge it.

"Let's try again," she said. "On *three* we'll push down with everything we have."

They poised themselves above the bar and placed their hands on the end of it.

"Uno, due, tre!"

Christina felt a lurch, and with their combined strength, they pushed the lever downward. The overhead lights went off and dim emergency lights lit in their place.

"We need to be prepared," Franco said. "Remember they have guns. He looked around the room and picked up the remains of the burnt rope. "This is all we have." He got on his hands and knees and dabbed his finger into a black gooey puddle. "And an engine leak."

"Serious?"

Franco stood to the side of the door with the rope in his hand. "Yes. All we can do now is wait and see how serious."

They watched as the puddle grew bigger, and then they heard footsteps pounding down the stairs.

Turino entered the engine room with a cigarette dangling from his mouth and a gun in his hand. He stopped and raised his gun when he saw Christina out of her ropes, but before he could react, Franco ambushed him from behind and wrapped the rope around his neck. Turino gagged and dropped the gun. Christina picked it up and they headed for the stairs, slamming the door behind them.

On deck, Stefano finished a cigarette and threw the butt overboard. He yelled for Turino.

Franco came up behind Stefano and held the gun to his back. "Turino's unavailable."

"Doria the Great has escaped." Stefano put his hands in the air. "Why am I not surprised?"

And then, the sudden, huge explosion reverberating underfoot.

Christina hit her head on a railing and landed on the wooden deck with a loud, painful thud. In a silent dreamlike state, she saw Franco's face hover over hers. Then Stefano's face replaced Franco's. In very slow motion, she watched Stefano take the gun and aim it at Franco.

Oh God, she prayed, *please don't shoot him.*

Her eyes would not focus. Her head throbbed. Through blurry eyes she saw Franco swipe at Stefano's legs. Stefano fell. The gun slid within Christina's reach, but she could barely move her limbs. She felt the weight of her body as though she had fallen into quicksand. Heavy silt trapped her, but with all her mental and physical strength, she moved her hand.

She raised the gun and pointed it at Stefano's abdomen.

Epilogue

Christina lay asleep in a hospital bed, while various monitors beeped quietly around her. She stirred, and then opened her eyes for the first time in twenty-four hours. She blinked a few times, and gradually the environment around her came into focus; an IV tube dripped into one arm and a bulky plaster cast covered her other one. Her burned hand had a white gauze bandage wrapped around it, and under her hospital gown a thick bandage secured her ribcage. She blinked again and saw Franco resting in a chair next to her bed. His head jerked as he awoke from a catnap.

"Dolcina." He gently nudged her shoulder. "How are you feeling?"

"Awful." She managed a small smile. "Is there any part of my body that's not bruised?"

Franco moved her hospital gown to the side and kissed her stomach. "I think your belly button is unscathed."

Christina laughed and then winced at the sharp jab of a broken rib.

Suzan and Dan entered the hospital room hand-in-hand. They playfully cleared their throats to get the lovers to notice them, and then Suzan gave Christina a gentle hug. "Hey, how are you doing?"

"I think I'll survive." Christina smiled and gripped Franco's hand. "What happened to Stefano?"

"He's in the hospital," Dan said. "Having surgery to remove a bullet from his spleen. If he survives, he's not only going down for arms trafficking but for hiring Arnold Hague to kill your friend Peter and Martin Denton too. We got a full confession from Hague."

Christina nodded. She wished it didn't feel so insignificant knowing who had killed Peter. He was still dead, and nothing would bring him back.

"Listen, kiddo," Dan said. "We'll let you get some rest. If you ever get tired of banking, the FBI will be glad to have you."

"She'll take that offer over my lead body," Franco said.

Christina tried not to laugh. "Over my *dead* body."

The others grinned, and then Dan left the room for a second. With the help of a hospital intern, he returned with a wooden crate, nearly six feet tall and four feet wide.

"Is this the present that nearly got me killed?" Christina asked.

"Don't ask me, I'm just the messenger." He handed the box to Franco. "We're outta here. I'll let Franco open it for you."

As soon as they were alone, Franco wedged the knife the intern gave him under the thick metal staples and worked them loose. He struggled for several minutes with the box, and then he pulled out an enormous painting.

"Wait." He slid Christina's glasses on her, and then he turned the painting around.

He had painted her life-size, in the green dress she had worn to the nightclub, sitting in the courtyard at the Hotel della Luna et Stelli, with the magenta bougainvillea swirling around her head. She examined the painting further and exclaimed at the detail. He even remembered to dot on the small freckles that appeared on her arms and hands when she spent too much time in the sun.

Her hands. What was that on her hand? Christina looked closer. Wrapped around the ring finger of her left hand was the exquisite diamond and ruby ring his grandmother wore in the portrait in his hotel.

A rush of emotions swept through her. Her eyes wandered down to the lower right hand corner, where he had signed the painting *Love, Franco*. Above Franco's signature, he had painted a small inscription with careful brushstrokes: *Will you marry me?*

Christina tried to get up from the bed to give Franco a hug, but the IV tube held her back.

Tears pooled in her eyes. "Yes, Franco, *Si, mio amore, si.*"

About the Author

Jill St. Anne is the pen name for Jill Zajicek Wickersham. She was an award-winning investigative journalist in college. After her undergraduate work, she received an MBA in International Business. Her most recent job in the corporate world was with Chase Manhattan (now JP Morgan Chase) where she worked in the Private Client Services department, helping the bank meet the financial needs of high-net worth individuals in Silicon Valley. She currently lives with her husband and young daughter in South Kensington, London, the San Francisco Bay Area and British Columbia, Canada.

www.jillstanne.com